ASHES, ASHES

*From page one, the chase is on –
and many will die. Unnecessarily.*

Forensic psychiatrist, Ms Barrett Conyors
knew that if Richard Glash weren't manacled to his chair, he would kill her. He had
likely imagined every detail of her murder
and then obsessively sketched the scene
hundreds of times. At forty-two Richard,
who'd spent all but four and a half years of
his life locked away ... had few interests,
other than drawing and killing.

ASHES, ASHES

Charles Atkins

Severn House Large Print
London & New York

This first large print edition published 2009
in Great Britain and the USA by
SEVERN HOUSE PUBLISHERS LTD of
9-15 High Street, Sutton, Surrey, SM1 1DF.
First world regular print edition published 2008 by
Severn House Publishers Ltd., London and New York.

British Library Cataloguing in Publication Data

Atkins, Charles.
  Ashes, ashes.
  1. Escapes--Fiction. 2. Suspense fiction. 3. Large type
  books.
  I. Title
  813.5'4-dc22

ISBN-13: 978-0-7278-7802-1

Printed and bound in Great Britain by
MPG Books Ltd, Bodmin, Cornwall.

For Harvey and Cynthia Atkins

One

Forensic psychiatrist Barrett Conyors knew that if Richard Glash weren't manacled to his chair, he would kill her. She stared across the steel table into his ice-blue eyes; he didn't blink. The six-foot-five, orange-clad man with his slicked-down, jet-black hair had likely imagined every detail of her murder and then obsessively sketched the scene hundreds of times. At forty-two, Richard, who'd spent all but four and a half years of his life locked away – the last decade here in super max at Green Haven Correctional – had few interests, other than drawing and killing.

Barrett had seen many of his drawings and paintings; just thinking of the gruesome images brought a fresh wave of nausea. Glash's pictures were brilliant – some freakishly photographic, others abstract – but always with the central themes of murder and murderers. He'd pick his subjects, such as a famous serial killer or a person from his past who he believed had hurt him, and he'd fill sketchpads with variations on a theme, like a classical composer ... only different.

What are you thinking? she wondered, wishing her stomach would calm, as he held her gaze and let his attorney, Carla Phelps, speak for him. And that, Barrett knew, was just one of the awful problems in her last-ditch attempt to keep Richard Glash right here, in a super max prison cell serving four consecutive life sentences for murders he'd committed the week following his eighteenth birthday.

'Tell me about the voices,' she said, braced for the objection.

'You already asked that,' Carla Phelps, his redheaded, green-eyed, thirty-eight-year-old attorney shot back. 'In fact you've wasted our time for the past two hours going over the same material. He answered once. He told you he hears voices. Now you're badgering.' Her voice was nasal, the syllables carrying a Boston twang she'd deliberately accentuate when pounding away at a witness ... or in this case, Barrett.

Glash stared as Barrett silently counted to ten. If he was contemplating her gruesome murder, she could come up with one or two versions of her own for the tastefully dressed and perfectly made-up Carla Phelps, a woman with bipolar disorder who Barrett had once treated on an inpatient psychiatric unit – another horrible complication on a long list of all the things that were going wrong with this case. The videographer in the corner of the room was another. Barrett had been ambushed by Carla, who'd insisted that audio was inadequate and that today's interview needed a video transcript.

'Ms Phelps,' Barrett began, knowing that every word she said, her facial expressions and every gesture were being captured to be later examined and dissected by the attorney. At least she'd had the foresight to wear her most conservative navy suit with a white button-down shirt – her courtroom uniform; its severity a deliberate ploy to play down her looks, which at thirty-three and enhanced by only a hint of lipstick still turned heads, often getting her mistaken for Angelina Jolie. But Barrett wasn't thinking about her appearance or how she had been outmaneuvered and out-dressed by Carla, in her lightweight gray silk suit and flawless makeup; she'd obviously dressed for the camera, a tacky but effective legal ploy. Juries were more swayed by appearances than anything else.

Barrett was frustrated and frightened. Richard Glash, with Carla's assistance, had figured all the angles that could get him transferred to a state hospital for the criminally insane. She had to keep her cool, and resist the urge to reach across the bolted-down table and throttle Carla Phelps; this was all her fault. 'We will be here for hours more, if I am unable to thoroughly evaluate Mr Glash's contention that he has become psychotic ... and developed schizophrenia – an unusual occurrence in someone in their forties.'

'Yes' – Carla's lip curled – 'let the record show that Dr Conyors has just asserted that my client, who has been diagnosed by a *true*

9

expert in the field as having paranoid schizo-phrenia, is lying and malingering.'

For two hours now there had been many of these asides for the video. Barrett knew that Carla was laying traps, thinking down the road that if this were viewed in court, it would appear that she was hounding poor Richard Glash – a man who following his release from a locked adolescent state psychiatric hospital went on a copy-cat killing spree that had left four social workers and one judge dead. His sixth intended victim had barely escaped. For that lucky woman it had been her second assault by Glash; the first when they'd both been children and he'd attempted to scalp her with a butcher's knife – he'd been four, she three.

Barrett ignored Carla, and still holding Glash's gaze, asked again, 'Tell me about the voices.'

'You can answer,' Carla said, and then smirked. 'I'm certain that Judge Garrett will rule this entire interview inadmissible any-way.'

Glash spoke, his voice deep and flat. It reverberated off the walls of the concrete room. 'I hear a man's voice.'

'What does it say?' Barrett asked, knowing she'd been over this before, but hoping for a change, some small inconsistency with which to trap Glash in a lie.

'It tells me to kill people.'

'Is it inside your head or outside?'

'Outside.'

'When did you first hear it?' she continued, noting how his answers never varied. Somehow, somewhere he'd gotten his hands on the answer book. Unlike most convicts who attempted to fake mental illnesses to get transferred to a forensic hospital or to buy a not-guilty-by-reason-of-mental-defect plea, Glash was holding tight to a good impersonation of a paranoid schizophrenic. Barrett was desperate to find the chink. She knew Glash did not have schizophrenia, and even if he did, he'd always known that his crimes were wrong. Richard Glash killed because that was his obsession.

'I've always heard it.'

'When were you first aware of it?'

'I've always heard it.'

'Yes, but when did you realize you were hearing voices?'

'Not voices,' his tone was pedantic, as though he were correcting a child who couldn't get the answer straight. His eyes focused on hers. '*A* voice. A man's voice that tells me to kill people.'

'Describe the voice,' she said, as the nausea returned; it was bad this morning.

'It's deep and raspy.'

Nice touch, she mused, *a bit of detail but not too much*. 'Did you hear it as a child?' She swallowed hard as salty saliva flooded into her mouth.

Carla shook her head, her short spiky hair glowing copper under the fluorescents. 'I can't believe the incredibly stupid line of this

11

questioning. My client has explained that he has always heard the voice. I think that would include his childhood.'

'Did you hear it as a child?' Barrett repeated, putting a fist to her mouth. She tried to take slow breaths. She started to dry heave, hiding it behind her hand.

'You're sick,' Glash stated.

Barrett felt sweat bead her forehead. 'It'll pass,' she said, hoping that saying it would make it so. 'Tell me about the voice.'

'Are you going to throw up?' he asked.

She shook her head. 'Tell me about the voice.'

'I've always heard it.'

'I see,' Barrett said, imagining how Carla Phelps must have groomed Glash for the taped interview. His shock of jet-black hair had been pruned and combed with a right-sided part. If he weren't in the prison jumpsuit with chains at his wrists, waist and ankles, he'd almost pass for normal. *Almost,* she thought, *but not quite.* Somewhere between the unflinching gaze and the flat voice you quickly sensed that something was off, like talking to a robot. Richard Glash had an illness – some might call it a condition – but it wasn't schizophrenia. He had a form of autism – Asperger's Syndrome – that was first diagnosed when he was three. He had no ability to feel for others, and couldn't grasp human interactions. Even gestures as simple as a handshake were impossible for him to understand. He was obsessive and prone to

12

violent attacks of rage if anyone attempted to vary his routines. As a result, he'd spent the majority of his last twenty-seven years in either solitary or super max.

She shifted her line of questions. 'If you've heard these voices—'

'*A* voice,' he interjected.

'Right, *a* voice, a man's raspy voice, why is it that you've only recently mentioned it?'

'Don't answer that!' Carla pushed forward in her chair. 'For the record, Dr Conyors is attempting to lead the prisoner.'

Barrett turned to the attorney, relieved that the nausea had subsided. 'I'm doing no such thing. I'm attempting to conduct a psychiatric interview with your client. Your constant objections and interruptions are inhibiting my ability to do this.'

'Dr Conyors, with all due respect,' Carla said, her voice dripping with sarcasm, 'I don't think it's my objections that are interfering with your ability to conduct an interview.'

Barrett was used to these kinds of attacks from attorneys. As a forensic psychiatrist she expected ploys meant to throw her off and to try and discredit her. But with Carla, this was now personal. The woman held a whopping grudge against her. Barrett knew that she blamed her for the break-up of her marriage and the loss of custody of her baby girl seven years ago. What had happened was tragic and way too common. Carla had developed a post-partum psychosis – a frequent occurrence in women with bipolar disorder. She had attempted to take her newborn from the nursery and leave the hospital in the dead of night. When stopped, wearing nothing but a paper hospital gown, she'd rambled about how demons were trying to enter her baby, and she needed to get her away. She was taken from maternity to the psych ward, and that's where the two women's lives had first intersected. Barrett, the chief psychiatric resident, took on Carla's case, and watched the woman's life – that had been so filled with hope and promise – totally unravel.

Now, as Barrett looked at the attorney she could see the hatred in her green eyes. 'I'll rephrase,' Barrett said. 'Mr Glash, who did you first tell about your voice?' She then looked at Carla.

'Go ahead,' the lawyer said.

'Dr Friess.'

'The consultant psychiatrist here?'

'Yes.'

'When did you tell him?'

'Three years ago.'

Of course, Barrett thought, just as word would have been spreading about the class action case being brought by Carla's Patient and Prisoners' Rights Group. Similar suits were then popping up all over the country. They alleged that prisoners with severe mental illnesses were being deprived of their Fourteenth Amendment Rights – Freedom from Cruel and Unusual Punishment. Carla's contention was that a group of identified prisoners – all convicted murderers – had

14

mental illnesses, and were not receiving adequate treatment in the prison. She had found the ear of a sympathetic Superior Court judge who'd issued a consent decree against the Department of Corrections. Either the department had to provide adequate and appropriate treatment in the prison system, or the four prisoners would need to be transferred to a state forensic hospital.

The videographer, a plump young man who seemed out of place in chinos and a polo shirt, signaled that he needed to change tapes.

Barrett glanced at the clock overhead, they'd been at this for over two hours. She was getting nowhere and it was just a matter of weeks, maybe even days, before the judge made good on his threats to transfer the prisoners, because Corrections had shown a stunning lack of response to his edict. This was her last shot at keeping Glash here where he had to be. As the camera's red light went back on, she shifted tactics.

'Enough about your voices,' she said.

'*Voice*,' he corrected.

'As you say. Tell me about your interest in murder.'

Carla nearly choked. 'What's that got to do with your diagnostic evaluation?'

She looked Carla dead on. 'If you continue to object to my every question I'll petition the court for additional interview times. Is that in your client's best interest?'

Carla glared, but knew Barrett was right.

15

This could drag on for days, and the last thing she wanted was to lose Judge Wilson Garrett's good will. 'You can answer,' she said.

This wasn't Barrett's first interview with Glash and she watched for the effect the change in topic would have. For the first time that day he smiled, over broad, even teeth.

'Tell me about murder and murderers,' she coaxed.

'What would you like to know?' he answered. 'I know everything that's ever been written. Who would you like to talk about?' His deep voice boomed in the small interview room, like a professor warming to a favorite thesis. 'Gacy? Manson? Hinckley? Starkeweather? Ramirez?'

'They are interesting,' she said, meeting his smile with one of her own. 'What do you know about the others in your case?'

'Everything,' he said, as both boast and statement of fact.

'I object,' Carla said. 'This is completely irrelevant and a waste of everyone's time.'

Glash turned to Carla. 'No it's not. I like these questions. This is what we will talk about. You will be quiet now.'

Carla opened her mouth to speak.

Glash cocked his head and repeated, 'Be quiet.' Carla clearly was at a loss.

He turned back to Barrett. 'There are four of us, as you know. You know a lot, Dr Conyors, and that's why we must talk about murder. You're an expert; you're famous.

You've been in the newspapers and I've seen you on TV. I'll begin. The other three are Jane Saunders, Dr Clarence Albert, and Allison Tessavian. We're all different, although three of us carry diagnoses of schizophrenia. Dr Albert and I have paranoid schizophrenia, Jane Saunders is schizo-affective bipolar type and Allison Tessavian has delusional disorder erotomanic type.'

As Barrett listened to his deep monotone, she had the sense of being lectured to. This was Glash's passion, or so she'd come to believe. He lived and breathed anything related to murder. Should he ever be released, or escape, he would immediately resume killing. She had no doubt of that.

'On June the twentieth 1992, Jane Saunders,' he said, as though reading from a script, 'who'd recently given birth to her third child, killed all three of her kids between nine forty-five a.m. and ten thirty. She then called nine-one-one to tell them what she'd done.' His eyelids fluttered, and his tone shifted to a dull falsetto – not a perfect imitation of Saunders' infamous call, but chilling: '*Something is wrong with my babies. God has taken them; it could have been the devil. They're all dead; they're not moving anymore, someone should come.*'

Carla stiffened, and Barrett wondered what the attorney must have been thinking. The connection with Jane Saunders was too close for comfort – both mothers who had become psychotic. Carla had never hurt her daughter,

17

but that was the fear that had driven her husband away and made him seek full custody. Barrett remembered the heartbroken man, an attorney who'd fallen in love with Carla when they'd both been in school. He'd sobbed in her office, and despite a half-hearted attempt to understand his wife's illness, he'd quickly and cruelly set about dissolving their marriage.

Glash continued, displaying a detailed knowledge of Jane's case, her arrest, the psychiatric evaluations, her failed attempt at a not-guilty-by-reason-of-mental-defect plea. He then discussed the recent bestseller written by her husband, John J. Saunders. 'Have you read it?' he asked Barrett.

His question surprised her. 'Yes,' she said.

'Tell me what you thought of it.'

For the first time Barrett caught a sense of emotion in his voice, an urgency, a desire to know. She was torn; her critique of a tell-all book did not belong in this taped interview. But this was the first time there'd been anything like a normally paced conversation with Glash. She couldn't risk losing this sliver of an opportunity. 'I thought it was sad and exploitative.'

'It sold over a million copies in hardcover,' Glash replied. 'The paperback is coming out September first. I think he'll use his wife's transfer and court case to generate publicity. Don't you agree, Dr Conyors?'

'That makes sense,' Barrett said.

'That's what I thought; we sometimes think

alike, Dr Conyors,' Glash said. 'Now let's move on to the case of Dr Albert...'

For the next thirty minutes Richard Glash displayed an encyclopedic knowledge of Dr Clarence Albert – the PhD microbiologist who five years prior had mailed powdered anthrax to the executives of Bioforward, a Jersey-based biotech corporation where he'd been employed for over twenty years. From there Glash shifted seamlessly to a retelling of Allison Tessavian's erotomanic fixation on the pop idol Justin Green. Allison believed Justin was in love with her; she'd stalked him and killed his then girlfriend, singer Melinda Coo.

Suddenly, Glash stopped talking.

The silence was eerie, just the low-pitched hum from the camera. Barrett found herself staring at the orange-clad man. He smiled. 'I've killed five people,' Richard Glash said. 'That's not a lot, is it, Dr Conyors?'

'It is,' she said, wondering where he was going, and knowing that everything he said or did had its own logic. But how to figure it out?

'No, it's not. How many people have you killed?'

Barrett felt the air getting sucked from the room. Of course Glash would know about her, and the recent high-profile case in which she had shot and killed Ellen Martin, and come close to putting a bullet between the eyes of Ellen's twin brother, Jimmy. She felt sick, and wanted to get this over with. Her heart raced; she didn't want to have to think

19

about Jimmy Martin, a man who'd stalked her, and murdered her husband, Ralph.

'Do you think that you killed Charles Rohr?' Glash asked, bringing up another one of her cases that had gone tragically wrong.

'He shot himself,' she replied.

'I know that,' Glash said, dismissively, 'but you were the reason, weren't you?'

'I can't discuss these cases.'

'I know that too. There are rules of confidentiality. But those people are dead, so it doesn't apply. I think, Dr Conyors, you've killed more people than me. And I'm in prison. That doesn't seem right. They call me a serial killer. You're one as well.' He shifted in his chair, the shackles jangled.

She felt him studying her. Just as he knew all about the other prisoners, Glash had done his homework on her. She wondered how much he knew about her, about her family. She pictured her younger sister Justine, who like her had been traumatized by Jimmy Martin. Justine finally was back at work in the hospital, seeing patients. Only yesterday they'd argued, Justine pleading with Barrett to have an abortion.

'How many people have you killed, Dr Conyors?' Glash repeated. 'What about when you were an intern at Yale and a medical student at Tulane? Did you kill any patients? They say doctors do it all the time, but they call it accidents and natural causes.' A pressure built in his voice. 'How many people have you killed?'

Barrett struggled to format a question, as she watched Glash's breathing grow more rapid.

'How many?'

Carla spoke. 'Richard, try to calm down.'

'Shut up!' he shouted at her, twisting in the chair.

'Answer the question, Dr Conyors. How many people have you killed?' He was straining, the muscles bulged and corded in his arms.

The videographer pressed back to the corner of the room, still filming, but terror on his face.

Barrett stayed rooted in her chair as Glash screamed his question. She was scared to death, but thrilled that she'd gotten him to show his true colors, and all caught on film. What would the judge make of this? Or a jury?

'How many people have you killed, Dr Conyors?'

The interview was over. Once Richard Glash's rage was triggered nothing would stop him from lashing out at anything and anyone in his path. At a forensic hospital, maintaining him would be a nightmare. People would get hurt ... or worse.

'How many people have you killed, Dr Conyors?'

And then the unthinkable. The steel chain that rooted him to the floor snapped.

Barrett was out of her chair as Glash lunged for her. A decade of martial arts training had not prepared her for the fury of his assault. He barreled into her chest and knocked her back, as guards swarmed the small room. They attacked with both pepper spray and a TASER gun. Glash twisted and screamed, his hands and legs still shackled. *'How many people have you killed, Dr Conyors?'*

Barrett's eyes welled up, her heart pounded, and the nausea returned as she cowered, watching the guards attempt to subdue Glash.

'Stop it!' Carla screamed, having removed herself to the corner by the door. *'You're hurting him!'*

'How many people have you killed, Dr Conyors?'

He screamed and struggled, as they zapped him repeatedly with the high-voltage TASER.

Pressed back against the wall, Barrett knew that the best course would be to get the hell out. She could see the guards getting hurt, one's face cut open from the steel chain; another got caught in the side of the head by Glash's flailing elbow. She tried to think back through the interview; nothing there would help, not even this. Carla would spin it and make this all a part of his mental illness. 'I don't know,' she said, loud enough to be heard.

The sound of her voice – or maybe the cumulative effects of the pepper spray and TASER – seemed to calm him. 'How many people have you killed, Dr Conyors?' he asked again, his body pressed down to the ground by five bleeding and winded guards.

'I don't know,' she repeated. 'Why is it so important to you?' she asked, bracing her hands against the wall and trying to stand.

'Don't answer, Richard,' Carla shouted.

He ignored her. 'You've killed more people than me. It's not right. They should lock you up, and set me free.'

Carla looked across at the videographer, and saw that the red light was still on the camera. *'Too* fabulous,' she whispered under her breath, and turning straight to the camera: 'For the record, the interview ended in Dr Conyors causing the prisoner, Richard Glash, a man suffering with paranoid schizophrenia, to become agitated. He was subsequently assaulted by five facility personnel and brutally attacked with both pepper spray and a TASER gun. This is a clear and graphic representation of how my client, a man with a serious and persistent mental illness, has consistently and violently been subjected to cruel and unusual punishment. I will, on his behalf, pursue this matter in the most aggressive manner.'

Two

Three days after the disastrous interview with Glash, Barrett gripped the cool surface of her desk and struggled to catch her breath. Rationally, she knew that she wasn't dying, but the surges of adrenalin that pulsed through her sent a different message. Her thoughts skittered from the fetus growing in her belly to Friday's terrifying evaluation. When he'd come after her, it had brought back terrifying memories of when Charlie Rohr had shot himself dead with a Marshals Service revolver not three feet from her. The image of Rohr's head jerking back as the bullet hit home... '*Stop it!*' she said, wondering if her voice carried outside the closed door of her new office. If it had, her secretary, Marla, would either ignore or timidly knock to see if Barrett needed anything.

'Calm down,' she told herself, trying to take slow, measured breaths. She used a technique her Wing Chung Sifu, Henry, had taught her: the good breath goes in; the jangled breath goes out. *Just observe, don't think.* She let random thoughts and images enter and leave: the pale blue of her button-down shirt against the navy of her blazer, the feel of her

24

belly expanding against the waistband of her khakis, her feet firmly on the floor, sensing their weight through the rubber soles of her walking shoes. She felt the air flow through her body, she kept her thoughts focused, and tried not to think about the child growing inside of her, the one that...

A red light flashed twice on her phone, and then Marla's voice said, 'Dr Conyors, Dr Houssman is on line two.'

'Thanks, Marla.' She picked up.

'Barrett, how are you?' The older man's voice worked better than any of her Zen techniques.

'Honestly?' she asked, picturing George with his thick glasses, sitting in the middle of his sun-drenched apartment, probably wearing one of several identical gray raincoats, about which as trainees she and her colleagues had speculated as to their purpose, wondering if he was either a flasher or had watched one too many Columbo specials.

'No, lie to me, I'm having a tough day,' he quipped.

'You? You're retired – at least, I thought you were.' Both of them were aware that Houssman, the eighty-four-year-old legend in forensic psychiatry, was busier now than he'd ever been, between working as a consultant, presenting at conferences and continuing to supervise trainees, who eagerly sought him out.

'I've been thinking about you,' he said, 'about the...'

'Abortion?' she said bluntly.

'Yes.'

'It's all set,' she said dully. 'A couple more hours, and it's over.'

'It's for the best,' he said.

'That's what everyone tells me. I just keep thinking about Ralph,' she said. Just mentioning the name of her dead husband Ralph Best – the talented musician whose last name she never took – filled her with a dull ache, like a piece of her was missing. Sometimes she'd imagine him playing trombone, hearing the fiery passages, as he'd shoot up and down the scales. 'Why couldn't it have been his?'

'I know,' George said.

'Let's talk about something else, I've got to just keep my mind off it.'

'I heard about what happened with Glash,' he said.

'It was horrible. I felt totally unskilled,' Barrett admitted. 'He was toying with me. I'll send you a copy of the tapes. It was four hours of ... I'm worried, George.'

'You're not alone.'

'If he gets transferred to Croton, he'll wreak havoc. He's incredibly smart and time holds no meaning for him. I can see him playing the good patient for as long as it takes.'

'Exactly right,' Houssman agreed. 'He knows the rules, and figures angles to make them work. He'll be perfectly well behaved and take all his medications. Then, his sham symptoms will disappear, and come the time of his six-month review he'll have his patient rights attorney argue for his release, demanding a less restrictive setting under the Olmsted Act.'

'I've been going through his old records,' Barrett said, 'looking for anything that can be used to keep this from happening.'

'What did you find?' Houssman asked, his voice more tentative than usual.

'Nothing with your name on it, and it kind of surprised me,' she said, keeping her tone light. 'He would have been high profile at the time of his arrest. I would have thought you'd have been the evaluating psychiatrist.'

'He was, and I wasn't,' Houssman said abruptly.

Barrett was struck by something in his voice. Since Barrett's fellowship in forensic psychiatry, he had played a big role in her life. Somewhere between mentor and the father she never knew – or rather, chose to forget. George wasn't saying something. 'And?' she prompted.

'I had someone else do the evaluation,' he answered simply.

If she hadn't had so much else on her mind, like that in less than two hours she'd be terminating her pregnancy, she would have pushed. George was leaving something out and she knew it. Glash's case was too fascinating for him to have given it away without good reason. As she looked across her Danish modern desk and through the large windows that gave her an expansive view of downtown Manhattan and the steel-gray East River, she thought back. Twenty years ago George would have sat where she was now. He'd been the founder and director of the forensic center, a job she'd held for the past two and a half months, and one she wasn't certain that she wanted. The furniture was all new, an expense Barrett had insisted upon, wanting to eliminate every trace of her past boss, supposed friend and clinic director Dr Anton Fielding, now under investigation by the university, the state and the feds for misappropriation of grant funds, and a serious ethical violation that involved the release of a homicidal patient – a man whose child Barrett currently carried. Thinking of Anton filled her with rage and a horrible feeling of being tricked, lied to and placed in danger.

'Barrett, I don't have to tell you this and yet ... if Richard Glash is ever released, he will kill at the first opportunity.'

'I know, this whole case isn't making any sense. Jane Saunders, and even Allison Tessavian, I can understand. Those women should never have been sent to prison. Their crimes were perpetrated while floridly psychotic, under the sway of their voices and delusions. I actually agree with the attorney – and the judge – on those two. At the time of their killings neither one thought their actions were wrong. Jane thought she was saving her kids from the devil, and Allison believed that Melanie Coo was having an affair with a man she believed was her husband. The fact that it was all delusion could have made a decent

28

case, but for whatever reason their attorneys didn't go there. But Clarence Albert and Richard Glash ... I'm scared, George. I'm at the point where I no longer know how the system works.'

'Or doesn't work.'

'The inmates are running the asylum...' she hedged.

'What is it?' he asked, immediately catching that she'd held something back.

'Do you know Carla Phelps?'

'The Legal Protection Project? I know of her, and I've read her articles. A smart cookie.'

'This comes under the heading of "I will have to kill you if you ever tell anyone what I'm about to say".'

'Barrett, you know that's a two-way street with us. You trust me and I trust you.'

'But this is a hands-down breaking of confidentiality ... she was my patient about seven years ago. I was chief resident on the inpatient unit and she got admitted from OB with a post-partum psychosis.'

'She's bipolar?'

'Very much so, and everything went bad for her. She'd never told her husband about her manic depression. He didn't take it well, and while she was still hearing voices and believing that devils were attempting to kidnap her baby, he filed for divorce and full custody of their daughter. She stayed on the inpatient unit for two months. We couldn't get her symptoms under control. By the time we finally did, she had almost no life to return to. When she finally left the hospital she was furious. She accused me of conspiring with her husband. At one point she believed I was having an affair with him.'

'I told you not to do that,' Houssman quipped.

'Cute, George.'

'What happened then?'

'No idea.' She paused.

'What?'

'That's not entirely true. I just remembered something. Did you ever notice how paranoid people sometimes get the thing they most fear? That people really will conspire against them ... hurt them, take away everything, especially when they come into contact with mental health professionals?'

'Yes ... so what happened with Carla Phelps?'

'As she was getting better and stabilizing on meds, her husband went forward with the divorce. He used her mental illness to get full custody of their daughter – claimed she was unfit and had put their child in harm's way as a result of her bipolar disorder – on some level that was true. Her hospital records were subpoenaed. Things I'd written were used to support his case, many taken out of context. My evaluation from the night she was admitted was pretty strong – something horrible could have happened to that baby. A couple months after she'd been discharged, I was approached by her husband's attorney. He wanted me to be an expert witness in another case ... they'd been so impressed with my workup on Carla. I asked what had happened. That's when I found out she'd lost nearly all her parental rights. They left her with weekly supervised visits. So let's just say that I'm not one of her favorite people. I'd love to not have anything to do with her.'

'Barrett, if this were any other case I'd say recuse yourself. The problem is, as director of the clinic, you're the buck-stops-here woman. This case is too big, too important to risk with someone else. If this goes south, it'll open the floodgates for thousands of copycat suits.'

'I know,' Barrett said. 'Every violent criminal will try their damnedest to become mentally ill.'

'You know, in principle I agree with a lot of what Phelps is trying to do. I just wish she wouldn't try to make her point with Glash. There was one phrase in an article of hers that jarred the hell out of me. Something like "no advance in civil rights comes without a price". She was making comparisons to the suffragettes and then to the civil rights movement of the Sixties. I think the quote was "there are always casualties in the fight for freedom; freedom is never free".'

'I read that,' she said. 'But we can't see it play out with Richard Glash. Have you ever seen his drawings and paintings?'

'Yes,' he said softly.

'I Googled his name. I found sketches and

drawings of his for sale, some on eBay some in galleries. They're very hot.'

'When he was a child—' Houssman stopped in mid- sentence.

'What were you going to say?'

'Not important. Barrett, I've got to get going. By all means send me the tape. I'll see if there's anything in it that will help. But whatever you do, whatever it takes, do not let them transfer Richard Glash to Croton.' He hung up abruptly.

'George? What the hell was that?' She was still holding the warm receiver. It wasn't like him; it made her anxious. She hit the intercom. 'Marla?'

'Yes, Dr Conyors?'

It was a slight annoyance that despite having told Marla – for the past four years – that it was OK to use her first name, she was still *Dr Conyors*. 'I'm going to need three sets of the Richard Glash interview tapes. Please get them copied ASAP and have a courier get a set to Dr Houssman.'

'I'll get right on it ... and Dr Conyors?'

'Yes?'

'Your sister and Detective Hobbs are getting out of the elevator.'

'Great,' she said, feeling a dull ache in her gut, 'send them in.' She hung up the phone, and put her head in her hands. 'Shit, shit, shit.'

The door opened; she didn't want to look up.

Justine Conyors, with her long dark hair

piled on her head and fixed in place with rhinestone barrettes in the shape of butter-flies, took one look at her sister and dryly commented, 'I guess none of my Rosemary jokes today.'

'Huh?' Barrett looked up at her beautiful younger sister in a summery lilac linen dress and sandals, and Ed Hobbs in jeans and a light-blue button-down shirt. Recent burn scars covered the lower right half of his face, but he was still handsome as ever in a tall, sexy-ugly way. The leather jacket over his arm was way too hot for the day, but a practical solution for his revolver.

'Don't,' Hobbs warned Justine, 'she won't find it funny.'

'Tell me what?' Barrett insisted. 'I can use anything funny.'

Justine smiled. *'Rosemary's Baby'*.

'You're sick,' Barrett said, and in spite of herself cracked a smile. 'Fabulous, I'm carry-ing the devil's child.' From anyone other than Justine, she would have been enraged – Bar-rett had been raped, and the three of them had barely escaped with their lives; Ralph had not been so lucky.

'Kind of,' Hobbs said, forcing himself to make eye contact. 'You ready?'

'Good question,' Barrett said, getting up and glancing down at her briefcase. She had a moment's pause, wondering if she should bring it along to the obstetrician's office for her vacuum aspiration ... her abortion.

'I don't think you'll need that,' Justine offer-

33

ed, knowing that now she needed to be the strong one for her older sister. 'Unless you're planning to get a bit of work done while you're in the stirrups.'

Barrett nodded, and let them lead her to the door; Hobbs on her left and Justine on her right. *Why does this feel like I'm being led to the gallows?*

As they passed Marla, Justine tried to keep things light, knowing how difficult this decision had been for Barrett. 'I love your new furniture,' she commented, having helped Barrett pick out the light wood office suite with its Asian feel and rough-textured upholstery.

'Nice carpet, too,' Ed added, keeping her moving forward, his thoughts a mixture of anxiety and dread. *What if she didn't go through with this? What then?* Ed snuck glances at Barrett. His feelings for her ran too deep for 'let's just be friends'. He'd fallen hard, like a teenage boy with his first bad crush. It wasn't a little in love, it was the whole damn thing, and up until three months ago, before all of the badness happened, he'd hoped the feeling was mutual. There'd even been one hell of a kiss. But that was old news, not just three months. He'd replayed that kiss a thousand times, her soft lips, her hair silky in his hands, the warmth of her skin, the press of her body against his. In that moment he could have pushed for more; he hadn't. Her husband had still been alive; she'd been angry and vulnerable. In hindsight he wondered if the kiss had more to do with getting back at her unfaithful husband than her true feelings for him.

The elevator doors closed, and Barrett turned to Hobbs. He felt her gaze, and blushed – not that anyone could notice under the angry scar tissue that had landed him the precinct-house nickname of the Batman villain Two Face. 'You OK?' she asked.

'Not great, how about you?' he said, daring to look deep into her gray-blue eyes.

'I just want this over.'

'Praise Jesus!' Justine added, aware of the tension between Hobbs and her sister. As a surgeon, just out of training, Justine took a professional's stance, looking at his scars. They'd done a good job with the skin grafts, and they still looked bad. They'd fade with time, but kids would always look up, and grab their mothers' hands tighter. People would stare, then look away and whisper. After 9/11, even though she'd only been a surgical intern, she'd worked on dozens of burn cases. She knew it wasn't just the physical scars that stayed, but the emotional ones that left burn victims trapped inside their homes, not daring to risk the scrutiny, the whispers and the repulsion. She liked Hobbs, and nothing would make her happier than to see Barrett and him hook up. But unlike Hobbs, who wore his scars on the outside, she knew that emotionally Barrett was skating close to the edge. She'd asked her sister what she felt for the detective. 'I love him,' Barrett had told her, 'like a friend. I thought there might be more. Now, I don't know.' Barrett knew that Hobbs's feelings ran deep, and she didn't want to hurt a man she cared about so deeply, a man who'd risked his life for her.

The elevator landed with a thud. The doors clanged open. As they walked through the lobby, half a dozen forensic psychiatrist trainees and social workers greeted Barrett. She mumbled bland responses, pulled on a pair of dark shades and dove through the revolving glass door.

Hobbs and Justine followed, as Barrett hailed a cab on the corner of 2nd Avenue and 34th Street. She and Justine got in the back and Hobbs sat next to the driver.

Justine held her sister's hand.

Barrett looked at her and at the back of Hobbs's head. Her thoughts careened off, glad that Justine and Hobbs were here to support her, and kind of wishing they'd just leave her alone. 'Thanks for coming,' she whispered.

'Of course.'

'And you haven't breathed a word to Mom,' Barrett said, looking her sister in the eye.

'No. Not a thing, although considering what she's been through, she'd be able to handle this.'

'I know,' Barrett said, thinking of their mother, Ruth. 'I just don't think she should have to. I just want this day to be over. I want to be through this. I want to...' her voice trailed off.

'What?' Justine asked.

'I don't know.' She tried to smile. 'I want to go away. Somewhere with a beach and an endless stream of alcoholic beverages.'

'If you want company,' Hobbs offered.

'Thanks, Ed,' she said, uneasy with his romantic hints. 'The way I've been feeling I need to be on that beach all by myself.'

'So who's bringing the drinks?' Justine asked.

'A robot,' Barrett answered. A cell phone rang.

'It's mine,' Barrett said, pulling it out of her over-sized black pocketbook. 'Yes?'

'Barrett?' It was Felicia Morgan, medical director of Croton Forensic – New York State's largest high-security facility for the criminally insane.

'What's up?'

'Something bad and I need you to drop whatever it is you're doing and get up here. I just got a call from the commissioner's office that the court has issued an end-of-the-business-day ultimatum on the *Tessavian et al v. The State of New York* consent decree.'

Barrett shuddered and immediately thought of Richard Glash. 'What's the ultimatum?'

'Worst-case scenario,' Felicia said. 'If the combined Departments of Corrections and Mental Health are unable to put in place comprehensive treatment plans for the four inmates by the end of the business day today, the judge has ordered that they are all to be transferred to Croton by eight o'clock tomorrow morning. Can you be here within the hour? You're the only who's evaluated all four of them, and if we have a chance in hell, we're going to need you to draft the treatment plans. This is a nightmare. You can come, can't you?'

Barrett saw the four-story, white-faced office building of her gynecologist come into view. She could feel the baby – Jimmy Martin's baby – growing inside of her. She wanted this to be over, didn't she? 'I'll be there,' she told Felicia.

'Thank God. I have an awful feeling about this, Barrett. Nothing has gone right with this case. I just know they're going to end up here.'

'I hope you're wrong,' Barrett said, and hung up. She looked at her sister, who'd overheard.

'You've got to be kidding?' Justine said.

'What's going on?' Hobbs asked, twisting around.

'No choice,' Barrett said. 'I have to postpone.'

'Are you crazy?' he blurted. 'You can't be serious.'

'Barrett,' Justine added, 'whatever it is they can do without you for a few hours.'

'It's a matter of public safety,' Barrett said, picturing Richard Glash and how he'd nearly killed five guards. She told the cab driver to take her to her condo on West 27th. 'I have to go to Croton.'

'Barrett, what's going on?' Hobbs asked.

'I can't go into details, but it's dead serious

and I don't have a choice.'

Hobbs looked her in the eye. 'You have a choice, Barrett. You always have a choice.'

She glanced at Justine. There was so much she wanted to say, and so much that she didn't want to put in words – because her sister wouldn't understand. Like the sudden wave of relief that fell over her as the cab pulled away from the clinic. The baby was still inside her; still safe, still alive. Jimmy Martin's baby ... her baby. Tears welled; she looked away from Hobbs and from her sister's worried face. But now she needed to focus on Richard Glash, to get to Croton and to not think about the baby, or her murdered husband or that having just turned thirty-three, this life was not the one she had planned for.

The cab pulled up to the corner by her building. 'I'll get out here,' she said, not wanting to look at either Hobbs or Justine. 'I'll call you,' she said, grabbing her pocketbook and automatically reaching for her briefcase, only to remember that Justine had told her to leave it.

'Call me tonight,' Justine said. 'We have to talk.'

'Sure,' Barrett said, wanting to get away. 'It's fine. I'm fine.'

'No, you're not,' Justine said, following Barrett out of the cab. 'Come here.'

'What?' Barrett said, ready to bolt down to the garage where she kept her Saab.

Justine grabbed her sister and hugged her

39

tight. She whispered in her ear, 'I love you, Barrett. We're going to get through this.'

Emotions vibrated through Barrett as she hugged her sister back and held on. They'd been through so much over the years. She hated that she was holding things back from Justine. But that had always been the arrangement; Barrett was the strong one, always doing the right thing for others. Turning down a Juilliard piano scholarship to go to medical school, or doing whatever it took to keep her marriage together despite Ralph's infidelities. Or like now, canceling her abortion to help out at Croton. 'I love you, too,' she told Justine. 'I've got to go.' And she walked fast down to the garage. She knew that she was doing the right thing – public safety over personal matters. So why, she wondered, as she pulled out her car keys, did this feel like she was running away?

Three

Carla Phelps ran a hand through her artfully spiked hair as she sized up Dr Nehru Bai, the young psychiatrist seated across from her at the inpatient conference-room table at Bellevue's locked ward. She weighed his every word as he laid out his case to the silver-haired probate judge as to why Marion Caldwell – her client – needed to be committed to a state hospital for long-term treatment.

'She's floridly psychotic,' he said, speaking fast with traces of a British public-school accent, 'with both auditory and visual hallucinations. She was admitted after she stopped taking her antipsychotic medication and was noted to have a deterioration in her overall functioning, most notably her hygiene. This is her fifth such presentation in just the last nine months. She's bouncing from hospital to hospital and needs a longer admission in a state facility to achieve stability.'

Carla bristled at his cockiness, at how he talked about his patient, not even acknowledging her presence. To him Marion was something other than human, not a real woman – certainly not entitled to her rights. Her green eyes sparkled as she thought about how to rip him – and his case – to shreds. To her right sat – or rather, fidgeted – Marion, a forty-nine-year-old woman with a disheveled mass of steel-gray hair, dressed in a hospital gown and bathrobe. She carried a diagnosis of schizophrenia and had spent most of her life in either a state hospital or a group home. She wanted to be discharged, didn't want to take the pills that made her drool and feel sedated and she most definitely did not want to be shipped back to the state hospital.

At the table on her left sat Lucinda Peters, Carla's latest pretty young legal intern who would spend a year with her learning to advocate for people with serious mental illnesses. Completing the inpatient commitment hearing were the probate judge – Selby Blake – the patient's sister – Beatrice Coles – and the hospital's attorney – Sam Dunne.

Carla waited for a pause in the arrogant young doctor's dissertation, and then attacked. 'So, Dr Bai, if I understand you correctly you believe that my client, who represents no acute danger to herself or anyone else, should be involuntarily committed to a long-term state hospital. Is that correct?'

The just-out-of-training psychiatrist swallowed hard. She knew this was only his second commitment hearing and he'd been warned about Carla. 'She can't take care of herself,' he answered.

'Based on what evidence?' Carla shot back.

The hospital attorney and judge both turned to face Dr Bai.

'She'd stopped taking her medications,' he replied.

'So does one-quarter of the American population,' Carla answered. 'Does that mean we lock up everyone who stops their anti-biotics too soon? Or in your profession, as I'm sure you're aware, over fifty percent of prescriptions will not be taken as prescribed. Should we lock up fifty percent of your patients? Is that what you'd like us to do?'

'She wasn't taking care of herself in other ways,' he said, casting desperate looks toward the hospital's attorney. 'And she's psychotic.'

'I hear voices,' Marion said, having been coached by Carla. 'I've always heard voices. Sometimes I see things that other people can't see. I've never tried to kill myself, and I would certainly never hurt anyone. God punishes sinners.' She stared intently at the psychiatrist. 'He knows everything that's bad. He keeps track. He watches me, and makes certain I don't do bad things.'

'Marion,' Carla interjected, knowing not to let her client get started on a rant, 'how much money do you receive a month?'

'Five hundred eighty-four dollars and twenty-seven cents.'

'That's right,' Carla said. 'And tell me, and the judge, how you manage to pay all of your bills with that small amount of money.'

Carla went on asking Marion a series of questions that made it clear that despite being psychotic, she could in fact take care of herself.

Carla then turned to the judge and the hospital's attorney. 'I am petitioning the court that not only should my client not be committed, but that she be allowed to leave here immediately. She is not imminently dangerous to herself or to anyone else and she is able to provide the rudiments of self care, as you've just heard.'

Marion's sister, a neatly dressed woman in her late fifties with bleached and permed hair, half rose from her chair. 'My sister is sick! She needs to be in a hospital. You need to keep her. You need to make her take her medications. You don't know what she's like when she's out and off her medications. She'll call me at three in the morning, asking me for money, screaming at me. You can't do this!'

Carla looked across at the judge and cocked an eyebrow. 'Here's the deal,' she said, turning her gaze to the hospital's attorney. 'If Ms Caldwell is not released this afternoon, I will file a wrongful imprisonment suit against the hospital first thing in the morning. Yes, she's psychotic and yes she probably won't take her medications – that in and of itself is not enough to keep her against her will, even under Kendra's Law. By keeping her you're infringing on her constitutional rights. Essentially, Dr Bai' – she fixed the nervous young psychiatrist in a withering gaze – 'you will find yourself named in a lawsuit that will drag on for years. You're holding a human being against their will. You're using your power and authority as a psychiatrist to infringe on

44

Ms Caldwell's basic rights. You've locked her up and coerced her into taking medications that are harmful to her body and that she doesn't want to take.'

'But she's sick!' Bai stammered weakly.

'Any further arguments?' the judge asked.

There was silence around the table. 'Good, if everyone would clear the room, I'd like a few minutes alone with the patient.'

Carla, during the break, walked with Lucinda through the inpatient unit. 'I hate these places,' Carla muttered as she stared through the wire-meshed window that faced the river.

'It's so unfair,' Lucinda agreed, trying to keep pace with her mentor, while not wanting to appear skittish around the patients – most of them in hospital gowns.

'I'd just like to wipe that smug look off that psychiatrist. Who the hell does he think he is? All of them playing God. Locking people away for years without a trial. They should all spend a few months in one of these places. Let them know what it feels like.'

'A taste of their own medicine,' Lucinda remarked, brushing a strand of silky blonde hair off her forehead.

Carla realized her usually serious intern had made a joke. This one has possibilities, she thought, but hesitated about disclosing any of her own history. There was a risk in revealing her manic depression, the three times she'd been locked up in a psyche ward just like this one. Look what it had done to her marriage – although in hindsight she thought Bill had

45

used her illness as a way to get rid of a pushy wife who'd become an embarrassment. At parties and law firm retreats where he'd flit from partner to partner like some ass-licking bumblebee, she'd never played the docile attorney's wife. Early in their five-year marriage she knew he'd never make partner. She knew she was the better attorney; she would be the one to go places ... or so she'd thought.

She took stock of Lucinda, from her serious navy skirt suit to the recently planted emerald-cut diamond that sparkled on her ring finger. 'Does anyone in your family suffer from mental illness?' she asked.

Lucinda looked away. 'My dad.' She didn't offer anything further.

'Has he ever been hospitalized?'

'He's dead ... shot himself.'

'I'm sorry,' Carla said, struck at how each of the interns she'd worked with over the past three years had their own stories of mental illness – just as she did. 'You know I have bipolar disorder,' Carla said.

'Yes.'

'Great, so much for confidentiality.' Carla chuckled. 'I know that people talk.'

'They do.'

'What do they say?'

'That you're driven. That you're determined to make a change. That you want to make things better and that you really care about our clients.'

'Stop blowing smoke up my skirt,' Carla said. 'What do they say that you don't want to repeat?'

Lucinda was about to answer when a heavy-set nurse in a pink uniform told them the judge was ready.

They reassembled around the table, and the judge solemnly told Marion, 'Ms Caldwell, you're free to leave the hospital at any time. Should you wish to remain that is also your choice.'

The young psychiatrist stammered, 'But she's psychotic. You can't let her go!'

Before the hospital's attorney could intercede the judge angrily responded. 'It's as Ms Phelps has said – your patient is psychotic and she probably won't take her medications; in fact she does not believe there is anything wrong with her. But she's not hurting anyone, including herself. Just because somebody's idea of reality differs from yours doesn't mean you can lock them away. Do you understand that, Dr Bai?'

Chastised, the psychiatrist nodded, as Marion, grinning widely, shook Carla's hand and then Lucinda's. 'Thank you so much,' Marion said, not letting go of Lucinda's slender hand, unbridled joy on her face, like a game-show contestant who'd just hit the jackpot. 'I had such a wonderful time with the judge; he's such a lovely man. You're both such lovely women; I hope you're not lesbians, because God hates fornicators. And he especially hates lesbians.'

'You're very welcome,' Carla told her. 'I'd recommend you ask the nurses to get you your clothes and get out of here as quickly as possible.'

'Yes,' Marion said, as Carla's cell rang. 'I've got so much work to do. God's work, in mysterious ways.'

As her client strode triumphantly to the nurses' station, to demand her clothing and personals, Carla answered.

Lucinda listened in.

'*Too* fabulous!' Carla said, and then noted the time on the LED readout of her cell phone. 'But we can't assume anything, we have until four thirty this afternoon to insure that nothing goes wrong – that's five and half hours. They're going to try to pull something together at the last minute. I can be back at the office in fifteen minutes. I want everyone in the conference room when I get there. We're right at the gate; it's just going to take a little more work to bust it open. I want everyone primed and ready to pull out all the stops. This is it. I am so fucking excited!' She clicked her phone closed.

'What's happening?' Lucinda asked.

'Judge Garrett is not happy.' Carla's grin was infectious.

'And?' Lucinda asked, watching her boss, and smiling herself.

'Corrections and Mental Health have until the end of the business day to comply with the consent decree.'

'And if they can't?' Lucinda asked.

'No doubt about it,' Carla said, 'they're not going to, and come tomorrow morning all

48

four of them will get transferred to a forensic hospital, but that's just the beginning.'

'How do you know they won't come up with something? They've managed to stall things this far.'

'It wasn't them,' Carla chuckled. 'Come, Lucinda, it's time to watch and learn.' They walked to the outer door of the inpatient unit. Carla looked back as the clerk pressed the release button for the lock. In the distance she saw Marion, who had rapidly dressed in two shirts, a stained plaid wool skirt and a dark overcoat. She was waving. Carla smiled and waved back.

'God hates lesbians!' Marion shouted, still smiling and waving.

'Oi, that one needs to get out of here fast,' Carla commented, as she opened the door. 'OK,' she said, needing to strategize and deciding that Lucinda could be trusted. 'This is how things work ... You have two bureaucratic state agencies – Mental Health and Corrections – that need to construct and implement complex plans for each of the prisoners by the end of the workday today. Aren't you curious as to why over the past two years they haven't been able to accomplish this?'

Lucinda stopped at the stairwell entrance. She had a perplexed expression. 'Yeah. That doesn't seem like such a hard thing. I'd just assumed they weren't taking things seriously. But that's not it, is it?'

'No,' Carla said, as she opened the stairwell door. 'Let me teach you about state government, and how you can bring everything to a dead stop. You start with a call to a union representative, preferably someone well connected and high up. On the Mental Health side of the field, let them know that very dangerous prisoners are being transferred to their facility. Prisoners that they are not equipped or trained to manage; prisoners that will invariably cause staff injuries, or worse. I think I used the phrase "people will get hurt; it's just a matter of time". On the Corrections side, I tell them, confidentially of course, that this is just the start of a massive shift from Corrections to Mental Health, so massive in fact that it is part of an administrative plan to eliminate over a thousand state positions in the Department of Corrections.'

As they got into the elevator Lucinda seemed perplexed. 'Is it? I wasn't aware of any of this...'

Carla threw back her head and laughed. 'I made it all up ... and for all I know it could be entirely true. What it did was start simultaneous rounds of grievances in the two agencies. Workers and their families were given instruction by their union to get their state representatives involved and ... that's step one.'

'There's more? This is amazing. Is this legal?'

'Of course it is ... just don't get caught. Next comes the importance of friends and knowing how to bury and "lose" paperwork. Because the consent decree is so high profile

50

you have the top brass in both agencies wanting to be involved. That means lots of people signing off on every document. Stuff gets lost, and because it's state government, no one thinks twice about the delays and the mistakes.'

'That's really devious,' Lucinda said, as they pushed through the revolving door in the hospital lobby.

'Not at all,' Carla remarked, as she felt the sweltering August sun on her face. She took a deep breath, and not even the smell of the hospital's dumpsters baking in the heat could dampen the glorious feeling of being on the cusp of something important – three years of hard work about to come to fruition. 'Lucinda, it's called doing what works.'

Four

Richard Glash gazes out the back of the air-conditioned Department of Corrections wagon as it transports him from the maximum security Green Haven Correctional Facility in Stormville to Croton State Forensic Hospital. It's early Tuesday morning. Handcuffed and shackled, an armed Marshal sits next to him; a second one drives and can be glimpsed through steel mesh. They wear name tags, but Glash labels them 'A' and 'B'. He calculates the amount of time they've been on the road; he ticks off seconds and runs equations that let him know how much remains of the thirty-minute drive. He visualizes a digital clock with glowing numbers ticking down – *twenty-two minutes, thirteen seconds*.

He enjoys the streaming sensations, and knows that his brain is superior to his guards', whose thoughts are likely tuned in to their breakfast or some trivial joke from last night's late show.

Glash realizes that he has more in common with computers than with other humans. He thinks of himself as a machine that can maintain several functions at the same time, as he does now.

'A' attempts to strike up a conversation. 'You got a beautiful day for the drive,' he remarks.

Glash never stops the running calculations of time remaining – *eighteen minutes, twenty seconds.* 'Yes,' he answers dully, 'the weather is lovely.'

'A' regales Glash about his weekend's camping expedition at a state park near the Ashokan Reservoir. 'God's country,' he says, 'unspoiled and no one around for miles.'

Glash monitors the conversation, and allows his mouth to answer with an occasional rejoinder. 'Uhuh ... interesting ... really? ... That's great.'

Like watching several TV monitors at the same time, Glash observes the moment, and where it fits into the story of his own life. He replays scenes that he's painted, carefully keeping them in their proper order, like photos in an album, preserving the details. He is four years old and enters a basement storage room of the family's candy business in the Lower East Side of Manhattan. His father – Peter – stands over the battered remains of his mother – Dorothea. The side of her head has been badly damaged; he can see bits of brain tissue through her shattered skull. Father holds an eight-pound steel hammer that he uses to drive the iron wedge that pries apart the wooden candy crates. The hammer is red with old paint and his mother's fresh blood. The colors are different, Richard observes, yet they are both still called red – *fifteen minutes, forty-one seconds*. It was Father's only murder, a deed that Richard surpassed a mere seven days after his eighteenth birthday. He catches himself jumping forward in time; it's important to keep the story in order.

'Won't be much longer,' 'A' speculates.

'No,' Glash answers – *twelve-minutes, zero seconds*.

He lets the scene shift. His mother now dead, his father goes to prison and four-year-old Richard becomes a ward of the state. He flips through the faces of the Youth Services social workers, the case managers and the judges. He sees them alive with their smiles and their promises of a new home with loving parents. He puts names to each of the perfectly remembered faces – *nine minutes, fourteen seconds*. He keeps them on a list, those he's killed and those yet to be killed. He chides himself for again skipping ahead in the sequence – *six minutes, nineteen seconds*.

They placed him with a family – a mother, a father and two older sisters. He starts to deepen his breathing.

'You feeling OK?' 'A' asks.

'Yes.' And he quietly pumps his breath fast and deep, while taking inventory of 'A': his clothing, his firearm, his reach, his weight. 'B' has unknown variables, yet Glash extrapolates similarities – both armed and dressed alike, therefore with a high certainty the firearms will be the same and in similar holsters.

'B' is taller, estimated age of forty-four; 'A' is five-foot-ten, estimated age of twenty-six and a weight of 204 pounds – *three minutes, fifty-eight seconds*.

Glash moves to the next picture. He is four and a half, watching a movie on the television set in the living room of his foster family. It's a Western starring Gary Cooper – a famous actor – *two minutes, ten seconds*. Indians surround a wagon train and attack. They wave tomahawks in the air. They scalp and kill – *one minute, thirty-two seconds*.

He is four and a half years old in his foster family's kitchen. No tomahawk in the knife drawer. He picks up a meat cleaver close in size and shape. But no painted handle with feathers and beads; it's black with two steel rivets that hold the big blade in place. He takes it from the drawer and leaves the apartment – *forty-two seconds*. He rings the buzzer on the next-door apartment; it's where Mary lives – she is three and has long blonde hair. She is three inches shorter than he is – she is not famous – *twelve seconds*. She opens the door because she knows it's him. Since moving in with his foster family, he and Mary have played together every day.

The Correction's wagon turns, a dark-clad motorcyclist on a vintage R series BMW zooms past in the opposite direction, gravel pings against the sides of the van. Glash, who has been hyperventilating for six minutes, begins to twitch. His arms and legs start to jump, seemingly uncontrollably. His lids flutter and his eyes roll back.

'A' calls out to 'B': 'Shit! He's having a seizure.'

'B' shouts back, 'We're almost there, hold on.'

Glash falls back hard as the van lurches forward. His movements grow more violent. 'A' shouts, 'He's hurting himself. Stop the van!'

The vehicle skids to a sudden halt. Glash has fallen to the floor; he is shaking violently, his legs and arms spasm angrily against his shackles. He's broken the skin on his wrists, blood oozes around the chains.

'A' leans over him to try and prevent his head from being injured.

Glash's manacled arms reach up. They quickly snake the chain around 'A''s neck and snap it with a bone-cracking certainty as 'B' unlocks the rear door. Glash liberates 'A''s firearm – a Smith & Wesson. He shoots 'B' a single time in the head. Using his mouth to steady the gun he shoots off his handcuffs, noting the sharp sting of the powder burn on his hands and the smell of burned flesh. He does not stop, as he fires two more shots to break the chains that restrain his legs. He jumps out of the back of the van. The air is warm, the humidity is low, the sky is a light cerulean blue and dotted with cumulus clouds. His feet are on the gravel driveway. Croton Forensic Hospital, where he spent two months being evaluated after his murders, is to his back; the visitor parking lot is in front of him. He searches in the distance and spots the black pickup truck. He then sees Carla Phelps and Lucinda Peters. He labels them 'A' and 'B'.

He quickly reaches down and liberates guard 'B''s firearm – he was correct; it is a similar, but older, Smith & Wesson – and with a gun in each hand, like Gary Cooper, he races toward his new 'A' and 'B'.

Five

It's 8 a.m. and Barrett hasn't moved from the Steinway D Grand in the deserted administrative building across from Croton, with its high chain-link fences topped with razor wire and dotted with guard towers – in reality looking far more like a prison than a hospital. She's not slept and still wears the blue button-down shirt, chinos and navy blazer she put on yesterday – a more casual outfit than usual, something suitable for terminating a pregnancy. For the last three and a half hours she has tried to block out everyone and everything by retreating into her oldest and greatest passion – music. It's her road not taken, the full Juilliard scholarship turned in for something more practical, a pre-medical degree, four years of med school, a year's internship, three years' psychiatric residency and a final year in forensics. Music has always been her passion, but sometimes – as her beloved piano teacher, Sophie, a holocaust survivor, would remind her – we make sacrifices for those we love.

It had been a day and night from hell. Yesterday, nothing they did could satisfy Judge Garrett. Faxed treatment plans for each of the prisoners sent to his office had been lost, important documents and prior evaluations had vanished from files. Felicia's secretary, who swore that a courier had been sent with hard copies of the treatment plans, realized – too late in the day – that they'd been sent to the wrong address. It seemed the harder she and Dr Morgan had worked, the farther they fell behind. At four thirty Judge Garrett had ordered a conference call with the commissioners of Mental Health and Corrections. Barrett and Felicia had listened in, saying nothing, as the judge hurled insults at the two officials, accusing them of incompetence and of interfering with the court. Net result, all four prisoners were to be transferred – immediately – with the judge's added warning that if adequate treatment was not provided, he'd go the next step and had threatened release.

'Please don't go,' Felicia had begged, as the two women, who'd been through training together, grappled with the magnitude of what needed to be done to prepare for the prisoners – a logistical nightmare. Felicia had worked through the night, freeing up four high-security rooms, moving patients, arguing with security guards, aides and enraged nurses who had been mandated to do doubles. When Barrett had last seen her rail-thin friend at 2 a.m. the black-clad director had joked, 'I get the prize – four grievances in eight hours.'

As Felicia had plowed through the nuts and

bolts of clearing rooms and arranging staff, Barrett oversaw the arrivals, doing the bulk of the intake evaluations herself.

Frustrated, frightened and tired, she couldn't help but think about the next to arrive – Glash. She pounded the keys with a Rachmaninoff *Prelude*. Her left hand easily negotiated the octave-and-a-half chords, her right drawing a haunting theme that filled the deserted auditorium.

As she flew through the opening passages she felt a hollowness left by her late-night interview with Jane Saunders. As Barrett had done the prosecution's expert evaluation of Jane, it was brief. Since her arrest and conviction three years ago Jane had retreated into a thick psychosis. She refused all medications, and with Carla Phelps advocating for her right to do that, there was little treatment that could help. Barrett had asked her if she ever thought about the children she had killed.

Jane had given her a wide-eyed stare from under her stringy mass of mousy hair. 'They're with Jesus. They're angels.'

'Do you see them?' Barrett had asked.

'Yes.' And Jane had giggled.

'What's so funny?'

'The children. They make me laugh,' Jane had said, her tone conversational. 'They're always playing tricks and getting into all sorts of trouble.'

'Are they here now?' Barrett had asked.

'They're all around me. They float. They're

angels. They're with—' and she'd stared at a spot in the corner of the room and started to sing *Jesus loves me! This I know...*' It was a sweet clear soprano, on pitch, and it had sent chills through Barrett. Gooseflesh had prickled and she could almost sense Jane's children circling the room.

Barrett had kept the interview short, it was more a formality to get Jane settled and to insure there was some semblance of treatment in place. She'd ordered medications – a tranquilizer for the hallucinations and a sedative to help her sleep at night. She'd refused both. She'd also written for therapy, which in Jane's current state would be ineffective. Truth was, Barrett reflected, as her fingers dipped into a tone poem by Erik Satie, Jane didn't want to leave her psychosis. She'd killed her children, and to have to face that truth ... too awful, better to stay crazy and believe they're angels.

With a start she realized that the piece she was now playing had been one of Ralph's favorites. She pictured him and the horrible day she'd gone to the morgue to identify him. It had been explained, at first, as a random hit-and-run – struck by a cab as he left a rehearsal. Later she'd learned that the only man she'd ever truly loved had been murdered by Jimmy Martin – her patient. Ralph had betrayed her, been unfaithful and more than once. Yet, even as their marriage was falling apart he could make her tremble with his touch. As angry as she'd been, she had still loved him.

Her cell phone rang; its musical clang cut through the music. She lifted her hands from the keyboard. It rang again. Before looking at the LED she knew who it would be. 'Hello, Justine,' she said.

'Hey sis, where are you?'

'Still at Croton.'

'Can't you go home?'

'Soon. Where are you?'

'At the hospital. Just finished an appendectomy on a four-year-old and waiting for them to set up the room for a bone-marrow biopsy. But say the word and I can get someone to cover and we can pop you right back over to Pat Harrison's office. She said she'd squeeze you in anytime.'

'I know ... I was just thinking about Ralph. This baby should have been his ... ours.'

'I know,' Justine said, 'but it's not, and no amount of wishing is going to change that. Barrett, we've got to get past this. You can't be thinking about having this kid.'

'I know.'

'So when can you get out of there?'

'Two more evaluations. I did the two women last night. I've got the guys today.'

'You know it's in the paper,' Justine said.

'No surprise. They're all high profile and the fact that they're getting transferred to a forensic hospital is a huge shot over the bow. This could open up the flood gates for every convicted felon to fake their way into a hospital.'

'It's not my business,' Justine said, 'but they seem pretty crazy to me. That one who killed her kids, the other one who drowned Melanie Coo – what's her name?'

'Allison Tessavian.'

'She thought she was married to Justin Green, right?'

'You know I can't.' Although she would have liked to tell Justine about the bizarre late-night evaluation with the platinum-blonde Allison, who was clownishly made-up with blue eye shadow and thick, pancake-size circles of rouge that totally covered her cheeks. Allison had rambled on about Justin Green: 'We have a mansion bigger than anything you can imagine. I have a white Rolls-Royce Corniche and four dogs – Mandy, Candy, Randy and Butterscotch. Justin just spoils me rotten. He's always bringing me presents and makeup and my jewelry costs more than you'll make in your entire life.' When Barrett had pressed for details about how she had drugged, kidnapped and then drowned Mr Green's real-life girlfriend – Melanie Coo – she'd refused to answer, merely stating, 'There's always trash throwing themselves at my baby. And you know what we Southern girls do with trash ... we take it out.' But Barrett, bound by rules of confidentiality, kept it to herself.

'OK,' Justine said, 'so you can't talk about that. Shall we say I tell Dr Harrison we'll be there at four tomorrow for your ... procedure?'

Barrett sighed; Justine was not going to let up.

'Come on, Barrett. If we don't get this done Mom will soon suspect. You don't want that, do you?'

'No.' Barrett pictured her mother, and wondered what she'd say if she knew. 'OK, tell Pat four. I'll be there ... Justine?'

'What?'

'Weird question ... if this were Mom, what would she do?'

'That's a tough one,' Justine said. Their childhood escape from rural Georgia was a family legend. 'And why are you asking?'

'I don't know. I just think how important we were – *are* – to her. She gave up everything, packed us in the car and just drove away. Do you ever think how our lives might have been if we'd stayed in Georgia?'

'Sometimes,' Justine admitted. 'But what little I remember of our father, it wouldn't have been good. Someone might have wound up dead – probably Mom. You remember the night he came and tried to take us back?'

'I have nightmares about it,' Barrett said, 'where he's banging on the door. Sophie and Max downstairs screaming up.'

Justine chuckled and imitated Sophie's Polish accent: 'Go away! Leave them alone. I call police. I call police!'

'Thank God she did,' Barrett added.

'That's about the only clear memory I have of him,' Justine said. 'You were older – do you remember anything good about him?'

'Not much, except being frightened all the time. Hiding in my bedroom, hearing him shouting ... knowing that he was hitting her. She was so young. She got married at sixteen. He was thirty-one. And she did just what her own mother had done: married young to a man who beat her and ... why am I thinking about all of this?'

'I don't know, Barrett. But I'm worried. Some part of you wants to keep this baby. And I don't believe in coincidences. You had an appointment yesterday and you decided not to keep it.'

'I couldn't,' Barrett said, but part of her knew that Justine had a point.

'Uh-uh ... so we'll keep it tomorrow?'

'Four o'clock.'

'Barrett, this is totally the right thing. I'll see you then. Love you.'

'I love you too.'

Barrett stared down at the keyboard as she felt a surge of panic rise. She put her hands to her face to slow her breathing.

It almost worked.

A siren blared. Barrett's head shot up. She glanced at the LED readout on her cell. Two minutes after eight. Two minutes after Richard Glash was scheduled to arrive.

She sprinted toward the front entrance, and pushed her shoulder into the heavy double door. She blinked against the hazy early morning sun and scanned the couple hundred yards to the squat brick Croton facility. Just outside its perimeter she spotted the

Correction Department's transport van directly in front of her. Her heart jumped when she saw the downed guard at the back of the van and the open door. 'Shit!' She looked toward the Croton entrance and saw a massing of security guards in their state-issue blue uniforms. But they weren't moving. She followed the general direction of their gaze and turned to the visitors' parking lot off to her right. There was a commotion by a black pickup truck. She saw the shock of Glash's dark hair, and then Carla Phelps with Glash's hand – presumably holding a gun – in the small of her back and a second revolver to the head of a long haired woman. He was forcing them into the vehicle.

'Why aren't they doing anything?' she muttered, but knew that the Croton guards weren't really cops, just entrenched state employees who measured their lives by how many more years they had to go before collecting their pension. And the van had stopped just outside Croton – she could almost hear them saying, 'Not our job.'

Barrett quickly plotted out the shortest distance to the pickup. Glash wouldn't know she was here, and sticking to the shrubs in front of the admin building she sprinted toward the lot. Moving fast on rubber-soled shoes, she couldn't ignore the incredible danger of confronting Glash. She thought about one of Hobbs's truisms: 'A dead hero is no hero at all.' She had no doubt that those two women might soon be murdered –

someone had to do something. As she cleared the edge of the parking lot she heard the truck roar to life. It must belong to Carla, she thought, although didn't she drive an Audi?

Still three cars away she wasn't prepared for the roar of the engine and the gravel spewing at her. He pulled out fast, throwing the vehicle into reverse; the tailgate was inches from her hiding spot; there was no time for thought. Barrett's reflexes, honed from her martial arts training, took over. In the split second it took for Glash to get the vehicle into drive, Barrett grabbed hold of the cold metal tailgate and vaulted into the bed of the truck. Using her arms and legs like springs she cushioned her fall, trying to make no noise. Her upper right arm landed hard on a steel bolt, ripping the flesh.

She stifled a scream. The truck's tires spun up gravel and then the vehicle shot forward and picked up speed. Barrett braced herself in the corner behind the driver and listened. She could hear the siren from Croton, but it was other sirens she was praying for. *Where the hell are the cops?* If she could have risked it she'd have looked back at Croton, to see if they were doing anything. Once Felicia knew of the escape the place would be swarming with cops – FBI, too, now that a kidnapping was involved. *Help is on the way*, she tried to tell herself. She thought of Hobbs, pulled out her cell and pressed the speed dial.

'Thank God,' she whispered as he picked up.

'Hello? Barrett?'

'Hobbs, I'm in deep trouble.'

'I can't hear you, speak up.'

'I can't,' she said, risking a raise in her voice. 'Listen, Richard Glash has escaped and taken two hostages. I'm in the back of his getaway vehicle, a late model black Ford four-by-four pickup truck. He's heading north.'

'What the hell are you doing in there? Get out!'

'I can't,' she said. 'The guards here just stood by and let it happen. No one did anything. Tell the cops to use my cell as a GPS. They've got to catch this guy. You have no idea the damage he'll cause. People are going to die.'

'Barrett,' Hobbs pleaded, 'get the hell out of there. At the first opportunity, leave your damn cell in the truck and jump.'

'Shit! Why didn't I think of that!' she said, now noticing a large, locked black toolbox, an array of neatly-tied bungee cords and three coils of blue nylon rope. Why would Carla have all of this in her truck?

'Think of it now. Does he know you're there?'

'I don't know.' She tried to hear through the steel wall that separated the bed of the truck from the cabin. 'I hope not.'

'I'm calling this in now. I'll be there as fast as I can.' He paused. 'I love you, please take care of yourself.'

Barrett strained to hear. 'What did you say?'

'No more risks.'

'I hear you.'

'And Barrett...'

'Yes?'

'Stop playing Rambo.'

Her teeth chattered. 'I'm so frightened, Hobbs.'

'I'm on my way.'

The line clicked dead. Careful to not set off the ringer, she switched the audio to vibrate, curled into a ball and prayed that help would come fast.

Six

A heady feeling coursed through Richard Glash, his body tingled and he wondered if it was what they called happiness. He felt light-headed and the two women next to him, the long-haired one who kept sobbing – pretty Lucinda – and the red-headed lawyer, reeked of fear and blood.

'Richard,' Carla half-screeched, 'you need to let us go. They'll come after us. You need to stop the truck and let us out.'

'Shut up,' he said, determined not to split his attention. 'I have two hostages. I only need one,' he lied, knowing that two hostages were perfect, an 'A' and a 'B'.

Lucinda was shaking, 'Oh God, oh God.'

Glash slammed his elbow into the side of her head. 'Shut up.' His bare flesh registered the feel of her silky hair, just like ... his head whipped around.

Lucinda recoiled. 'I'm sorry,' she whimpered.

'Blonde.' He turned back to the road and scanned everything, the smells of the women, the newly cleaned upholstery of the truck. Blue skies up ahead, the lurch of the road beneath the speeding vehicle. His brain ticked off the seconds and the miles that separated him from Croton. He wondered briefly about the other three prisoners who were to have been transferred, and ran through the names, addresses and phone numbers of everyone connected to their cases. They were all famous – Jane Saunders, Dr Clarence Albert and Allison Tessavian – high-profile killers who'd been on television shows. Entire books had been written on Jane, the most recent the bestseller by her husband that Richard had discussed with Dr Conyors.

Glash knew that the only reason books had not been devoted to him was that his career had been cut short, almost before it had begun. That would not happen again.

A cell phone rang; it played the tune *Take Me Out to the Ball Game*. It was Lucinda's.

'Give it!' Glash ordered.

The tearful young woman fished it from her pocketbook.

Glash ripped it from her hand, his finger snagging briefly on her diamond. 'That's an engagement ring,' he said, as he hurled the cell out of his window. He looked at Carla. 'Give me your phone.'

'I don't have one,' the attorney said.

'Give it, or I shoot her in the head.' He put guard A's sidearm to Lucinda's temple; he cocked the trigger. And then, still holding the gun, he began to stroke her hair with the back of his hand. 'It's pretty,' he said. 'Soft.'

'Don't! Leave her alone,' Carla shouted.

'Here.' She gave over her cell.

That too went out the window. 'They trace those,' Glash said. 'I can't be caught ... yet.' He pictured the quickest route to the first address on his list. He calculated the travel time – *twenty-two minutes*. He had to focus, but other locations and other possibilities flashed to mind. He pictured his last visit from Mary. She wore a long blonde wig, not far from the color of the woman next to him's hair. It was pretty and soft. He'd once asked Mary to take off the wig to let him see. She'd done that for him. He knew she didn't want to, and yet she had. That had been four years, two months and three days ago, and he'd thought about it daily. It gave him a squishy feeling in his stomach, and made his cock get hard. He wanted to touch the scars, to...

Another cell rang. His eyes darted to the glove compartment, but that wasn't where it had come from. His ears strained for the source; not from inside the cab, but from outside, from the back. He stared into the rear-view mirror. He could see nothing, just the top of the locked tool chest.

He searched the road up ahead – no cars in sight. He was not being followed and took a sharp left that jolted the truck off the road and on to a dirt path that led into a dense wood.

Barrett froze. She couldn't believe her cell had rung; she'd turned off the ringer. She prayed it had not been heard as she pried open the plastic cover on the back and ripped out the battery. She knew her prayer had gone unanswered as the truck bounced off the road and headed into the woods. Braced in the corner, her immediate thought was to get out fast. Hurt all over, the gash in her upper right arm had soaked through her shirt.

Hobbs was right. She was insane for doing this. If she survived she'd go into therapy and do whatever it took to stop taking these crazy risks. But that would be another day. Right now she had to get away. As the truck bounced over the dirt road she sidled on her belly toward the tailgate. She reached up, knowing that she'd be visible through the rear-view mirror, and unlatched the gate. She tried to push it down with her hand; it wouldn't budge. Quickly, she turned over and kicked at it with both feet. It popped down, and trying not to think about the danger, she tucked and rolled out, landing hard on the rocky ground. The breath was knocked out of her, and searing pains shot to her brain from her right shoulder, her right hip and something bad with her knee. A wave of nausea rose from her belly. *At least you didn't hit your head.* She listened for the truck and when she couldn't hear it a sickening realization dawned. She glanced up and saw it had stopped not thirty feet away.

Glash was moving fast, but not toward her. He'd dragged Lucinda Peters out of the cab by her hair and was ordering Carla to follow them. Lucinda started to scream and Glash cuffed her violently.

Barrett struggled to her feet, trying to get her bearings and to push past the pain. She turned to run.

'Don't, Dr Conyors. I'll shoot her in the head right now.'

His flat voice cut through her; the slim chance that she'd been undetected was gone. She also knew he wasn't making hollow threats. She stopped, and turned on her throbbing knee, every ounce of her being telling her to run.

'Throw me your cell phone, Dr Conyors.'

Barrett unhooked her phone from her pants and tossed it to Glash. She looked at Lucinda's panicked face and at the way Glash was handling her as though she were something less than human.

'This is good news,' he said, as he crushed the cell under his prison-issue boot. 'Turn around, Dr Conyors, and lie flat on the ground. Carla, lie next to her.'

'Richard,' Carla started to plead, 'don't do this. Please don't hurt anyone. It's just going to make things worse for you.'

Glash erupted. He let go of Lucinda's hair; the young woman fell to her knees as Glash grabbed Carla, threw her to the ground and began to pistol whip her. *'Don't tell me what to do!'* he shrieked, as the attorney attempted to shield her face with her hands. But soon, a sickening blow to the head made her fall unconscious.

Barrett, realizing that he might kill them all, blocked out the pain and barreled toward him. Before he could raise the firearm and get a clear shot she rammed into his body and jammed her injured elbow into his solar plexus. It should have been a crippling blow; it wasn't. He grabbed her wrist and twisted it behind her back. His gun hand snaked around her neck in a sleeper hold. His six-foot-five frame held her immobile. She felt his arm tighten around her throat, shutting off the oxygen to her brain. She struggled and kicked, and fought the panic that told her she was about to die. She pictured her mother and Justine. *You were right, Hobbs.* And then everything grew dark.

Barrett's eyes opened to the sickening sound of gunfire – a single shot. She struggled to orient herself. She was seated upright in the truck. It had been turned around and in front of it was Glash, not ten feet away, standing over Lucinda Peters; Carla, still unconscious, was to their right. The girl wasn't moving. Barrett's hands were tied tight behind her back. Her fingers felt the hard plastic of ASP restraints. *Where the hell did he get those? Were they in Carla's truck? And what would she be doing with them?* Those thoughts disappeared when Glash turned and made eye contact with Barrett. 'Watch me,' he said. From his back pocket he took out a large, stainless steel meat cleaver.

She tried to look away. She did not want to

see this, an image he'd painted hundreds, maybe thousands of times. He looked at her; his blue eyes bore straight into hers. 'Dr Conyors, do not turn away. Do not close your eyes. Watch me. If you don't I'll kill the other one. Watch me!'

'No, Richard.'

'It's already dead,' he explained. 'It won't feel it.'

It was a sick bargain, but the best she had. 'OK, Richard,' she said, thinking he'd probably end up killing them all. In a weird way, she understood why he wanted her to watch, as he grabbed hold of Lucinda's long blonde hair and began to do the thing he'd painted all those hundreds of times. With no emotion, he looped Lucinda's hair over his right hand and with the left proceeded to bring the cleaver down hard below her hairline.

The sound of metal on flesh and bone was like a woodcutter chopping logs, only duller and wetter. Barrett's eyes never moved but inside she felt a sense of horror, of things beyond her control.

He worked quickly. When he was done, he stared at the young woman's bare and bleeding scalp. He reached down and grabbed her left hand. He examined her engagement ring and then pried it off and dropped it into a pocket.

She watched as he walked over to the still unconscious Carla, hoisted her up and then deposited her on the seat next to Barrett. He

76

belted her in and then reached down and popped open the glove compartment. Inside, Barrett glimpsed half a dozen identical plastic cell phones. She suddenly realized that this could not be Carla's truck. He slammed the door and she watched him in the rear-view mirror as he walked away and talked on the phone. She strained to hear, his voice low and monotone. At one point she could hear dimensions and measurements. '"A" is five-foot-three, red hair that is three to four inches over her forehead and short, like a man's haircut on the back and sides. Green eyes. Her shirt is white, mother-of-pearl buttons one-point-three centimeters in diameter; made by Perry Ellis...' This went on as he inventoried each item of clothing and the physical attributes of both her and Carla. He ended that call and then punched in a second number and left the phone on top of Lucinda Peters' scalped corpse.

He climbed into the cab, his shoulder brushing painfully against hers. He looked at Barrett, his breath warm on her face. 'You will remember that?' he asked.

'Yes,' she said, her mouth dry. She was barely able to speak, nearly paralyzed with fear. 'Who were you talking to, Richard?' she asked.

He looked at her. 'You'll figure it out.' He put the truck into drive and rather than heading back to the secondary road, he turned around and plunged them deeper into the woods.

'Where are we going?' Barrett asked, wondering if he'd answer, or beat her the way he'd beaten Carla ... or kill her.

'How many murders does it take to be famous?' he asked, his tone almost conversational.

'I don't think there's an actual number.'

'It's interesting, don't you think, how we both know a lot about killers?'

'Yes,' she answered.

'It's something we have in common.'

Barrett's body ached and her brain wanted to forget the horrific images she'd just been forced to witness. What was he getting at? What did he want from her? 'Yes, we have something in common. I would like to know where we're going.'

'To kill John J. Saunders,' he replied. 'Jane should have done it. I'll do it for her.'

Seven

Hobbs was on the verge of losing it. *How could this have happened?* He glared across the light-filled office at Dr Felicia Morgan, Croton's rail-thin medical director. Her phone hadn't stopped ringing; she was on it now. Dressed in black, she seemed agitated and uncertain.

'The FBI will be here within half an hour,' she said, putting down the receiver and running a hand through her short-cropped hair. Three other lines were blinking red. She blew out a slow stream of breath and glanced at Hobbs. 'One is the governor, two is my boss, the commissioner, and three is Channel Eight.'

'Go with your boss if you have to and forget the other two.' He knew she had priorities, knew that as an NYPD detective this wasn't his jurisdiction, but right now he couldn't care less. What mattered was Richard Glash kidnapping two women with Barrett in the back of his getaway vehicle over two hours ago, and as far as he could tell there wasn't a fucking thing being done about it. He cracked his neck, feeling every muscle tense in his body.

His cell rang and for a brief moment hope surged. Was it Barrett?

'Hobbs?'

It almost sounded like her. 'Hey, Justine.'

'Tell me she's OK.'

'How did you find out?' he asked, the sound of her desperation fueling his.

'I got this horrible message on my answering machine – I was in surgery so I couldn't pick up. She was whispering and she sounded really scared ... what the hell is happening?'

'Your sister,' Hobbs said, trying to keep the fury from his voice, 'decided to throw her pregnant ass into the getaway car of a psychopath who'd just taken two hostages. When did she call?'

'Just after eight.'

'Nothing since?' he asked, hopeful that there was still a chance she'd not been discovered.

'No.'

'Shit!'

'What?' Justine asked.

'It doesn't matter,' he said.

'Ed, please tell me. I'm about to lose my mind.'

'It's not good, none of this is good. I was having them use her cell phone to locate their position. It went dead twenty minutes ago. Not that far from here.' He felt a burning rage. The delay in getting them to trace the call, the minutes it took to bring the state troopers up to speed, the criminal incompetence of the Croton guards – the fifty minutes

80

it took him to drive from Manhattan, only to find the trail cold. He wanted to jump in his Crown Vic and chase after her. But where?

Justine sobbed. 'We should have pushed harder. If we'd made her have that damned abortion, none of this would have happened.'

'Sure, try getting your sister to do anything she doesn't want to.' He struggled to keep his tone light, but if Barrett had been there, he didn't know which he'd do first, throttle her or kiss her. 'Justine, I got to go. If you hear from her call me right away.'

'Promise you'll do the same.'

'You got it,' and he hung up. 'So tell me about Glash,' Hobbs said to Felicia, who'd just finished a rough call with her commissioner. Hobbs couldn't yet figure if this intense-looking woman, with her dark clothes, trendy glasses and short hair, was friend or foe.

'Barrett is pregnant?' Felicia asked, having overheard Hobbs's conversation. 'I had no idea.'

'You didn't hear it from me,' he said. 'Please tell me everything you know about Glash.'

The door opened and a frail-looking older man dressed for a cool day or a Bogart movie in trenchcoat, gray fedora, black wool pants and pressed white shirt, entered without being asked. 'I'd probably better do that.' He looked at Hobbs through thick glasses that distorted his pale eyes, like a goldfish looking out of a bowl; he took off his hat, scanned the various surfaces in the room, and placed it carefully on a stack of journals by the door. 'You must be Detective Edward Hobbs,' he said, without extending his hand. 'I'm George Houssman, I don't know if Barrett has ever mentioned me.'

'She has,' Hobbs said, wondering what the semi-retired professor was doing here.

'Good.' Houssman looked at Felicia and nodded. 'By your expression, I'm assuming he's not yet been caught?'

'No,' she said, glancing down at the flashing red lights on her phone.

'Leave that alone, then,' Houssman instructed. He looked at Hobbs. 'Have a seat, young man.'

Hobbs was about to argue, but something in the old guy's manner – authority and something maybe more vulnerable – made him pull up a metal-framed armchair.

'You have no idea,' Houssman began, not sitting, 'of how I hoped this day would never come. And now Barrett ... He'll come after me, too.' He looked out of a barred window at the grounds below. In front of Croton's main entrance yellow crime-scene tape ringed the transport vehicle that had carried Glash. The bodies of the two Marshals were only now being covered in white oilcloth bags.

'Why would he go after you?' Hobbs blurted, struggling to stay in his seat.

Houssman paused, still looking out of the window. He nodded his head. 'At least my wife is dead.'

82

'Please spit it out,' Hobbs said, not caring if he sounded rude, 'if you know anything about this Glash.'

Houssman turned and looked at Ed. There was something appraising in the way he examined the tall detective with his scarred face. 'She's like a daughter to me,' Houssman said. 'I understand your urgency, but what I have to say is something I've kept secret for nearly forty years. Now I have no choice. Richard Glash, if he's not stopped, will come after me, my two daughters and my grandchildren. He will systematically kill everyone he believes has ever done him wrong. You see, for a very brief period, Delia – my wife – and I took in Richard Glash as a foster child, with the hope of one day adopting him.'

Felicia, in awe of the esteemed pioneer in forensics, was about to speak and then stopped herself.

Houssman glanced at her. 'This is no time for niceties, Felicia. You wanted to ask why none of this is mentioned in Glash's records.'

'Yes,' she said.

'I didn't want it to be there, and this all happened long enough ago when it wasn't so difficult to eliminate an uncomfortable detail or two from a medical record. Glash's juvenile records are still sealed. On the list of things that must be done immediately is getting them and scouring them for every name and address connected with his early life. All those people, like me and my family, are in mortal danger. No more interruptions. I'll go though the facts quickly' – he looked at Hobbs – 'because the last thing you want are the reminiscences of an old man.'

'Thank you,' Hobbs said. He looked intently at Houssman, his heart bounding in his chest.

'Delia, and I couldn't have children,' he began.

Hobbs groaned to himself, sensing a long and pointless story.

'So we took in two foster children, the offspring of a woman who had killed her husband and was sentenced to serve thirty to fifty years. She had no other family, the children were young and it seemed a good option. It worked out well and a year later we adopted the two girls, our daughters – Stephanie and Alice.' Houssman caught Hobbs's eye. 'I will go fast,' he assured him. 'Our two girls were well adjusted; we'd taken them in when they were three and five. So when I came upon the case of Peter Glash and realized that this four-year-old would be a ward of the state and needed a foster family, I thought that this might be the final addition to our family. I was cocky in those days, convinced that sociopathy was far more nurture than nature. Richard was a good-looking boy, although we knew right off he was also special.'

'As in retarded?' Hobbs asked.

'Hardly, on standard IQ tests Richard scored high in the genius range. He was aloof and quiet and from the time he was old enough to hold a crayon or marker, he'd exhibited savant-like artistic abilities. His strangeness I put down to his intelligence and his early home life. I rationalized that if my wife and I pulled him from a bad environment, we could alter the course of his life for the better. I was horribly wrong, of course.'

'What happened?' Hobbs asked.

Houssman blinked three times; he grimaced, the edges of his thin lips drew up as though he'd just tasted something bad. 'My wife was sewing when Richard knocked on the Sullivan's door. Their young daughter – Richard's playmate – answered it. He attacked her. Delia, to her dying day, never recovered from the shock of that child's screams and what she found. Richard Glash had taken a meat cleaver from the kitchen and tried to remove Mary's scalp. Later, we'd discover that his inspiration had been a Western. It looked interesting to him, so he wanted to try it. It's a miracle he didn't succeed in killing that little girl. Delia got slashed trying to pull him off. She described it like he was some sort of animal.'

'You couldn't have known,' Felicia said.

Houssman glanced at her; his jaw was tight. 'Of course not, and then again ... I had evaluated his father. I should have been more careful.'

'What was the father like?' Hobbs asked, realizing that in a few seconds Houssman had given him more useful information than anyone else in the past two hours.

85

'Not what I'd expected,' Houssman continued, pleased that Hobbs was asking the right questions. 'I went into his evaluation believing it to be a straightforward crime of passion. An older husband discovers his younger wife has been cheating and in a fit of fury bludgeons her to death. His attorney decides that it has the makings of a not-guilty-by-reason-of-mental-defect plea and the case gets sent my way for an expert opinion.'

'And?' Hobbs prompted, wanting to speed the old man up.

'Peter Glash could not have done anything in passion. He was cold, and his every action was carefully considered. A man incapable of blind rage. I remember thinking that he embodied the age-old truth: revenge is a meal best served cold. The murder of his wife was deliberate. It occurred weeks after he'd discovered her affair with a purveyor who made deliveries to their candy business. There was no evidence of psychosis. He told his story repeatedly without changing a detail. No psychiatric diagnosis fit. He was not schizophrenic or manic depressive. In hindsight, his diagnosis was likely the same as his son's.'

'Which is?' Hobbs asked.

'Asperger's.'

'What the hell is that?'

'Look,' Houssman said, 'I promised not to bog you down in details so let me give you what's useful. It's a form of autism that does not include mental retardation. It's far more common in boys and frequently travels through the men in a family. No one knows where it comes from – there are many theories. The core defect is an inability to comprehend social interaction. People with Asperger's are typically very obsessional; things need to be done in a specific way, at a specific time. If they're prone to violence – and the vast majority are not – their anger is often triggered by a variation in routine or by being told "no". To an outsider it could be as trivial as putting the pillows on their bed in a different manner, or leaving a window open a hair's breadth more than usual. Peter Glash's reason for killing his wife was that women are supposed to be faithful to their husbands. She strayed from his rigidly held belief, and because of that she needed to die at his hand. He had some biblical quotes he'd spout. I recall something about stoning harlots.'

'What happened?'

'He went to prison, of course. That would have been nearly forty years ago.'

'Is he still in?' Hobbs asked.

'I wouldn't know,' Houssman replied, 'but it's easy to check.'

'Any more about Richard Glash?' Hobbs pressed.

'Felicia, I assume you have his records on hand?'

'Just the prison and arrest records. I need a court order for everything before his eighteenth birthday. I did get these,' she said, pushing a large sealed cardboard box marked 'inmate belongings' to the edge of her desk. 'It came ahead of the transport wagon.' She looked up at Hobbs and then at Houssman. 'I didn't open it for fear of contaminating any potential evidence.'

Hobbs had no such qualms and flicked open the red Swiss Army knife he used as a key chain and ripped through the red-and-black striped tape. Houssman looked on as Hobbs rapidly unpacked the contents and laid them out on Felicia's desk. First a stack of artist's spiral-bound sketchpads. 'Jesus,' he muttered as he flipped through page after page of nightmarish murder scenes. 'I know this one,' he said, looking at a charcoal sketch that depicted the excavation of the crawl space beneath John Wayne Gacy's house. Partially exhumed corpses and skeletons broke through the surface of their shallow graves. A sweat-covered Gacy was caught in half-profile, stooped over, a young man's naked body off to the side.

'Before his mother's murder,' Houssman commented, 'Richard drew animals. I have sketchpads filled with them. Anyone seeing them assumes they were done by a skilled adult artist and not a three- or four-year-old. He drew the family cat and without being taught he'd switch styles from realism to cubism, to Japanese line drawing. I can only assume he'd seen examples on advertisements or maybe his parents took him to museums. Some you'd swear had been drawn by Picasso or Matisse. That all changed after his mother's murder.'

'That's when he started drawing murder scenes?' Hobbs asked, coming to an image that fueled his spiraling anxiety.

'That's Barrett,' Felicia gasped, stating the obvious. 'What's wrong with her?' The picture, drawn in rust-colored pencil, showed Barrett's high cheekbones and almond eyes, but her complexion was marked with open pustules and oozing sores that dripped blood. The whites of her eyes were shot through with angry veins; her full lips were cracked and bleeding. 'What else is in there?' Houssman asked quickly, wanting Hobbs to flip past the accursed drawing. What followed wasn't much better: other faces, some they recognized, others they didn't, all similarly pocked and diseased.

Hobbs felt sick. His head spun and at first he didn't recognize the buzzing of his cell. He flipped it open on the second ring. 'Yes?' his mouth felt parched. It was a buddy of his, Carl Briggs – a State Trooper.

'Ed, you're not going to like this.'

Hobbs braced for the worst.

'We found your lady friend's cell smashed to bits in the woods outside the Titicus Reservoir ... and we've got a homicide.'

Hobbs could barely speak. 'Is it her? Is it Barrett?'

'I don't think it's her,' Briggs said, 'not from what you described. It's a young, female Caucasian, long blonde hair – or at least she used to have. Our perp decided to play cowboys

89

and Indians with her. Identification tag has her as a Lucinda Peters – state employee with some department I've never heard of.'

'Where are you?' Hobbs asked. 'I'll be there as fast as I can.'

'Wouldn't bother,' Briggs added.

'Why?'

"Cause I just got the call that we got homicide number two not ten minutes from here in Katonah. And Ed, whatever this guy's up to it's clear he wants publicity and he's moving fast, 'cause both here and with the stiff in Katonah the first call he made was to the press. They beat the feds, and they beat us. It's a fucking zoo! We're all going to be TV stars.'

'They have an ID on stiff number two?' Hobbs asked, feeling a sick tingle in his fingers and toes.

'Yeah, kind of a semi-celebrity, name of John J. Saunders. His wife's the one who killed the kids a few years back.'

'You got the address?' Hobbs wrote it down. 'Thanks, man.'

'Don't mention it.'

Ed hung up, took a look back at the cardboard box of Glash's belongings, and headed toward the door. Glash still had her; she was still alive; she had to be.

'I'm coming with you,' Houssman said, grabbing his hat and following Hobbs out into the corridor.

'Are you insane?' Hobbs replied, picking up his pace, not wanting to be saddled with the

90

eighty-four-year-old psychiatrist.

'Be reasonable,' Houssman answered, catching up with him. 'We've just scratched the surface on Glash. I have more to tell you and I can do it while you drive. And unlike Barrett, I know not to put myself in the line of fire. What was she thinking? She's a fucking psychiatrist, for God's sake! And did I hear correctly, that Glash killed Jane Saunders' husband?'

'What?' Hobbs asked, slowing slightly. 'What does she have to do with this?'

'Quite a lot, I'm afraid,' he said, pushing past Hobbs as the skirts of his long gray trenchcoat flew out around his ankles. 'I'm definitely coming with you. We don't have much time. Everyone I care about has been placed in mortal danger, so keep moving.'

'You got it,' Hobbs said. 'So what's the deal with John and Jane Saunders?'

'Possibly our first break,' Houssman said, not slowing. 'Glash was one of four prisoners getting transferred, Jane Saunders, Dr Clarence Albert and Allison Tessavian are the other three ... oh my God!'

'What is it?' Hobbs asked, finding himself having to step up his pace.

'The pictures he drew of disease. Clarence Albert...'

Before he could get out the words Hobbs made the connection. 'He was the scientist who mailed anthrax. Oh, shit!'

'Let's just get there,' Houssman said. 'I'll tell you everything I know.'

Eight

Tall like his son, but skeletally thin, Peter Glash stooped through the low doorway as he left his still-warm BMW motorcycle locked in the squat shed garage. He walked across the trash-strewn alley to the four-story loft building on Lower Delancey that had been in the family since the turn of the century. Not given to emotions, he worried if all their planning had been for nothing. He pulled his cell out of the breast pocket of his leather jacket and stared at the LED screen. Even though it indicated there had been no calls, he pressed the back button just to check – nothing.

At Croton, he'd seen the van that was supposed to be bringing Richard, but had been unable to glimpse anything through the small barred windows as he'd roared back to Manhattan, stopping every ten to fifteen minutes, just to check. Had he gotten away? Had he tried to call? The small round mirrors on his bike had told him nothing as he'd shot past the van – was Richard even inside? Perhaps there'd been a last-minute switch and it was one of the others – like Dr Albert.

Peter didn't want to dwell on all of the

variables in his son's plan. Too many 'what ifs?'. What if Dr Clarence Albert was just a paranoid psychotic or a liar, and not a genius? The man wasn't right in the head, thinking the government was filming his every move. What if everything he'd promised was just the fantasy of a madman? Or what if they'd delayed Richard's transfer? Or discovered the pickup truck and the cell phones? What if they routinely scoured the parking lot for cars that weren't supposed to be there? But the thought that tortured him, that had tortured him for decades, was *What if Richard never gets out?* He flipped open the cell again – *let him call, please let him call.* He stared at the screen, as though willing it to happen would make it so ... nothing, just traffic noise and the sounds of cut-rate commerce on the other side of the wood and metal fence that hid the alley from Delancey.

Peter unbolted the side door that led into the five-room apartment where he'd lived his entire life. His great-great-grandfather had bought the iron-fronted building with the money from years of street peddling. In the past, the two upper floors had been rented out to immigrant families – first the Irish, then the Jews – and then his grandfather had expanded his candy business, passed it on to Peter's father and it had been going strong until the day Peter went to prison. Peter could still hear the school children cramming into the shop, their grimy hands clutching pennies, waving them over the counter. Him behind with his brothers, Frank and Edward, measuring out lengths of button candy, or counting licorice whips – two for a penny, five for two. He never liked those kids, never trusted them, always trying to steal, their little hands going where they shouldn't. Even his own brothers couldn't be trusted, although Frank at least had kept up the building during his ten years in Elmira. Then again, Frank owed him, and knew not to cross him.

He walked through the dark but tidy kitchen and went into the gated and boarded-up store. Shafts of light pierced through the wood and the metal gates. Peter stared at the floor and pictured Richard – his son – as a toddler, curled up under the counter with the tabby cat. His pudgy hands always working on another picture ... always drawing. He was a beautiful child with piercing blue eyes and jet-black hair, just like his mother – the harlot. The smallest thought of her, brought from Romania at great cost ... his hands balled at his sides – 'Harlot! Whore!' The words sank into the walls. It was all her fault – Dorothea's, the whore.

The cell rang.

'Hello?'

'Father?'

'Yes, Richard.' Hope surged.

'Thank you, Father.'

'You're welcome, son.' Peter could barely breathe. So many questions he wanted to ask. But all he could think was that Richard was free, he was finally free.

'I have two hostages. I will give you their information now. Do you need to get a pencil and piece of paper?'

'No, son ... go ahead.'

'The first is a little famous; her name is Dr Barrett Conyors. She's five foot eleven inches, she has short dark brown hair and blue-gray eyes – although that won't matter.' He continued with a detailed account of everything Barrett was wearing. 'You'll need more accurate information and I will get it for you.' He then described Carla Phelps. 'I'm going to be on TV,' Richard said after finishing relaying his hostages' statistics and clothing.

'Yes, son.'

'I'm going to be very famous.'

'Yes,' Peter agreed, the phone pressed tight to his ear. He felt an unknown emotion, like a pressure filling his chest.

'I have to go now ... Dad. I'll call soon.'

'Yes, son ... and Richard?'

'Yes, Dad?'

'I'm very proud of you. Please be careful.'

'I will.'

And they hung up.

Nine

In the back of a Chrysler van with her hands in APC restraints and her legs duct-taped together, Barrett strained to stay upright and keep from being further injured as Glash drove away from the Saunders' house. What she'd been forced to witness was seared into her brain, Glash the connoisseur of murder. Every detail was a perfect recreation of Jane's murder spree, only instead of her young children, Glash had slit the throat of her husband, a man who'd been making a living out of his wife's tragedy. She could still picture his face plastered on the back of the glossy book jackets that spilled from boxes piled in his living room. She'd read somewhere that he'd gotten a million dollar advance for *Whatever Happened to Grown-Up Jane?*, a book that portrayed him as the victim of a wife whose mental illness had spiraled out of control. What he'd neglected to tell was how he had systematically ignored the advice of all the psychiatrists and doctors who had treated Jane.

She choked back a wave of bile as she pictured John J. Saunders pleading for his life. She could have told him it would do no good.

Seconds later his throat was slashed from ear to ear, like a gaping second mouth. Glash had then dipped his forefinger into the rushing blood and painted the walls of the living room with apocalyptic verses: *'And I saw when the Lamb opened one of the seals, and I heard, as it were the noise of thunder, one of the four beasts saying, Come and see'*. As horrific as it was, Barrett, who'd spent hours examining the photos of Jane's crime, knew that Glash had done his homework. The walls had once again dripped blood in the Saunders' home; same words in the exact same places. A wall for each of the horsemen, Glash had worked fast, dragging Saunders' corpse like a fleshy inkwell, not stopping until he'd penned the final verse: *'And I looked and behold a pale horse: and his name that sat on him was Death, and Hell followed with him. And power was given unto them over the fourth part of the earth, to kill with sword, and with hunger, and with death and with the beasts of the earth'*. She wondered what the crime-scene team would find when they did their luminescence tests. No matter how much fresh paint had been slopped on those walls, the old blood would still light up. She could almost see their expressions of disbelief; Glash's efforts would be within millimeters of the original.

She pressed her back against the side of the van – their new vehicle. Glash had abandoned the pickup in Saunders' garage and taken his Town & Country minivan. Ironically, the seats had been removed and the back loaded with more boxes of his book, as though he'd been stopping at home in the midst of a publicity tour. She strained to hear what was happening up front. She heard Carla's voice: 'Richard, it's not too late.'

Glash said nothing.

'I know how you must feel,' Carla continued. 'I've been through this too, different, but not that different.'

'What do you mean?' he asked.

'I have a young daughter,' Carla said. 'Her name is April and because of Dr Conyors, and other doctors like her, she was taken from me because I was in a psychiatric hospital.'

'What's wrong with you?' His voice was a monotone.

'They said I have bipolar disorder.'

'Do you?'

'Yes.'

'Then they were right to take away your daughter.'

'How can you say that?' Carla asked.

'Some say Jane Saunders has bipolar disorder; she killed her children. I killed her husband. I don't have bipolar disorder. I shouldn't have been locked up.'

Barrett angled her legs and pressed back so she could glimpse Glash and Carla. She shuddered as she caught a blue eye staring at her in the rear-view mirror. 'He was famous,' Glash said.

Barrett realized he was talking to her. 'Who was famous?'

'John J. Saunders, he wrote a book and was on television. That makes him famous.'

'I suppose so.'

'He'll be more famous now.'

'Yes,' Barrett said, puzzling at where this was going, and thinking it had something to do with his insistence on her watching him murder Saunders and poor Lucinda Peters. 'You're famous,' she said, trying to test a hypothesis.

'Not very, but I will be,' he answered. 'Now shut up, both of you.'

Barrett lost track of time as Glash drove – it seemed like hours. At one point he pulled off the road and carried Carla back and dumped her next to Barrett. He then threw a blue plastic tarp over them. Minutes later he drove into a gas station and filled the tank. Before leaving the vehicle he spoke. 'If either one of you tries to escape or makes a sound I'll kill everyone here and set fire to the pumps. I like fire. It's pretty.' He didn't wait for a response.

Barrett glared at Carla in the dim light that filtered through the blue plastic. She was furious. 'This is your fault,' she whispered. 'People are dying because of you.'

Carla looked at Barrett, their faces uncomfortably close. 'It's so easy for you, isn't it? Go around judging everyone,' her voice was a hissing whisper, 'playing God, deciding who gets locked up, who can be a fit mother. It must be quite the burden, Dr Conyors, to be so important.'

'What happened to you wasn't my fault,' Barrett said, knowing that like it or not her fate was tied to Carla's.

'I'm sorry,' Carla replied sarcastically, 'it must have been someone else telling the judge that I was gravely disabled and should have only supervised contact with my child.'

'That was only meant for while you were still manic and delusional.'

'And who decides that? Am I manic now?'

'No.'

'Just checking,' Carla said. 'Seeing as we're both probably going to die,' she continued, 'I always wondered if you had something going on with my husband. You do remember Bill? Tall, handsome, supposed to be with me till death do us part. He always made a point of saying how "attractive" he found you. Were you fucking him?'

'Get real,' Barrett said. 'Any other questions?'

The two women, both bruised and similarly restrained, glared at each other inside their blue plastic tent. A moment of realization passed between them.

'We are so screwed,' Carla said, her anger replaced by surging fear.

'I know, and we can't fight like this,' Barrett said.

'You're right. It's just I've hated you for so long ... Truce. What does he want?' Carla asked, the anger gone from her voice. 'It can't be just killing for killing's sake. Otherwise we'd both be dead ... wouldn't we?'

'That's what I'm trying to figure out,' Barrett whispered. 'His fascination is murder, but there's more to it. Why is he leaving cell phones with the bodies and why is he making me watch?'

'He wants to be famous,' Carla said, and quickly shut up as Glash opened the passenger door.

They stayed silent as he drove. The daylight that illuminated their makeshift tent faded, and eventually they were in total darkness.

The vehicle lurched to the right and left the highway for a secondary road. Minutes later the wheels began to bump over an unpaved surface. Barrett heard gravel ping against the undercarriage; pressure grew in her ears as they gained altitude. Then they came to a stop.

The two women tensed. It felt too quiet. They huddled motionless, not daring to move.

The rear doors opened and Glash ripped off the tarp. He was carrying a shovel.

'Please God, no!' Carla whimpered, seeing the shovel and assuming the worst.

Glash looked at Barrett. 'Do you know where we are?'

Barrett shivered in the cool night air, her eyes, now accustomed to the dark, took in the strange scene, a deserted wood-framed cabin in the middle of a pine forest. A crescent moon shone a silver light down on the clearing. Glash rested the shovel against the side of the vehicle and grabbed Barrett by her restrained legs and roughly sat her up in the space between the open van doors.

At first she was about to say 'no', but something about the mountain setting was familiar. They'd been to the Saunders' home, and so thinking through the other two – Allison and Dr Albert – she said, 'This is Dr Albert's cabin.'

'Yes. Good. What did he do here?'

'He manufactured anthrax spores,' Barrett replied, feeling like this was a test where she'd better come up with the right answers.

'Yes. Good.' Abruptly, he picked up the shovel and walked toward the cabin. Then he turned right and vanished into the woods.

'Carla,' Barrett whispered, 'I have business cards in my jacket pocket, but I can't get to them. See if you can reach in and get one.'

'If he sees us...' Carla said, as she repositioned herself closer to Barrett.

Barrett leaned forward, allowing her blazer to gape open. Carla's restrained hands fumbled inside the lining, her fingers feeling for the small state-issue business cards.

'I got it,' she said, clasping a single card between her fingers.

Barrett looked up and scanned the woods for Glash. 'Drop it.'

'It's too bright,' Carla said, as the too-white card glowed in the moonlight.

Barrett repositioned her bound feet to cover the card.

'Now what?' Carla asked.

Barrett heard movement, and then Glash

appeared in the clearing. He was holding a metal box the size of a carry-on suitcase.

'Richard,' Barrett whispered, 'I have to urinate. It's been hours. I've been trying to hold it in and I don't want to soil myself.'

'Yes,' he said, 'I should have thought of that.' He threw the shovel into the back of the van, and put the box on the passenger's seat. Then, without saying anything, he reached in and grabbed hold of her legs.

He had caught her by surprise, and she struggled to keep her rubber-soled shoe over the business card. As he pulled her out the back and scooped her up, the card fluttered to the ground. She prayed he wouldn't see it. If he did, he'd immediately know that she was trying to leave a trail – or at least a clue. He carried her to the edge of the woods, put her down on a large rock and proceeded to rip the duct tape from her pant legs. 'Don't try to run away,' he said. 'Your hands are restrained. You won't succeed and then I'll have to kill her.'

'I won't run,' Barrett said, and realized that she really did need to pee.

He walked behind her, wrapped his arms around her waist and unzipped her pants and pulled them down. There was nothing sexual, even when he grabbed her cotton panties and pushed them down to her ankles. He stepped back, never taking his eyes off her.

She thought to ask him to turn around, but knew that might be pushing her luck. She squatted and emptied her bladder on the leaf-covered ground. Her calves ached, but it felt good finally being able to move her legs. When done, she stood up and he dressed her.

'Walk back to the vehicle,' he ordered. 'It's easier that way.'

Her heart pounded as she headed back, her eyes fixed on the business card that glowed silver in the moonlight. Trying to keep her body between Glash and the card, she realized how risky this was. At the rear of the minivan, she put her foot over the card. 'Can you help me up?' she asked.

'Yes.' He bent to scoop her up, and as he did she kicked the card gently under the vehicle.

'Thank you,' Barrett said, wanting to keep his eyes off the ground.

'You're welcome,' he answered automatically, and looked at Carla. 'Your turn. I'll take you to urinate.'

Barrett tried to calm herself as she waited for Glash to return. She was relieved that he'd not tied her legs again. She thought about trying to make a break for it, but knew that if she did, it wasn't just her own life she'd jeopardize; Glash would make good on his threat and kill Carla.

He returned, roughly dumping Carla back inside. He grabbed her by the back of the neck and pulled back her navy blazer. He did the same with her white blouse, as though he were reading the labels.

'What are you doing?' Carla asked, as he pulled back the fabric and seemed to dig into her neck.

He didn't answer. 'Who made your jacket?' he asked, looking at Barrett.

'Donna Karan,' she said, wondering what interest Glash had in their outfits.

'And your shirt?'

'It's Ralph Lauren, oxford cloth.'

'It looks like a man's shirt,' he said.

'It is, I like the fabric and I bring them to my tailor to get them fitted.'

'What about your shoes?' He looked at Carla and then back at Barrett.

He continued making them itemize their clothing and their sizes. When he was satisfied, he slammed the doors.

The two women looked at each other in the dark as they waited for him to get back in the vehicle. Instead they heard him talking. 'What the hell was that all about?' Carla said.

'Not a clue,' Barrett said, straining to hear what he was saying.

'I need the coordinates,' he said. 'Good. This will be the last one before I become very famous. Now pay close attention, I have more details that you need.' He listed all the items of clothing that the two women were wearing.

'Who's he talking to?' Carla whispered.

'I don't know.'

'He has an accomplice?'

'Has to,' Barrett said, and then quickly asked, 'That first pickup truck, was that yours?'

'No.'

'So he just happened to find a parked vehicle with the key in the ignition and everything he'd need to take hostages in the back.

Shit!'

'So who is he working with?'

'You were there this morning,' Barrett said, 'did you see anyone, anything at all?'

'I don't think ... wait a minute, there was something,' Carla said. 'Lucinda pointed it out, a man on a motorcycle. Some kind of vintage bike that Lucinda's fiancé wanted ... a BMW. I just figured it was someone who worked at Croton, going home.'

'Did you get a look at him?' Barrett whispered.

'He had a helmet on and leathers.'

'Can you be sure it was a man?'

'No,' Carla admitted, 'but he – or she – seemed pretty tall.'

'Ssh!' Barrett warned as Glash opened the driver's door.

He got in and looked back. 'Have you two figured out what comes next?'

There was something different in his tone that made Barrett think of a small child wanting his mother's attention. Hoping to appease him, Barrett played along. 'Well, Richard, you've done something that had to do with Jane Saunders, you've just picked up something from Dr Albert's...'

'Yes,' he said, 'very good ... now what will I do?'

'That leaves Allison Tessavian. You intend to do something related to her case.'

'Yes, but can you figure out what? I want to see how smart you are.'

'Something that will make you famous,'

Barrett said, realizing that Glash's fascination wasn't just with murder and murderers as she'd previously thought, but with the fame that came with high-profile cases.

'*More* famous,' he corrected. 'I'm a little famous now; more famous in the morning; more famous than that in the afternoon. Who's the most famous murderer of all time?' he asked abruptly.

'I'm not certain,' she said, suddenly taut with fear.

'Guess,' he ordered.

'Cain from the Bible, Charles Manson ... Adolph Hitler...'

'Good,' he said, satisfied. 'They're all very famous. But they're not the biggest killer of all time. You know who is?' he asked.

'I don't,' she said, relieved to hear him turn the key and start the engine.

'It's God,' he said. 'He kills everyone. Everyone dies.'

'Yes,' Barrett said.

'You know,' he said, 'God tells man to kill each other.'

'I don't think that's true,' Barrett said, realizing too late that disagreeing with Richard was not smart.

'It is!' he shouted, and twisted back in his seat. 'God tells man to go to war!' His face was contorted and spittle flew out with his words. 'He tells him to stone the whore. God wants man to kill. He wants me to kill. It's all in the Bible. It's a fact, Dr Conyors, that people kill for God. God is very famous, isn't he?'

'Yes, Richard,' she said, hoping to calm him down, knowing that one of his rages could easily lead to their deaths.

'I'm going to be as famous as God...' He was breathing heavily and staring back at them.

She met his gaze. Seconds stretched. He didn't blink; neither did she. She felt frozen and sick; knowing her every move was being evaluated. Any careless word or action could be the one that brought about her death or Carla's.

Abruptly he spoke: 'Now shut up and go to sleep ... *now!*'

She and Carla sank to the floor, their legs tangled in the blue tarp. Barrett could feel Richard watching them. She'd never felt so vulnerable and so frightened; with them bound and on the floor, he could do anything. She met Carla's gaze, the lawyer's eyes glittered in the dark. The two women held their breath and waited. Finally, the vehicle began to move.

Ten

Hobbs watched as Houssman got patted down prior to entering the maximum security Bedford Hills Correctional Facility. It was 8 a.m. and already he could tell it was going to be another scorcher. Why the old guy continued to wear his long gray trenchcoat Hobbs had no idea. He suspected it had something to do with why every time they passed a restroom Houssman would disappear. The one time Hobbs had needed to relieve himself he'd found Houssman at the sink, washing his hands for what seemed a very long time. Maybe the coat was a barrier between him and ... whatever he needed to wash off his hands. Obsessive quirks aside, Hobbs was glad he'd let Houssman tag along. He now understood why Barrett – goddamn her – held him in such high regard. George had exhibited a brilliant way of throwing out multiple possibilities as they'd scoured Glash's prison records and examined the murder scene at the Saunders' house. His first comment when they'd viewed Lucinda Peters' scalped corpse was, 'He's been wanting to do that since he was four.'

'Your point?' Hobbs had asked, his gut

109

twisting over this poor woman's murder, not even ten minutes from Croton. Glash was losing no time in getting started.

'It's characteristic of Asperger's,' Houssman had instructed, not taking his eyes off the young woman's mutilated head. 'They're highly obsessional and once fixated, they can't let it go. It's the reason Glash is so dangerous: everyone who he believes has hurt him, he'll go after. It doesn't matter how many years or decades have passed. That's why I have no doubt he'll come for me. But that's not what worries me.'

'What is?'

'His way to get revenge is to hurt and to kill the families of all those who've hurt him. When he comes for me, if he's not caught and killed, he'll go after my children and my grandchildren.' Houssman swallowed hard. 'What's odd here,' he continued, 'is that he's twice attempted to scalp and kill the same woman. She was our next-door neighbor's youngest – Mary Sullivan – although that might not be her name anymore.' He turned to Hobbs. 'We need to find her, but why did he murder this poor young thing using the method reserved for Mary...? Oh,' he said softly. 'I hadn't seen that...'

Hobbs looked in the direction of the dead woman. His eye caught on the torn skin of her ring finger. 'He's taken her ring.'

'Yes.'

'Why would he do that?' Hobbs asked, not able to take his mind off Barrett and the peril she faced, scared sick about the significance of the ring; it hadn't been that long ago that another killer had gone after her with twisted fantasies of marriage and kids.

'I don't know,' Houssman said, 'but there will be a reason.'

It had been an exhausting and frustrating night. Glash had eluded the authorities, and despite a vast network of roadblocks throughout Westchester and Putnam County, he'd not been spotted. With the police scanner on, Hobbs and Houssman had spent the early morning snatching a couple of hours of upright and nightmare-filled sleep in the Crown Vic parked outside the Bedford Hills facility. Every few minutes Hobbs would startle awake, his mind racing with horrific images – Glash's drawings, the blood on the walls, Saunders' gaping neck. To calm himself, he'd focus on Barrett; remember the feel of her in his arms, the taste of her lips. He would rescue her and she would love him. But then the other thoughts came: *What if she's already dead?* Each long minute was a kind of agony, the urge to go after her, the desperation at not knowing which way to head. 'You have to wait, Hobbs,' he'd tell himself. 'Close your eyes, try to sleep.' And around and around, until dawn began to break.

When Houssman awoke, he commented, 'My ankles are swollen.' With a groan he bent down and pressed a finger into the puffy flesh over his black stretch sock. 'Dependent edema. You get any sleep?' he asked.

'Not much.' And they'd watched the clock, waiting for 8 a.m., the earliest Hobbs had been able to pull to get inside the prison.

Now, at the security checkpoint, it was Hobbs's turn. He unholstered his steel-gray Glock, exchanged it for a receipt, and spread his arms and legs for the pat-down and wave with the metal-detector wand.

'They were in the same cell block at Green Haven for over three years,' Houssman remarked, referring to Dr Clarence Albert, as he waited for Hobbs. 'If the two of them connected, they'd have plenty in common.'

'Like?' Hobbs asked, as the guards buzzed them through the first of the security gates.

'Clarence Albert, depending on your view, falls somewhere between a condition called delusional disorder, paranoid type, and paranoid schizophrenia. I was asked to consult as an expert witness for the defense about five years ago. His lawyers wanted to try an insanity defense. They weren't happy with what I found, so they ended up paying for my time and hiring another expert.'

'Yeah, keep going till you get the answer you want,' Hobbs commented, as they followed their escort to a service elevator.

'Exactly. A hired gun, but I don't do that. I had no doubt the man was mentally ill and that his paranoia, and belief that the company he worked for and the government were actively conspiring against him, were largely responsible for his actions. But that doesn't buy you an insanity plea. He wanted people to suffer. He wanted to make them sick in an extraordinarily cruel way. He knew it was criminal; he didn't care.'

'So how are they alike?' Hobbs asked, as they were escorted down cement-walled corridors to the prison's behavioral health unit.

'How aren't they?' Houssman began. 'Their IQs are both high in the genius range. They both believe large sectors of society have deliberately harmed them. They've both killed, and like Glash, if Albert were ever released there is no doubt that he would kill again.'

They were led through a final locked steel door and into a cellblock that had been retrofitted with a nurses' station and a small central medication room.

They were asked by a young Latino man in a white uniform to sign in. He then led them to Clarence Albert's cell.

Hobbs got his first glimpse of the prisoner through the small wire-mesh window as the nurse let them in. Albert was seated bolt upright on his bed staring at the door. His long, graying hair was slicked back over his scalp, bald patches visible between the oily strands. He was dressed in brown pajamas and wore wire-rimmed glasses that had a thick wad of surgical tape across the bridge.

'Thank you for agreeing to meet with us,' Hobbs began. He extended his hand to Albert. The microbiologist looked at it, but did not shake it.

'I was supposed to be moved yesterday. I

was supposed to go to a hospital,' Albert complained in a wheezing, asthmatic voice. 'They say that some of the rooms in Croton have windows.' He looked around his eight-by-four room with its cot, sink, toilet, portable television and radio and small bookcase crammed with textbooks and dog-eared science journals.

'The governor canceled the transfer,' Houssman said.

'Because of Richard Glash,' Albert stated. It wasn't a question.

'Yes,' Houssman replied. 'That's why we're here. You know him.'

'I knew him,' Albert replied warily. 'What has that got to do with anything?' He looked down at the linoleum-tiled floor, as though he were trying to conceal the smile spreading across his thin lips. 'Has he done something ... I mean, other than escape?'

'You've seen the news,' Houssman stated, as Hobbs watched, letting the older man steer the interview.

'Yes, but that doesn't tell me much, does it?' Albert replied. 'You're here and you think I know something. That I can help you catch Richard Glash.'

'Correct,' Hobbs said, feeling his anger start to surge. 'But I'm wondering if we're wrong and this isn't a waste of time.'

'I'm sure it is,' Albert agreed. 'Just a big waste of time. My time, your time.' His eyes shot up to the corner of the room, and he stared intently. 'Their time.'

114

'Who are you talking about?' Hobbs asked, his patience stretched thin, not in the mood for this guy to squirrel out.

'Don't pretend you don't know. You're all part of it. But you can't see everything.'

Houssman interjected. 'Dr Albert, we don't have time for that right now. I'm prepared to give you information you won't have heard on the news. Information that you'll want to know.'

Albert perked. 'I'm listening.'

'Richard Glash has killed four people that we know of since his escape. Two marshals, a legal aide and John J. Saunders.'

'How did the aide die?' Albert asked, his eyes bright, seemingly greedy for the gory details.

'Shot and then scalped,' Houssman replied, meeting Albert's gaze.

'Scalped ... interesting...'

'Why?'

'You know why, Doctor. Or is that the game we're playing? You want me to tell you what you already know? Seems like a waste. We've both seen Richard's drawings. He's quite a talented fellow. I think you would do well to not underestimate him.'

'Were you two friends?' Hobbs asked, his fists balled, and the knuckles cracked.

'One doesn't make friends in here. We were acquaintances. I found his company interesting. We'd play chess. I miss that. He's the only person who ever beat me at chess. We were well matched.'

'You asked about the aide,' Hobbs said, knowing that Albert was holding back. 'What about Saunders? Don't you want to know how he died?' And to himself, *You fucking piece of scum!*

Albert smiled. 'I'm assuming he was killed the way his wife killed the kids.'

'How could you know that?' Hobbs shot back.

Albert shook his head and turned to Houssman, his tone contemptuous. 'You're going to have to do better than that. It doesn't take a detective or a shrink to know what makes Richard tick.'

'Correct,' Houssman said. 'It's clear he kills with purpose and deliberation. He killed John J. Saunders for Jane. That's why we're here. What murder will Richard Glash attempt for you?'

Albert took a deep, wheezing breath. 'Such a good question. There are so many people I wouldn't mind seeing dead. If looks could kill, you'd both be flat on the floor. If looks could kill,' he said again, staring up at the corner of his room, 'would anyone be left alive? I don't think so.'

Hobbs felt his frustration mount; every second that passed kept Barrett in terrible danger. He wanted to throttle Albert, to pin his head against the wall and make him hurt. 'If he killed Saunders for Jane, then it seems likely he'll start mailing anthrax with hugs and kisses from you.'

Houssman eyed Hobbs and watched Albert

for his reaction. The PhD microbiologist never took his eyes off the corner of the room. His lips pursed and he smacked them open and closed several times. 'You are shooting in the dark, aren't you, Detective? Now the question you need to answer for me before we go further is this: if I know something – and that's a big if – and if I tell – another big if – what's in it for me? Because if you're right, and if I talk, seems likely I'll be getting some anthrax of my own in the mail. Richard holds grudges.'

'You want to go to Croton?' Houssman asked.

'I did.'

'I can make it happen. I can let the governor's office know, in no uncertain terms, that it is the appropriate place for you.'

'Well, Dr Houssman, I'm not so certain I still want to go there.'

'What's changed?' George asked.

'It's not bad here...' Albert said. 'Lovely nurses and medication. It seems quite safe.'

'Safe from what?' George persisted.

Albert smiled. 'You are worried, aren't you?' He hesitated, seemingly undecided whether or not to say more. 'You should be, but I'll give you this much: Richard won't be using anthrax.'

'Why not?' Hobbs asked.

'It takes too long,' Albert replied. 'He'd need the equipment to aerosolize it, and quite frankly other than the fear factor; it wasn't that effective, was it? Ten percent of those I'd intended to kill are still stinking up the face of this planet.'

'As I recall,' Houssman said, 'anthrax was just your opus. Wasn't that how you put it when you were arrested?'

'Yes,' Albert smiled, 'you remembered.'

'You had something else in store, but never told anyone.'

Albert kept quiet. The grin had returned.

'You find this funny?' Hobbs asked.

'Yes, very amusing. You don't have a clue, either one of you – they're all out there, like breadcrumbs. You just need to follow them before all the birds swoop down and carry them away.'

'You told Glash what you'd planned after the anthrax,' Houssman stated.

'We played chess. He'd show me his drawings.'

With a sickening realization Hobbs understood the sketches they'd seen. They were of Barrett, and others, dying from some horrible disease. His stomach knotted and his jaw clenched. He had to let Houssman handle this, because he was a heartbeat away from pummeling Albert.

Houssman switched tactics. 'He'll steal your thunder. It will be his name, not yours, attached to whatever happens. The fame will be his.'

'So be it,' Albert said. 'That's one place where Richard and I differ: he wants to be famous; I just want certain people dead – that we share.'

118

'What is he going to do?' Houssman asked point-blank. 'What is the murder he'll commit for you?'

'It's not *a* murder,' Albert said. 'Think bigger. Think biblical.'

'If you help us, we'll see your transfer goes through,' Houssman urged.

'I don't think I want it. Because if Richard succeeds,' Albert mused, 'I think I'll be safer here.'

'You're telling us there's nothing you want?' Houssman asked, desperate.

'Oh, there's things I want ... but you're not the ones who'll be giving them to me.'

'This is bullshit!' Hobbs shoved his face inches from Albert's. 'I think what we should do is put you back in the general population and spread the word that before you did the anthrax thing, you were arrested for diddling little boys. I think the gang on cell block C will give you quite the welcome.'

'You can't do that,' Albert said, his eyes wide. 'I wouldn't last a day.'

'Not my problem, and it would be easy for me to do,' Hobbs bluffed. 'After all, Glash took your attorney hostage.'

'Carla Phelps?' Albert asked, his eyes bugging out through his glasses. 'Why would he do that? She wasn't part of—'

'Part of what, Clarence?'

'Nothing. I didn't say anything.'

'But you did,' Hobbs pushed, 'and if you don't spill it fast, I'll get you into general pop. by the end of the day. Just think of the things they're going to do to you. They won't even care that you're old and scrawny. Are you picturing it, Clarence? You know what they do to old men who play with little boys?'

The gangly microbiologist put a finger to his glasses and stared back at Hobbs; his breath was fast; he wheezed. 'You can't do this to me. Please, don't.'

'Just answer the fucking questions,' Hobbs said. 'That's all you have to do.'

'I have rights,' Albert stuttered, his resolve faltering. 'You can't do this.'

'You have no fucking rights!' Hobbs shot back, in his face, spittle landing on Albert's glasses. 'And they sure as hell won't care about your rights as they're shoving a dick down your throat and another up your ass. Unless they just decide to cut you up first. But in my experience, Clarence, they'll do both.'

'Stop it! Leave me alone!' he said, his hands holding the sides of his head.

'Give it up, Clarence!' Hobbs spat back. 'One call and you're off this ward. I'll make sure you get the cell mate you deserve.'

'OK...' Albert's eyes darted around the cell, from Hobbs to Houssman to the corner. 'Before I was arrested I ran a piece in *The Times*, it was dismissed as the "rantings of a madman"; everything's in there.'

'No riddles,' Hobbs ordered, not caring that he was breaking every rule of interrogation. All he could focus on was Barrett.

'I swear,' Albert said, 'it's all in there.'

'Of course,' Houssman said, 'it's coded.'

Albert nodded rapidly. He hazarded a look at Hobbs. 'People are so stupid. It's been there all the time just waiting for someone to come and dig it up.'

'Dig what up?' Hobbs demanded.

Albert blinked and looked confused. He stared at Hobbs, who was still less than a hand's width from his nose. 'No!' he shouted. 'You can't do this! Guard! Guard!'

Hobbs didn't move as the burly nurse entered the room.

'Make them leave,' Albert pleaded. 'Make them go away!'

'Stay back,' Hobbs warned the nurse. 'Where should we dig?' he persisted. 'What is it you've buried?'

Albert shrank back on the bed; he turned his head to the wall. 'Make them leave. I don't care what you do to me. You can't threaten me. I have rights!'

Hobbs was seconds from leaping on Albert. Houssman tapped him on the shoulder. 'We'll get nothing else. Let's take what we have.'

'He's not telling us everything,' Hobbs snarled. 'You're going into general pop., Clarence. There's no deal unless you tell us everything.'

'I don't care,' Albert shouted into the wall. 'I don't care. Do what you want! None of it matters.' He sounded scared and uncertain, but then like a switch turned in his head he started to sing, 'Ring around the rosy, a pocket full of posy. Ashes, ashes, we'll all fall down.'

Hobbs was freaking as he and George retraced their steps through security and then back to the Crown Vic. His thoughts were racing and they kept flying back to Barrett and the huge question: *Was she OK?* He slammed the door and picked up the scanner. He looked at Houssman. 'It just keeps getting worse, doesn't it?'

Houssman nodded as Hobbs tracked down his superior – Captain Felix Schmitt. He shared their interrogation of Albert as Schmitt kept up a running stream of invective. 'Fuck, Hobbs. If that's even half right we've got to call in the pricks at Homeland Security, 'cause now you're talking goddamn weapons of mass destruction. Shoot me now. WMDs! Fuck! You think he's serious?'

'Hell yeah,' Hobbs said, as a muscle spasmed under the scar tissue of his jaw. 'But there's more. Before Albert got arrested *The Times* ran his manifesto.'

'I remember,' Schmitt said. 'They didn't want to, but we thought it would draw him out, make him take risks.'

'It kind of worked; problem is there was more to it than met the eye. He could have been just running off at the mouth, but I think he slipped up a bit. That manifesto is coded. Any chance you could get Geri Atwell to take a look at it?' he said, referring to the department's top cryptologist.

'You got it. Anything else?'

'Yeah, although it feels like way too many people got their hands in the soup. Who's heading up the FBI?'

'Tom Anderson,' Schmitt said.

'At least that's decent.'

'You want me to call him for you?' Schmitt asked.

'Naah, give me his number. I want to see what he has. You can make the call to Homeland Security.'

'I figured ... Hobbs?'

'Yeah?'

'This Albert, you think he told Glash how to do the anthrax thing?'

'I think something worse. He said Glash needs to dig something up. We might have some time. I just hope we get to him before...'

'God,' Schmitt said, 'this is the last thing this city needs.'

'What makes you think he'll head for Manhattan?' Hobbs asked, suddenly picturing his two little girls and his ex-wife out in Queens.

'It's his MO, right? He holds grudges; there's a lot of people on his list living here.'

'Right, let me know if you hear anything. I've got the scanner on, but it sounds like Glash is playing things for the press.'

'Big time,' Schmitt agreed. 'He somehow got his hand on a stack of prepaid cell phones and is leaving them like homing beacons with his bodies.'

'What about the getaway vehicle? They said it was left in Saunders' garage?'

'Yeah, it gets better. The VIN number was filed off. We'll get an ID on it; it's just going to take longer.'

'He's not working alone,' Hobbs said.

'Looks that way,' Schmitt agreed. 'Trouble is, like with your Albert, it could be anyone. Glash has been in four maximum-security facilities over the last twenty-plus years. He's shared cells and cell blocks with thousands of inmates.'

'What about visitors?'

'We've pulled the logs.'

'Letters?'

'Seems most of those he threw away before his transfer – like he was cleaning house.'

Hobbs then asked the question he'd been dreading. 'How much blood was in the getaway vehicle?'

'Not a lot. At this point we're cautiously optimistic that he's not killed the two remaining hostages ... one of them – that doctor – is a friend of yours, right?'

'Yeah,' Hobbs said.

'That really sucks.'

'You've no idea.' Hobbs finished the call and hung up.

Houssman looked at Hobbs. 'At least they think she's OK,' he said.

'For now.' Hobbs stared out of the windshield at the tower-ringed prison. 'Why does Barrett do shit like this?'

'Which part of it?' Houssman asked. 'She's complicated and I think what she's been through in the past few months has hurt her

124

very badly. She lost her husband, she very nearly saw her sister get killed. She was...'

'Raped,' Hobbs said. 'You know she's pregnant with that monster's baby.'

'I do. I was wondering about that. I knew she was scheduled to have it terminated yesterday.'

'Didn't happen,' Hobbs said angrily. 'Justine and I had her in the cab and at the clinic when all this started to happen. There was no talking to her.' He stared ahead as tears tracked down his face. 'She *had to go to Croton*, no delay, no let them figure things out without me. And now...' Hobbs choked on the words.

'You think of her as more than just a friend,' Houssman stated.

Hobbs nodded, hating to appear weak, but knowing that if he tried to speak his voice would crack and he'd start bawling.

Houssman, sensing the struggle, filled the silence. 'I think a lot of this has to do with me ... on a number of levels. Barrett knows my two girls – I shouldn't call them that anymore; they're both married professionals with children. I'll be a great-grandfather in two months.'

'I don't understand what that has to do with this,' Hobbs said, trying to regain his composure, trying not to dwell on all of the horrible things that had happened to Barrett. He felt whipped and scared; he wanted to protect her, to love her, and he wasn't able to do either.

'I told you that my girls were adopted; their

mother was a drug-addicted prostitute who had tried to get her life together and had ended up killing her husband and sometime pimp. When Delia and I took them in it was something of an experiment. I know that sounds terrible when talking about children, but there it is.'

Hobbs took a deep breath. 'What does this have to do with Barrett?'

'I'm breaking her confidence by telling you this. But you should know. The reason she hadn't terminated the pregnancy already is that a big part of her desperately wants a child. She's getting older. She has no husband. Apparently she and Ralph had difficulty conceiving.'

'She never told me that,' Hobbs said, feeling jealous that she'd share this with Houssman and not with him. 'I just assumed she was waiting.'

'The fact that she's now pregnant is not something she takes lightly. She thinks this might be her only chance. She looks at my girls – you'd never know that both of their biologic parents were convicted felons. Alice is a pediatrician and Stephanie is a top Manhattan designer. She knows that Jimmy Martin is dangerously disturbed, as was his sister. But they were also severely tortured by their sadist of a father. So is Jimmy's craziness genetic, or is he just the twisted product of years worth of systematic beatings and rapes?'

'She told you this?' Hobbs asked.

'Yes. She's been tormented over what to do: everyone around her telling her one thing, knowing it's probably the right thing to do but ... what if the child she's carrying is her only chance?'

'She can't be serious,' Hobbs blurted. 'If she has Jimmy Martin's baby, he'll eventually find out. Even though he's locked away for the rest of his godforsaken life, there's still a lot of money in the family. Any baby of his would be the natural heir.'

'She knows that,' Houssman said softly.

'She thinks she could keep it secret? Is she insane?' Hobbs couldn't believe what he was hearing, that Barrett was seriously contemplating giving birth to that monster's child.

'Ed,' Houssman said, 'there's a lot of insanity running around right now ... not just in her.'

'What do you mean?' he asked.

'You and Barrett have been through a series of terrible experiences – you nearly died in that fire. The body and the mind both take time to heal; it's part of a natural process.'

Hobbs cracked a smile. 'You're saying I'm nuts.'

'I am, and I think your feelings for Barrett extend well beyond whether or not she terminates her pregnancy.'

Hobbs looked away.

'You're in love with her.'

'Yup,' he said. 'And I don't think she feels the same. Plus, now that I look like a side-show freak ... If anything happened to her, I don't know what I'd do.' He turned and bit the inside of his mouth to try and stem the tears. It didn't work and they came again, silent and heavy.

'Let's not think about that,' Houssman said.

'Yeah, right. My brain isn't fucking working,' Hobbs said, wiping his face with the back of his sleeve. 'So Glash is going to go after whatever Albert buried. I know his property upstate was searched pretty thoroughly, that's my first guess. You want me to drop you off somewhere?'

'No. I think I'll ride along.'

'You are a tough old bird, aren't you?' Hobbs said, taking a deep breath and turning the key in the ignition.

'Don't let the years fool you. They're just a number. And Ed...'

'What?'

'We've got something in common. Someone we both love is in terrible danger, and I don't think I could stand not doing everything possible to save her.'

Ed said nothing as he turned on the flashers and stepped on the gas.

Eleven

Two hours after leaving Albert's cabin in the Adirondacks, Glash pulls Saunders' silver Town & Country minivan into a thicket that affords him a panoramic moonlit view of the sprawling gingerbread-trimmed and turreted late-nineteenth-century Bella Vista Resort in the Catskills. He stares in the rear-view at his two hostages; they are either asleep or feigning sleep. It doesn't matter; he gets out, checks their restraints, again binding the psychiatrist's legs with duct tape. 'Don't try anything,' he whispers, 'or I'll kill you both.' He feels certain they'll not escape in the estimated twenty-seven minutes he needs to achieve his objective. He unlocks the passenger door, opens the glove compartment and removes one of the three remaining prepaid cell phones.

He'd nearly crossed this murder off his list – too risky. But the fact that the pop star – Justin Green – is vacationing here, in the same hotel where years earlier Allison Tessavian abducted and killed his girlfriend, is too perfect. His father told him that Justin was here; he'd read it in the *Post*. Killing Justin Green will make his father proud. It will feel good to make his father proud.

Justin Green is extremely famous. Richard knows that when you kill famous people, you get to share their fame, like Mark Chapman, who killed John Lennon, and Andrew Cunanan, who shot Gianni Versace. He pictures the stopwatch in his head. He clicks it once to start it running.

He feels the Smith & Wesson in the right-hand pocket of the hunting jacket that belonged to Saunders. In the other pocket he has an eight-inch kitchen knife – also Saunders'.

A porter steps through the front door of the hotel as he approaches. 'Good evening, sir.' He holds the gilt-stenciled door.

Glash looks through the door, sees that there is only a single female clerk at the front desk; no one else. He puts a smile on his face as he stabs the porter – estimated age of thirty-two, weight one seventy-five – under his ribcage. The knife plunges straight into the man's heart. Glash drags the limp body under a row of ornamental shrubs – *twenty-five minutes, twelve seconds.*

He checks to see that there is no blood on his jacket. He walks across the polished marble lobby. The clerk looks up. She is young – estimated age of twenty-three – of mixed race and wears a white shirt, black vest and a tie with the hotel's trademark red and green tartan. 'Good evening,' she says.

Glash puts on a smile, as his long arms shoot over the polished counter and grab the young woman – estimated weight of one hundred and twelve pounds.

She tries to scream, but Glash's powerful hands wrap around her throat. He feels the rattle of air over her vocal cords as he squeezes. Her trachea pops, crunches, and then he snaps her neck. It makes him think of a chicken bone. He now has twenty-four minutes.

He shoves her body back across the counter and lets it drop out of sight. He goes behind and looks at the computer screen. He punches in the name – Justin Green. *Twenty-three minutes, two seconds*. He identifies his suite, and knows that the pop star will have at least one security guard with him. He also knows that the security guard did not stop Allison the night she kidnapped and then drowned Melanie Coo, and it certainly won't stop him – *twenty-two minutes, thirteen seconds*.

Twelve

At mid-morning the heat was oppressive, even in the pine-shaded heights of the Adirondacks. Hobbs felt caked in sweat and dust and he wondered how Houssman was holding up, but the old guy didn't complain – more importantly he continued to offer important insights as they joined dozens of Homeland Security and FBI agents in the search of Albert's Mechanicville property.

The three-room cabin had been thoroughly searched five years earlier, and in the interim, local teens and hunters had come and gone, breaking the padlocks installed by Albert's relatives. Hobbs had taken one look at the interior, seen the used condoms and a stained and disintegrating mattress now home to field mice and moles, and he'd despaired of finding anything useful. After two days with little sleep, little food and too much caffeine, his nerves were frayed and he kept picturing Barrett and Glash's horrific drawings of her. He hated that she hadn't confided her feelings about the baby to him. Why couldn't she have? What did it mean that she hadn't? Maybe if he'd known, things would have gone differently.

He eyed the growing number of law enforcement personnel, and ticked off at least six different agencies – FBI, Homeland Security, state and local police, OHSHA, and himself representing the NYPD. If he wasn't so revved and scared he'd be cracking jokes, probably with Tom Anderson of the FBI – currently under the cabin with a flashlight – about the Homeland Security Agents, like, 'How many Homeland Security does it take to screw in a light bulb? ... A hundred; one to screw it in and ninety-nine to screw it up.' It was a circus, with more cars pulling in every couple of minutes, and the choice of ring-master couldn't have been worse.

'Maybe you didn't hear me right,' Martin Cosway said in a nasal and abrasive Brooklyn twang, as though reading Hobbs's thoughts.

Hobbs tried to keep his face neutral as he confronted the man who'd once reported to him on the NYPD as a rookie detective. There had been no love lost on either side. Cosway, a short weasel of a man, was in his early forties, dark hair slicked back with shiny pomade that went out in the Fifties. Cosway knew that Hobbs had everything to do with his not making it through his probationary period. He'd left the force without giving notice with an internal investigation pending and had jumped at a position with the then fledgling Department of Homeland Security. A political animal in a black suit and tie, he'd found fertile soil and clawed his way up. Glued to his side, gulping a bottle of water, was second-in-command, Corbin Zane, red-faced and balding with the build of a high-school linebacker gone soft in the middle.

'This is a fucking waste of time,' Cosway said, wiping sweat from his brow.

'Nothing here,' Zane echoed, looking for a glimmer of approval in his boss's eyes. His blue cotton shirt was soaked through with dark half-circles that reached from under his arms almost to his belt.

'Hard to know if he's been here,' Hobbs admitted, angry as hell at the myriad tire tracks that had disturbed the clearing in front of the cabin. If Glash had been here, any trace had been obliterated. It felt like a fucking Easter egg hunt.

Houssman, standing next to Hobbs, seemed oblivious to the dynamic between Hobbs and Cosway. 'Think paranoid,' he said. 'Albert owned this property for over twenty years. He's up here in this cabin ... what's he doing?' Houssman scanned the clearing, his eyes skipping over the law enforcement types, who were mostly focused on the area immediately around the building. 'Damn shame so many people are disturbing the scene.' He looked up at Cosway. 'I know you're in charge, but in my sixty years of being involved with investigations I've never seen a potential crime scene compromised so severely. You might want to do something about that. Get it down to just essential personnel.'

Hobbs suppressed a chuckle, as Cosway flushed and Zane choked on his water, doubled over and coughed.

'I know how to do my job, and I don't appreciate getting sent on wild goose chases by has-been cops and retired professors,' Cosway shot back. 'And if I wanted essential personnel only, you'd be the first to go.'

Houssman ignored him and peered deep into the woods. 'You won't find anything in the cabin. Anything there would have been found years ago. Come on, Ed.'

Leaving Cosway behind, Houssman plunged into the woods. 'What a moron,' he muttered, examining the shrubs and the ground for signs of recent disturbance.

'You picked that up fast,' Hobbs replied. 'If they put Cosway in charge ... shit!'

'What?' Houssman asked.

'Unless he's had a total personality change since he left the force – and if he hadn't left on his own he'd have gotten kicked off – it's not good.' Hobbs swatted at his neck, his hand came away with a blood-smeared mosquito.

'Look, someone has been through here.' Houssman was holding a snapped branch while peering into a thicket of chokecherry and bramble.

'You're right,' Hobbs said. 'Question is, was it one of these bozos or Glash?' And he pushed his way through the underbrush, noting how easily it parted.

Houssman trailed in his wake, letting the dense foliage close behind him. About six feet in the two men found themselves in a circular clearing. 'Bingo!' Hobbs said as they stared down at a recently unearthed metal hatch that had been buried under a few inches of loose dirt.

'Normally, I'd get the crime-scene photographer,' Houssman said.

'I hear you,' Hobbs said, as he bent to examine the small mounds of fresh-dug earth that surrounded a manhole-sized steel hatch. Taking out a pair of vinyl gloves he opened the hatch, releasing a musty smell of old books. He unhooked a small Maglite from his belt and shone it down into the opening. 'Looks like a steel oil tank that got buried and converted into a make-shift bomb shelter ... Somebody's been here.'

He angled back so Houssman could take a look as the powerful beam of light passed over fresh scuff marks in the dust: a bare mattress, an electric lantern, neatly stacked boxes of canned foods and bottled water and a wall of plastic egg crates filled with books and leaflets.

'I'm going in,' Hobbs said. 'Stay out here and let me know if anyone's coming.' He produced a pair of latex gloves from his pocket and put them on.

Houssman didn't argue as Ed lowered himself feet first.

Hobbs landed with a dull thud; he could just stand upright in the center of the oblong metal room, which sloped down on the sides. The interior had the feel of an end-of-the-world hideout, complete with an unused chemical toilet, oxygen tanks, and a re-breather mask. Some of the reading material had spilled on to the floor. Its disarray was a wrong note in the otherwise meticulously tidy space. He looked through the book titles, mostly microbiology and genetics. There were also several cloth-bound notebooks. He opened one and saw pages of tiny hand-writing interspersed with careful illustrations and hand-charted graphs.

'What is it?' Houssman asked, as he tried to follow Ed's movements.

'I've got a sick feeling.'

'Yes,' Houssman said. 'Whatever it was that Glash needed, he's been here, got it and left.'

'Check this out.' Hobbs handed up the notebook to Houssman.

'Interesting,' he said, flipping pages.

'Do you understand it?' Hobbs asked.

'It's a Bioforward laboratory journal. Most companies would frown on a researcher removing them.'

'There's dozens of them down here,' Hobbs replied.

'I imagine they're all there, except the one that Glash took.'

'That's what I'm thinking,' Hobbs said, taking a final sweep of the interior with the light.

As he climbed out, Houssman was trying to decipher the careful handwriting and complex equations. 'Albert worked for Bio-forward,' he said slowly. 'He was specifically involved in trying to develop next-generation

137

antibiotics that could handle multiple resistant strains of bacteria.'

'I don't like how that sounds.'

'No. It won't be good. Albert would have had years to work on perfecting super bacteria that no drugs could stop.'

'Bacteria are living things,' Hobbs remarked. 'Albert has been locked up for over five years. You don't think he kept live strains down there?'

Houssman peered down the hatch. 'Not likely. Bacteria need food ... or you have to freeze them.'

'So what then? What was Glash looking for, an instruction manual?'

'Possibly, although we'd better be careful about jumping to conclusions.'

'But if it's a how-to, then maybe we've got some time. Maybe...'

'Maybe *she's* got some time,' Houssman said.

Hobbs shook his head. 'Cosway's a menace. I didn't tell you why I wanted his ass kicked off the force.' Still wearing gloves, he closed the hatch. 'It was a domestic dispute that turned ugly. The crack-head boyfriend has his girlfriend and their two kids hostage. I'd tracked down his mother and she was on the way to try and negotiate. It seemed like we'd be able to bring things to a good solution. We had an open line; the kid was more scared than angry and knew he'd made a series of stupid mistakes. The SWAT team was in place, just in case. When his mother got there

I went down to brief her. Cosway must have been waiting for me to leave. The minute my back was turned, he gave the order to storm the apartment. The kid panicked, he shot his girlfriend and then took himself out. The children saw the whole thing. I was with his mother...' Hobbs let out a slow breath. 'In the investigation Cosway didn't back down. He lied, and got caught at it. Said I'd ordered the SWAT team to take action. When that didn't work, he started spouting a load of crap about not negotiating with kidnappers.' A sudden revving of engines shut out the hum of the heat bugs. Hobbs's head whipped around. 'What's going on?'

They retraced their steps back to the cabin as several vehicles roared to life. Sirens blared.

Hobbs ran toward Cosway and Zane's Town Car, which was kicking up dust as it headed toward the road, a blue light pulsing on its dash. He planted himself directly in front of the vehicle. They slammed to a stop, nearly hitting him.

'What the hell is going on?' Hobbs shouted, as Cosway lowered the window.

'Fucking waste of time!' Cosway yelled back. 'Our boy's killed again. It's all over the fucking news!'

Hobbs's gut twisted; he braced for the worst. 'Who?'

'Justin fucking Green! Two hours from here! Glash wasn't here at all. While you've been blowing smoke up our asses Glash just killed four more people. He's making us look like morons. Now get out of the fucking way! And when this is over, Hobbs, I'm going to see to it personally that you take the fall for this. Move!' he shrieked, as Zane put the car in gear.

If Hobbs hadn't jumped out of the way he had no doubt that they'd have run him over. 'Shit!' he shouted, watching them roar off in the dust. His heart pounded; he'd never felt more desperate. Four more people; one was Justin Green, who the hell were the other three? He watched the dust cloud rise from the growing caravan of six black Homeland Security vehicles, an unmarked FBI sedan and four state cruisers.

'Idiots,' George Houssman said, as he bent on stiff knees to retrieve something from the ground where Cosway and Zane had been parked. 'Not been here at all. Look at this.' It was Barrett's card.

Hobbs took the card, and hastily reassured himself that she was OK and that she'd deliberately left a clue. That was followed by the crushing realization that Glash was hours away. And he'd killed four more ... *who were the other three?*

'You can't think about her,' Houssman said, trying to calm Hobbs's mounting panic. 'We have to assume she's OK, and even if God forbid she's not ... we can't get distracted. Justin Green would be the last one accounted for,' he said cryptically, as FBI agent Tom Anderson joined them.

'It's a nightmare,' the seasoned veteran with his balding circle of graying blond hair commented. He took a look at Barrett's card, and immediately understood its significance. 'So what else did you find? More importantly, where do you think he's headed next?'

Houssman stared in the direction of the fading sirens and the thick trail of dust rising through the woods. 'He's completed murders for Jane Saunders and Allison Tessavian. So it stands to reason that now he'll try to put in motion Clarence Albert's catastrophic vision.'

'The drawings in his notebook,' Ed Hobbs said, his mouth dry. 'It's what he's been planning. We should have pushed Albert harder.'

'It wouldn't have worked,' Houssman replied. 'He was shutting down. But I think whatever Glash took he'll need time and someplace where he won't be disturbed.'

'Any suggestions where?' Tom asked.

'It won't be chosen at random.'

Hobbs's cell rang. It was Atwell, the cryptolography expert who'd begun work on Albert's manifesto. 'You were right,' he said. 'It's encrypted and it has a shifting alphanumeric key. It's crackable, but the code randomly changes every five to ten symbols. How fast do you need it?'

'Now,' Hobbs said. 'Actually, ten minutes ago.'

'I hear you. The little I've deciphered has a weird biblical twang. Something about Egypt.'

'Plague,' Houssman said. 'Of course ...

That's what the shelter was for. Albert was planning to release a resistant strain. Oh, dear God ... that's what he meant: "ashes, ashes, we'll all fall down".'

Thirteen

Barrett woke from a fitful sleep to the steady hum of the van's engine, and the hard pulse of the tires moving fast. She was exhausted, her fingers were numb and her shoulder throbbed. She ran her tongue over cracked lips and glimpsed daylight through the blue plastic that Glash had again thrown over her and Carla. He'd fed them granola bars and would periodically give them sips of bottled water. He repeatedly reminded them of how little it mattered if they lived or died. But if that were true, Barrett wondered, why hadn't he gone ahead and killed them? It seemed a chore for him to be dragging them around. So he obviously had some purpose for them.

She looked toward Carla, who was curled in a fetal position, her head a couple of feet from Barrett's, her mouth duct-taped, both of her eyes blackened with fresh bruises that spread down her face. Barrett watched for the rise of her chest to know that she was still breathing. Earlier this morning Barrett had felt sure that Glash was going to shoot her. He'd pistol-whipped Carla, who'd screamed as he'd forced them to witness yet another act of carnage. Worse, he'd seemed to offer them a choice, as if they were his accomplices and not his hostages.

He'd returned to the van with a handsome young man, dressed in his underwear, bound and gagged. He'd told Carla, 'You pick. Him or you.' It had taken Barrett a few seconds to understand who this latest victim was ... Justin Green. How Glash could have managed to kidnap the pop star she had no idea, and it filled her with fresh terror. If he could get to someone like Green, who probably had security guards, how would anyone be able to stop him?

Carla had refused to answer Glash, and he'd beaten her. She'd finally managed to sob the word, 'Him.'

And that's when Glash proceeded to drown the teen idol in a large plastic bucket of water in the back of the van.

The poor man's athletic body had thrashed and kicked, his head held under by Glash's meaty hands. Water had splashed out, soaking them all; that's when Carla had screamed.

The third murder Barrett had been forced to witness. She'd felt numb, disconnected and not quite real, as she saw the life flow out of the beautiful young man with his poetic eyes. Snippets of pop tunes that had kept him in the public eye for nearly a decade shot through her head – *Wake up, Baby Baby* and the infectious *Let Me be Your Candy*. She'd bought that album online, unable to shake the tune from her head, admiring the pop star's use of baroque themes, harpsichord and all, updated and electrified.

'Please don't,' she'd mouthed as Glash had looked straight at her. He was like a child wanting his mommy to see him dive into the swimming pool – *Mommy, Mommy, watch me!* He needed an audience. It was the only reason she could find to explain why she was still alive. Yet that didn't seem like reason enough.

She twisted slightly away from Carla and on to her back – her shoulder started to throb. Through the edge of the tarp she glimpsed blue sky. The van had left the smooth highway surface and they were now going over a pockmarked road. Overhead she saw trees and the tops of buildings. One redbrick structure caught her attention, the architecture similar to the turn-of-the-century buildings on the sprawling grounds outside of Croton.

The van stopped and she braced herself. Carla was now awake and struggling to breathe through her nose.

She heard the doors open; her heart pounded; a wave of warm air swept under the tarp, billowing it upward.

Glash ripped it off and looked at her. She tensed and didn't speak as he studied her and then Carla, whose face was contorted as she struggled to take in breath through her nostrils. He seemed to be deciding something.

Was this the moment he'd decided to kill them? She realized that somehow she had stopped being afraid, her fear replaced by a kind of numbness, as she stared back at

Glash.

'If you scream again, I'll kill you,' he said to Carla, and then he viciously ripped the duct tape from her mouth.

She gasped. 'Please don't kill me,' she pleaded. 'I have a little girl. Her name is April. Please don't kill me.'

'Shut up,' he told her, but quietly. He looked at Barrett. 'I'm going to untape your legs. If you run, I'll kill her, then I'll kill you.'

'I won't run,' Barrett said.

'Good.'

As she looked behind him she recognized where he'd taken them. She saw several deserted buildings that comprised the abandoned Albomar State Mental Hospital. It was one of several sprawling facilities that at the heyday of long-term institutionalization of people with psychiatric illnesses would have housed thousands of patients. It was here that Richard Glash had spent the majority of his childhood. In a weird way, he'd brought them home.

He reached over and dragged Carla by her legs to the back doors of the van. Barrett watched as he hoisted the bound woman over his shoulder and holding a gun in his free hand, ordered her out.

She blinked against the blinding sunlight and felt her knees start to buckle.

'Stay in front of me,' he told her, and directed her up the stairs into what had once been the children's residential hospital.

He took them through a service entrance. A

chain and padlock had been removed and there was a gaping hole in the door where the lock had been.

Her mind spat out questions. *How would he have known the building was open? Why was the building open? Who the fuck was helping him?*

There were working lights inside, which didn't surprise her, as the state hadn't yet decided what to do with these old deserted buildings. She also knew that there'd be some kind of skeleton maintenance and grounds crew. Often they were given small houses rent-free somewhere on the sprawling acreage. The thought gave her a glimmer of hope, but if Glash had the wherewithal to get Justin Green, she doubted he'd overlooked something this basic.

'Open it,' he instructed, as they came to a gray steel door.

She pushed hard and found herself staring down a hallway lined with metal doors, each leading into a small square patient room. The doors had been painted different bright colors, someone's attempt to personalize the cold and scary place that had been home to hundreds of seriously disturbed children. She heard the outside steel door close behind her.

Carla's head shot up from Glash's back as she stared at the door, 'Oh God...'

Glash ordered Barrett into a glass observation room with a padded rubber floor across from the nurses' station. 'Face the wall.' She heard him enter behind her. And through her periphery saw him drop Carla on to a bolted-down metal cot.

He left and locked them in.

Barrett turned and let out a long breath. Through the two-inch thick, shatterproof glass she watched Glash disappear down the hallway. When he was gone she tried the door. It wouldn't budge.

Carla was sobbing. 'We've got to stop him. He's going to do something horrible.'

'I know,' Barrett said, thinking again how this was all Carla's fault. But like her fear of Glash, something had happened to her anger. She found it hard to even look at Carla, her face horribly bruised, her hair matted down with blood on one side where he'd gashed her skull with the butt of his gun.

'He's going to kill us all,' Carla said. 'I know it. Everything I worked for. He's going to undo it all. People will say he's why people with mental illnesses should all be locked away. They're going to say we're dangerous. I should have known. I should have believed him. I just thought he was paranoid or grandiose. I thought it was all fantasy.'

'What are you talking about?' Barrett asked, realizing that as Glash's attorney Carla might have learned something important.

'He's going to kill us all,' she repeated. 'It's what he wants. It's all he ever wanted.'

'Ssh!' Barrett ordered, as she heard the outer corridor door open. Glash had returned carrying a television set he'd taken from the Saunders' home. He placed it on the counter of the nurses' station so that the two women could see the screen. He turned it on and holding the remote flipped through the channels. The reception was bad, as the cable had long ago been disconnected. He found a local station and then another out of Manhattan, and a third that was mostly snow, but they could make out the sound. Two were carrying stories of the manhunt and the murders; the other was a kids' show with singing puppets. He disappeared back into the nurses' station and returned with two smaller and older TV sets; he put them on, and fiddled with their antiquated chrome antennae. The manhunt for Glash and his murder spree crackled through two, while the puppets – that came in the clearest – sang about the importance of washing your hands. They'd found Justin Green's body and the pop star's face, and clips of his recent videos, were interspersed with interviews of FBI agents and aerial photos of the crime scene at Croton.

Glash seemed disinterested in the news or the puppets as he set down the large metal box he'd retrieved at Albert's cabin. He took a screwdriver and using it like a chisel, hammered off the lock.

Fascinated, Barrett watched through the glass as he fished out a black-and-white notebook. He flipped it open and for the next couple of hours, he read through it page by page, oblivious to the cacophony of the TV sets tuned to different stations. As he read, he tapped his fingers on the edge of the counter, his mouth moved and he appeared to be counting very rapidly, as though what he was reading was written in a language that had more to do with math than English. Eventually, he came to the last page and shut the notebook.

He looked at Barrett. 'I'm going to be very famous.' She could just hear him through the glass and above the televisions. 'I'm already more famous than you are. I'm not as famous as Justin Green. Not yet.' He looked at her wrists, still shackled in the black plastic restraints, and walked up to the door. 'Are your hands hurt very badly?' he asked.

His apparent concern took Barrett completely unawares. 'They're OK,' she said, flexing her long fingers.

'If you couldn't write I'd kill you now. You write well. You get published. You'll write about me before you die.'

His matter-of-fact tone and the way he stared at her through the window left little doubt. 'Why are you doing this?' she asked.

'I thought you knew that, Dr Conyors.'

'Just to be famous? Why would you kill all these people? They've never hurt—' she stopped herself.

'Say it,' he ordered. 'You were about to lie to me. I don't like it when people lie to me.'

She kept silent.

'Don't lie. They *have* hurt me. They've hurt me and lied to me ever since I was little. You were trying to hurt me, but I don't think you lied. You wanted to keep me locked up. Now

150

I'm free and it's my turn to make people hurt. Everyone who's ever lied to me, who told me that my foster family would love me, or that the new hospital they were sending me to was just as good as a real home. They all lied, and soon they'll all die. You'll die, as will your sister and your mother,' he stated without emotion. 'I will too, but it's not a hundred percent certain. I might not die.'

'Monster,' Carla muttered. 'How can you do this? After what I did for you, how can you do this? I tried to make things better. I tried to help you. I never lied to you. I never tricked you. I never told you anything that wasn't true. Why are you doing this to me?'

'You need to shut up,' he said. 'I don't need you to write. I might not need you at all.'

Carla bit her lip; tears streamed down her face, and her eyes darted frantically. 'Don't you care about anything, Richard? I have a little girl who I'll never see again. Think about what happened to you; you're doing the same thing to me and my little girl.'

Barrett braced herself. She knew he was armed, and if he didn't need Carla, killing her would mean nothing to him.

Surprisingly, he turned and walked away. He stopped halfway down the corridor and pulled out a cell phone.

Barrett strained to hear who he was talking too. She thought back through many hours spent evaluating Glash, and couldn't come up with a single person who he'd ever identified as a friend. His own family, just a couple of uncles, wanted nothing to do with either him or his murderous father. So who was on the other end? And what were they doing? She thought back through the last forty-eight hours, the pickup truck in the parking lot, the brutal scene at the Saunders' home, finding Justin Green's location, the smashed locks downstairs. Whoever was on the phone was setting the course. But it was impossible to hear through the glass and din of the TVs.

He hung up, and turned his head. 'I'll be back,' he said, raising his voice over the TVs. 'I need new clothes. I need to look nice for my girlfriend. I'm going to ask her to marry me. Now that I'm famous, do you think she'll say yes?'

Barrett looked at Carla. 'Do you know anything about this?' she whispered.

Carla shook her head.

Barrett tried to think of any woman who'd had contact with Glash. All she could come up with was that sometimes murderers get fans who send them letters. Was this his accomplice? 'I didn't know you had a girl-friend,' she shouted back.

'Famous people have no trouble getting dates.'

'That's true,' Barrett answered.

'What should I buy?' he asked. 'What should I wear?'

It took her totally off guard, and then she realized that Glash, who was wearing an ill-fitting pair of pants and a torn tee-shirt he'd stolen from Saunders, had spent the majority of his life locked up in either a psychiatric hospital or a maximum-security prison. Buying clothes was something he'd never done. 'For pants you should get jeans or khakis, maybe a blue shirt to match your eyes.'

'What kind of shoes should I purchase?'

'Sneakers, walking shoes or maybe work boots.'

'What color?'

She understood that despite his incredible artistic talents and complex planning abilities, the simple act of picking out a wardrobe was throwing him. 'Black or white sneakers – don't get any other colors – and if you do get work boots they should be black or tan.'

'Thank you.'

'Richard,' she called after him.

'What?'

'Buy a comb.'

He nodded and walked away.

As he disappeared, Barrett's gaze fell on Albert's notebook; whatever was inside figured heavily in Glash's scheme. Now she thought of Justine and her mother, and threw herself at the door handle. She strained and pulled. It was useless.

'I'll help you,' Carla said.

And as the televisions flashed awful images – Justin Green; Glash; the hotel in the Catskills; an Andy Griffith rerun; the bloody walls of the Saunders' home; recent photos of Barrett and Carla; concerned cops; even the governor – the two women, with their hands still bound, exhausted themselves.

'We've got to stop him,' Carla sobbed, banging her now bloody fists against the door handle. 'He's going to kill us. I'll never see my daughter again.'

'We can't think like that,' Barrett said. 'As long as we're alive we've got a chance. I also think you kind of got to him with that.'

Carla sank to the floor. 'I can't believe that I let this happen ... you tried to warn me. But I've spent so much time hating you. You could have said anything and it wouldn't have mattered.'

'I know,' Barrett said, and realizing that she was getting nowhere with the door, she sat down next to her on the floor. 'I should have gotten myself pulled off the case when I saw you were the attorney. But I couldn't; it was too important and I'd already evaluated all of them. Plus...'

Carla gave a half smile. 'You couldn't trust it to someone else, could you?'

'No.'

'To me, when I realized you were the expert for the state, it was my chance finally to get back at you. I wondered if in some twisted way you wanted another crack at me. Or maybe this was God's weird joke to throw us together. All these years I've thought about what happened, and then when I saw you, and realized that you'd try to stop the transfers, it was my chance for payback. I wanted you to fail. I wanted you to feel a fraction of the hell you put me through.'

'I know it's kind of late in the day,' Barrett

said, 'but I am so sorry for what happened, and for whatever role I played in it.'

Carla nodded. 'When I left the hospital, my marriage was over. I could have dealt with that, but having my parental rights terminated was devastating. Everything I'd ever wanted was gone – even my career.' She laughed bitterly. 'Bill and I had agreed when we got married that I'd put my law career on hold while he got his started. When I left the hospital all I could think about was how I'd kill myself. I'd intended to take all of the pills I was given when you discharged me and overdose; it seemed fitting. I even wondered if you'd feel guilty, knowing that I'd ended my life with the very medications you'd prescribed.'

'I never meant to hurt you,' Barrett said, feeling tears start to well.

Carla bit her lip and shook her head. 'Do you know how angry that makes me? If you could feel the rage I've had to carry. How many times I listen to psychiatrists talk about doing everything in the patient's best interest. You have no idea what kind of power you wield. With just a flick of a pen you can have someone locked up, or have a conservator appointed so that they can't handle their own money or where they choose to live. But it's all in our best interest. In the course of a few weeks you took everything from me. Years of my life gone. How can you do that to someone?'

'I'm so sorry, for what happened,' Barrett

said.

'I think you are,' Carla said, trying to keep her temper under control. 'But that's just it, nothing changes. I've had three manic episodes in my life: one in college; one after I'd spent three weeks studying for the Bar exam, which I passed on the first try; and the third after I gave birth to April. I spent so much of my life being frightened and afraid of the illness. Not in the way you think, but more because of how people treated me once they found out. It's like you suddenly become something less than human, not quite a real person. I never told Bill. I was afraid he'd leave me. Obviously, I was right.'

'What happened after you left the hospital?' Barrett asked, feeling battered by Carla's story, and the part she'd played.

'I came close to committing suicide. But as I was setting out to do it, I actually thought about something you'd told me.'

'Really?'

'Yes, you'd tried to give me hope, to say that in time and with the medication I'd get back on track. That there was no reason I couldn't practice law, have a family. As you were saying those things to me, I was so filled with hate, not to mention being way over-medicated. But when I got home – or should I say back in my parents' house and the bedroom I'd grown up in – I heard it a different way. What you'd done to me, I knew you were doing to others. And not just you ... but every shrink in every hospital. How many times a day do women lose their children because of this? Or people have all their civil liberties stripped because they happen to hear voices or are paranoid? It was like a light went on, and I knew that yes, I would pull it together. I would practice law, and I would make sure that what was done to me, would become a thing of the past. Killing myself would have just made things worse – *Oh, the poor mental patient, they were right to take away her kid, to lock her up.* When I hear people talk about what's "in my best interest" it makes me furious.'

'I've noticed,' Barrett commented. As she said that her stomach cramped and she started to dry heave. All that came up was a bit of the last granola bar and some saliva.

'Are you sick?' Carla asked.

'No,' Barrett said, still hunched forward, waiting for the feeling to pass and thinking about what Carla had just told her. 'I'm pregnant.'

Fourteen

With one hand on the wheel of the Crown Vic and the other holding his cell, Hobbs tried to calm Justine on the other end of the line, as he drove through the lush green pine forests of the Catskills. His nerves were frayed, he was beyond exhaustion, and the words coming out of his mouth rang false: 'She's going to be OK,' he said, 'we're going to bring her home.'

'When we do,' Justine said, trying to keep up her end, 'can we lock her up for a while?'

Next to him was Houssman, his face covered with stubble, his gray fedora abandoned on the seat next to him, and his wispy white hair shooting out at crazy angles. He scanned a map of New York State, trying to trace where Glash had been and might go next.

Justine had called, desperate for information, wondering, like many, why the Department of Homeland Security had been placed in charge.

'What aren't they telling us?' she asked.

'I can't say,' Hobbs said, doing his best to stay out of the way of Cosway and his sidekick Zane. He had let Tom Anderson, the FBI agent, phone in their discoveries from

Albert's cabin hours earlier – the recently disturbed bomb shelter and Barrett's card; proof positive that Glash had been there. Listening in, Hobbs had heard Cosway's dismissive response. 'Old news,' he'd said.

Hobbs had slammed his fist into a tree, needing the pain to keep from screaming into the receiver, *'You fucking incompetent!'* Thank God it had been Tom on the phone and not him. The FBI agent had his phone on speaker and had calmly told Cosway that the FBI would handle the kidnappings and the murders, but there was compelling evidence that Glash wanted to pick up where Albert had left off. 'Isn't that why Homeland Security is involved? This looks like bioterrorism.'

'Let me clarify,' Cosway had screamed back, 'we're not *involved*; we're in charge. This comes under the National Incident Management System; I am authorized by direct order of the Secretary of Homeland Security to oversee what has been determined to be a national incident. Is that understood, Agent Anderson?'

Tom had stuck his middle finger up and waved it in front of the phone. 'Yes, sir.'

'Good, I'll send a team back to do a proper search of the shelter. I certainly hope you didn't disturb the scene.'

Now, with Justine still on the line, Hobbs was desperately trying to tell her that everything was under control, that Barrett was going to be safe and this was all a bad dream. But with a cold trail, an incompetent commander who viewed hostages as expendable, and a killer who sought destruction of biblical proportions, he didn't have a lot of reassurance to give.

'Just tell me she's going to be OK,' Justine begged.

'I'll do everything I can.'

'I know you will, Ed. I'm just so scared. You'd tell me if you'd found her ... dead?'

'I think she's OK. She's smart and resourceful, and if there's a way for anyone to figure out how to get away from this guy, she'll do it.'

'But would she?' Justine said. 'Or would she figure it was her duty to try and stop him? Look at what she did.'

'I know ... Justine, I'll call you if I find anything. Where are you going to be?'

She gave him her cell. 'I'm at the hospital. It's all anyone is talking about. It's on every station. People think Homeland Security is involved because of Clarence Albert and the anthrax mailings.'

'They wouldn't be wrong,' he said.

'Shit!'

'Exactly,' and feeling like his head was going to explode, he hung up, and made the turn up the sweeping drive to the Bella Vista Resort.

While Ed wanted to avoid any contact with Cosway, there was no mistaking the man being interviewed by a news crew as they drove up to the grand, castle-like Victorian hotel where earlier that morning Justin Green had been abducted and murdered.

Houssman looked through the windshield. 'Ed, stop the car. This feels wrong.'

'Tell me about it,' Hobbs said, his frustration at boiling point as he took in the multiple media vans and reporters tramping through the grounds, mucking up the crime scene. 'Idiots! Morons!' Then he watched Cosway smooth back his shiny hair as he fielded questions.

'Whatever Glash set out to do here, is done,' Houssman said. 'We'll find nothing of use, just more bodies. We've got to think ahead of him. I think I've got an idea as to who might be his accomplice. I realized I've been making an assumption that could be wrong.'

'Which is?'

'That Glash had no contact with his biologic father – Peter.'

'Isn't he in prison? He killed his wife ... oh, shit!'

'Exactly ... nearly forty years ago. He bargained down to second degree; I doubt he served more than ten to fifteen.'

'Is he even still alive?' But Hobbs already had his cell out and was dialing the department's liaison with Corrections. He identified himself and gave his shield number, while punching Peter Glash's name into the Crown Vic's on-board computer, and the Department of Corrections' prisoner locater.

Within minutes they'd learned that Peter Glash had been paroled nearly thirty years ago after serving less than ten years of an eighteen-year sentence. Hobbs held his breath as he asked, 'Do you have his current address?' He pushed the button for speaker-phone.

'We have his last known,' the woman said, 'it's fifteen years old.' And she read it out.

Houssman scribbled it down on the edge of his map. 'Let me have your cell,' he said.

Peering over his thick lenses to see the buttons, Houssman punched in Felicia's number. 'It's George Houssman,' he said as she picked up. 'Do you have Glash's visitor's logs?'

'Yes, give me a minute to find them.'

'Read me every name along with the dates.' As they waited, Houssman fished out a steno pad from a well in the passenger-side door.

'Think we'll get lucky?' Ed asked.

'I don't know.'

Hobbs cranked up the AC as they waited. He stared through the windshield and im-agined how good it would feel to smash his fist into Cosway's smug face. 'I think you're right about this being a waste of time. That address for Peter Glash, it's in the Lower East Side of Manhattan.'

'Yes,' Houssman said, 'the family owned a business there, the entire building actually.'

'Not a bad place for a hideout.'

'No, indeed.'

'Care for a drive to Manhattan?'

'Of course.'

Ed backed up and did a quick, gravel-spit-ting U-turn. Houssman glanced through the back window at Cosway. For the briefest moment he thought the Homeland Security agent had spotted them. 'I'm assuming you're deliberately not sharing our new-found insight with the energetic Mr Cosway?'

'A correct assumption.'

'Dr Houssman,' Felicia's voice came over the speaker, 'I've got the list ... is there any word on Barrett?'

Taking a cue from Hobbs's earlier call, he said, 'She's a smart woman, she'll know better than anyone how to work with Glash; I think she'll be OK. Now read me the list, and don't leave anything off.'

Hobbs nodded, gritted his teeth and floored it.

Fifteen

'There's a ninety percent certainty that I will die,' Richard Glash told Barrett as he drove. He listened for the sound of her typing. 'Did you get that?'

'Yes,' she said, her back pressed against the van wall, a small Sony laptop duct-taped to her bound legs. It was night and they'd been driving for half an hour. Glash was dressed in a navy blue security guard's uniform; he'd also put on a pair of thick, black-framed glasses. He was insisting that she record his every word. Despite the hours she'd spent formally interviewing Glash prior to this race to hell, it was only now that she truly saw who and what he was. Some of what she'd learned had shocked her, starting with the revelation that George Houssman had for a brief period been Glash's foster father. Revealing that was one of the few times Richard Glash had shown anything that could have passed as a gentle emotion. She couldn't see his face, but as he talked about George she'd wondered if he were crying.

'He was supposed to love me and take care of me,' Glash had said. 'He didn't. He and his wife, Delia, sent me to Albomar. They were

164

supposed to adopt me like they did their daughters – Alice and Stephanie. That's what they told me. I was four years old and I believed them. Did you get that?' he'd said angrily. 'They were supposed to be my mommy and my daddy.'

She'd decided it was best not to comment. This was Glash's world as he saw it. The fact that he'd nearly killed his next-door playmate didn't figure into his reality. Occasionally, she'd hazard a question.

'Why did you attack her?' she'd asked, referring to the little girl.

'I wanted to see. It wasn't at all like in the movie.'

'When you were eighteen you went after her again,' she said, years of interviewing criminals having trained her to not flinch but go straight to the heart of things.

'I wasn't done,' he'd said, his tone dry. 'I needed to finish it. You have to finish what you start.'

'Are you done now?' she asked. 'Did you finish that with Lucinda Peters?'

'Yes. And if I don't die I'm going to get married.'

'Really?' Her thoughts raced as she saw a connection with the tragic Lucinda, her scalping and Glash's repeated references to a girlfriend. She would have asked for more details, but he brought the van to a stop and turned off the engine. Her breath caught as he got out and came around to the back of the van. She tracked the soft tread of his footsteps and startled as he opened the door.

She looked at him, dressed as a guard, disguised with glasses and wearing a single black glove on his right hand. 'You want to know what I'm going to do, don't you?'

'Yes,' she whispered.

'Soon.' And he abruptly reached across and forced a balled-up gym sock into her mouth. She didn't struggle as he ran a strip of duct tape around her head, turned off the laptop, closed it and then threw the tarp over her. But before he did that, she glimpsed a large, squat, concrete commercial building. He'd left the van in the far corner of the lot, out of the range of the overhead lights. She could make out the first few letters of an illuminated sign – BIO. He'd brought her to Bioforward; the biotech firm that had employed Clarence Albert for over twenty years. Whatever Glash had retrieved from Albert's property had led him here.

With Glash gone, she struggled against her restraints; her legs cramped and her right shoulder sent stabbing pains whenever she twisted. The numbness that had fallen over her evaporated as she realized the deadly peril facing anyone in that building who stood between Glash and whatever he hoped to find. She had to do something. She didn't know how long he'd be gone, and pushing through the pain she bent down as far as she could and frantically worked away at the tape that bound her legs.

★　★　★

Glash calculates the distance between the parked van and the service entrance to Bioforward. Five years since Albert worked here. Glash wonders if the information he's decoded will still be applicable. His entire plan could fall apart in the next five minutes. He knows that once he enters the building, his every movement will be captured on video. Albert said there would be a single security guard. That's the first mistake. Through the lobby door Glash sees two, dressed just as he is – Albert was correct about the uniform – 'A' and 'B'; they're watching TV. He places a smile on his face, approaches the door and knocks.

'A' walks up to the heavy glass door and looks at him warily without opening it.

Glash flashes a Bioforward picture ID – it belongs to Clarence and was in the metal box; Glash has changed the photograph. 'I'm supposed to be training.'

'I didn't hear anything about a trainee,' 'A' replies without opening the door. He turns back toward 'B'. 'Colin, you know anything about a new guy training tonight?'

'As though they'd tell us,' 'B' answers.

'Right.' 'A' unlocks. 'I don't know what they want us to do with you, but...'

'I'll figure something,' Glash says, pulling the trigger on the Smith & Wesson – *four minutes, twelve seconds.*

As 'A' drops, a startled 'B' draws his gun; and an alarm sounds.

Glash instantly cuts his time in half – he is

approaching failure mode – *one minute, fifty-five seconds*. Was Albert wrong about the rest? He barrels toward 'B', firing as he goes.

The guard dives under the metal desk; worst possible move he could make. Trapped, he tries to shoot at Glash's feet. He clips him in the right shoe; it grazes the skin off two of his toes.

Glash takes aim and puts a bullet in 'B"s head. He glances at the security console; a moment's indecision. Too much is at stake – *one minute, zero seconds*. He pictures Mary the last time she came to visit – she was wearing a blonde wig; she let him see the scars underneath. The siren pulses – Albert was wrong about the number of guards. It was five years ago. The probability that he was wrong about other things is increasing rapidly.

He reaches down and pulls B's body from under the desk. He tears the security badge off and runs down the corridor to the right. Sirens blare and pulse. Lights flash. He swipes the badge through the digital reader outside the laboratory where Albert worked. The door clicks open. Albert was right about that – *forty seconds*. Probability of success is now thirty percent. He bolts to the far side of the room to a refrigerated vault with a computerized keypad. His fingers tap out the ten digits. The lock does not open – *twenty-seven seconds*. Blood seeps through his shoe and on to the floor. He tries the code a second time – it does not open. He steps back, aims at the lock. Fires three shots; two just bend the plate, the third cracks the bolt. He yanks back on the door – *ten seconds*. It opens. Cool air rushes out as he looks into the shelf-lined room. He is out of time – *minus five seconds*. Police will soon be swarming the building – failure mode. He scans the shelves and comes to a series of small cryogenic freezers. It's five years since Albert worked here: high probability that what he hid was long ago removed and destroyed. He reads the serial numbers on the freezers, finds the one he needs – that hasn't changed. He unlatches the lid releasing a frosty steam from the liquid nitrogen. Inside are rows of vials and tempered glass ampoules. With his gloved hand he reaches deep inside – *minus forty-two seconds*. Probability of success ten percent; chance of capture or kill – fifty percent.

Thoughts of failure cloud his mind. He has miscalculated. *Even if they're still here, what chance that they're still viable?* Seconds tick; his fingers find a slight movement in the floor of the tank. He punches down hard with his gloved hand on the edge, sending the other side shooting up. Dozens of carefully arranged biological samples tumble down. Some shatter and spill their contents into the icy bath below. He doesn't care. Potentially toxic fluids dribble down his arm and into his glove, because there, barely visible through the smoke, is a small sealed metal box. He grabs it, shoves it inside his pocket and runs – *minus one minute, twenty seconds*. He hears a single siren in the distance, and ignoring the pain that shoots up from his bleeding foot, he races down the corridor, out the door. He catches the flashing light of a police cruiser and then a second not far behind turning off the main road and heading into the industrial park.

He sprints across the parking lot to Saunders' van. He is deep into failure mode – *minus two minutes, eleven seconds*. He glances in the back to see that Dr Conyors is still under the tarp as he turns over the engine and with his headlights off makes a dash for the parking lot exit. He sees the first cruiser heading toward Bioforward. He turns in the opposite direction. He glances in his rearview to see if they are following. They aren't. They're headed toward the pulsing alarms that emanate from Bioforward's open door. He circles the periphery of the industrial park – hears more sirens as he turns on to the main road. No choice but to head toward them in order to get back on to the highway. He turns on his headlights, keeps his speed well within the limit and counts the cruisers as they speed past – *one, two, three, four* ... Probability of escape, seventy-five percent. Probability of success, seventy percent. He pictures Mary, he'll ask her to marry him, she has to say 'yes'. Maybe she'll want to have children. It would be nice to have children ... a wife.

Once past the last cruiser, he reaches across to the glove compartment and takes out a cell phone. He dials Channel Eight's news hotline. 'This is Richard Glash,' he says. 'I've

170

killed two guards at the Bioforward Corporation in Elizabeth, New Jersey. Itaken something that belonged to Dr Clarence Albert. I'm going to be very famous. Try to guess what I have. Try to guess what I'm going to do.' Then, in a monotone, he sings, *'Ring around the rosy, a pocket full of posy. Ashes, ashes, we'll all fall down.'* He rolls down the window and throws out the phone.

And for the rest of the ride, he thinks about Mary, children and the sexy, tingling feeling he gets when thinking about her wig and the scars underneath it. Maybe she'll let him feel them ... she did before.

Sixteen

Hobbs banged the still raw knuckles of his fist on the gated metal door of the Delancey Street building. It was 5 a.m. on Thursday morning, the sun was half up, and the street stank with yesterday's garbage baking in the sweltering ninety-eight-degree heat. Houssman tipped back his gray hat and looked up at the façade of the four-story, iron-fronted structure. All the windows had been barred and the storefront had sheets of plywood in the window, with heavy steel mesh shutters pulled down to the ground. Over the store was a rusted sign that read *IDEAL CANDY COMPANY – To the Trade and to the Public (established 1912).*

Hobbs caught a vibration through the soles of his feet. 'There's someone in there.' His right hand was on his sidearm, his muscles taut. His mind racing through the *what ifs.* Like what if Glash was on the other side of that door, a gun to Barrett's head? Or a gun pointed straight at him? He caught the sound of something moving, too heavy to be a rat ... at least, not the four-legged kind.

Houssman stepped back from the building and over to a gated alley. He pointed, through

172

the metal slats. 'I think that's where the apartment is.'

Hobbs rang the bell for the fifth time. He banged his fist on the door. 'Open up. I can hear you in there. It's the police.' Every fiber in his body tensed; this was wrong. He should have back-up, but that would let Cosway know his suspicions. And if Barrett were held hostage inside it would mean her death.

Houssman reached a bony hand through the alley gate and lifted the latch. 'There's another door back here,' he said, letting himself into the narrow alley. In front of him was a ramshackle wooden garage, to the left was the brick wall of the building and to the right was a tall, chain-link fence covered with weeds and ivy that separated it from the tenement next door.

Hobbs joined Houssman and banged his closed fist on the wooden door. 'Police, open up!'

'Quiet!' a voice hissed from the other side. The handle turned and a sliver of dark appeared. A gray-haired man with water-blue eyes peered through the crack; he blocked the opening with his body. 'What do you want?'

'Mr Glash?' Hobbs asked, trying to see inside as Houssman joined him.

'Who wants to know?' And then Peter Glash caught sight of Houssman. 'What are you doing here?'

'Hello, Peter,' Houssman said. 'I wasn't certain you'd remember me; it's been a long time.'

'If this is about Richard, I don't know anything. You took my son away from me. Now leave me alone. I've had enough trouble. I don't want the neighbors to know I have anything to do with him.'

Hobbs flashed his shield and placed a booted foot against the door. 'Do you, Mr Glash? Do you know where your son is?' He applied pressure, feeling the old man on the other side resist.

'Go away,' he said. 'I have nothing to do with Richard. I don't want you here.'

'Mr Glash, we need to talk to you. I'd prefer we not do it in the alley. Let us in.' A hand joined the foot, Glash started to falter.

'What if I won't?'

Hobbs eased off. 'I'll be back in twenty minutes with a search warrant. I'll have this building swarming with cops. And I'll get you thrown in jail for interfering with a multiple homicide and kidnapping investigation.'

'Why are you doing this to me? Why do your people persecute me? I haven't done anything.'

'I didn't say you had,' Hobbs said, his hand back on the door, applying pressure. 'Now let us in.'

'This isn't right, you can't do this.' But Peter Glash stepped back.

Hobbs didn't hesitate, as he rapidly took in the surroundings. His ears attuned to any sound, his eyes in wide focus, not wanting to miss anything in the shadows or the periphery. He quickly noted the immaculate and sparse kitchen, waxed and yellowed linoleum flooring, old chrome and Formica furniture, a single bare bulb illuminating the space. He let the door swing wide open, seeing the impact that had on Glash.

Peter Glash recoiled as sunlight spilled across the floor. His eyes darted toward the opening, as though expecting others to be watching. 'This is police harassment. I don't know what it is you hope to find here. I have nothing to do with my son.'

Hobbs stepped over the threshold, taking stock of Glash: tall, like his son, and looking younger than his seventy-one years. The resemblance to Richard was striking, both with the same staring blue eyes and gaunt faces. Only where Richard was stocky and muscular his father reminded Hobbs of a tall, bony bird.

Houssman trailed in uninvited behind Hobbs, leaving the door wide open.

'You killed his biologic mother ... your wife, nearly forty years ago,' Hobbs stated. 'That's something of a connection.'

'She was a whore!' he spat.

'When's the last time you saw your son?' Hobbs asked, stepping across the kitchen, making eye contact but keeping alert for any other sound or movement.

'Thirty-eight years ago.'

'Since your release you've never visited him?'

'No.'

'When did you last write to him?' Hobbs

asked, forcing eye contact, knowing in his gut he was lying – he had to be. Although the logs they'd had Felicia pull would back his story – Peter Glash had never gone to visit his son.

Glash hesitated slightly. 'Never, now leave me alone.'

'Why the pause, Peter?' Hobbs asked, pushing back the desperation – there was something here.

'What are you trying to do to me?' Glash spat back. 'I'll get my lawyer. This is harassment. Where are you going?' he said, realizing that Houssman had wandered to a closed door on the far side of the kitchen. 'I didn't say you could go in there!'

'Why?' Hobbs sniffed the air. 'What don't you want us to see?'

Houssman tried the handle. 'It's locked.'

'Open it,' Hobbs ordered.

'This is harassment. I'll call my lawyer. I'll sue you.'

Hobbs snapped, in a flash he'd crossed the last few feet that separated him and Glash. He grabbed the older man by the neck of his button-down shirt and pushed him up against the wall. 'Open the fucking door!' he shouted into Glash's face. 'Do it now!'

Peter Glash stared back at Hobbs. He didn't flinch. 'Go ahead, beat me. It won't be the first time I've been beaten by cops. You think this will make me help you? It won't. I've been watching the news and I've seen what Richard has been doing. You're mad because you can't stop him.'

176

'What do you know about him?' Hobbs shouted, twisting the course fabric tight around Glash's throat, cutting off his air.

'I don't know anything,' he wheezed, his hands batting ineffectively at Hobbs.

In the meantime Houssman was rifling through the kitchen drawers. As he came to one next to the sink Glash became agitated; he struggled fiercely to twist away from Hobbs's grip.

Houssman pulled a torn manila envelope from out of the drawer. He peered over his glasses at the address. He dumped the contents on to the kitchen table.

Glash glared at him.

'You lied to us, Peter,' Houssman accused. There, on the table, was a neatly folded letter with a faded Polaroid photograph of a teen-aged Richard Glash. The address was the Albomar youth facility. Houssman picked up the letter and started to read.

Dear Father,

I'm happy that you are no longer in prison for killing my mother. I am not mad at you and I understand why you killed her. I think they will keep me here until I am eighteen. I am told they have to let me go then. They lie and so I can't be certain if this will happen or not. I cannot predict the probability; I think it is greater than fifty percent. Although, I do agree, as you stated in your last letter, it is impossible to predict probability accurately unless you know all of the variables.

'That's private,' Glash hissed.

'No.' Hobbs smashed Glash hard against the wall. 'That's called *probable cause.* Now where the fuck is he?' he demanded.

'I don't know,' Glash replied; he was smiling. 'Go ahead and beat me. It won't do any good. I don't know where he is.'

Disgusted, Hobbs let go, walked to the locked door and kicked it in, splintering the wood around the lock. It was Glash's bedroom, drab and tidy, but what snagged his attention was a framed photograph of father and son in the grounds of the state hospital. It must have been taken soon after Peter Glash's release from prison. They were both smiling, but the expressions were forced and grimacing.

Hobbs grabbed Glash again, wanting to keep an eye on him, and pulled him along as he proceeded to search the building. He knew that Peter Glash was lying, but as he and Houssman went through the three rooms of the tiny apartment and into the largely derelict storerooms, he could see no trace of Richard. His despair mounted. There had to be something. 'Don't you care that your son is killing people and has taken two women hostage?'

Peter Glash stood still, watching the cop and the aged psychiatrist search his home and his business.

'I do care,' he sneered.

Hobbs gave him a warning look, he sniffed

the stale air. 'Something died in here.'

'I have a rodent problem,' Glash replied, and pointed out sticky glue traps at regular intervals around the periphery. 'See,' he said, looking at one on which a desiccated rat body was affixed. 'We've always had rats ... As for those two women ... they're not here, and Richard's not here; he's too smart for that. But I'll tell you this; they're both as good as dead.'

Hobbs felt something snap.

'Ed, no!' Houssman shouted, as Hobbs shoved Peter Glash against the wall. 'Ed! Don't!'

Hobbs didn't even feel Houssman's bony hands on his back, trying to pull him off. His eyes bore into Glash's as his fist slammed into his gut.

'Tell me where he is!' Hobbs screamed as he backhanded Glash's gasping face, making hard contact with nose and cheek.

Houssman's hat tumbled to the floor as he kept trying to pull him off. 'Ed, don't. This isn't the way. Maybe he knows things, but she's not here. They've not been here.'

Ed looked down at Peter Glash, and saw his nose was bleeding and his eye and jaw were red and starting to puff up. He wanted to scream, the emotions too powerful – rage and fear.

'He won't tell us anything,' Houssman said. 'And beating him isn't going to help. If it was, I'd say keep at it. Richard Glash isn't here ... But I think I know where he is. I should have realized it sooner.'

'Where?' Hobbs asked, getting off Glash, feeling as though his knees might buckle.

Houssman looked at Peter Glash. 'I'll tell you in the car. Let's get out of here. I don't think we have much time.'

As they headed out Glash followed them. 'You're in so much trouble. I'm calling my lawyer. I'll sue you. I'll sue you both!' And he slammed the door and bolted it.

Peter Glash's heart pounded. The right side of his face throbbed and he was still gasping from the blow to his gut. He didn't move at first and then he hurried from the apartment into the deserted storefront. His eye spotted the dead rat – he knew that he'd come close to catastrophe. The rat had been a good touch. He sniffed the air as he peered through a chip in the painted windows. He caught the scent of death as he watched the detective and Dr Houssman. He waited for them to drive away.

'Too close,' he muttered, as he pulled out a cell phone, identical to the ones being used and then discarded by his son. He punched in a number. There was no answer. He tried a second number. Again, nothing.

On the third try, he heard, 'Yes, Father?'

'The police were here,' he said, and, knowing that the mention of Houssman's name could send his son into a violent rage, he kept silent about that. 'They're gone, but it's close. They didn't believe me.'

Richard Glash said nothing at first. 'Did you tell them where I am?'

'No, but there's a probability they've figured it out.'

'How is that possible if you didn't tell them?'

'They saw the picture of us at Albomar.' Peter prayed his son wouldn't question him further on that.

'Is everything ready?'

'Yes.'

'All three of them?'

'Yes,' he answered, 'I got the last one this morning. She was jogging, and from the back she looks just like your lawyer. I dressed her just the way you said.'

'Good. I'll call you when I'm ready for them. I have one more thing I have to do. Then it's time. And Father?'

'Yes, Richard?'

'Thank you. I'd never have been able to do this without you. The probability would have been zero.'

As Peter Glash hung up, he felt something moist on his cheek. He assumed it was blood, from the cop's beating. He stared into an empty glass display case and caught his reflection. He could see the start of a large black eye, but what he'd thought was blood were tears. The first he had ever shed.

Seventeen

Barrett stared through the glass wall of the locked observation room, her eyes flipping between the three snowy television sets. Her wrists, still restrained, ached, but at least Glash had removed the tape from her legs.

Carla slept fitfully on the padded floor behind her and she saw no reason to wake her. She'd been like that since Glash had brought Barrett back from Jersey. What he'd revealed to her on the ride back was monstrous; it had shattered through her numbness, filling her with near-paralyzing panic. He'd insisted that she write it down. 'I will culture Dr Albert's plague strain,' he'd said, 'and then I will pour it into the Ashokan Reservoir, which supplies eighty percent of New York City's water.'

As he'd talked, she could barely think. Could such a plan succeed? The reservoir water was too cold; the bacteria wouldn't survive, and wouldn't they become too dilute to actually infect anyone? And in their current frozen form perhaps they'd already been destroyed. Albert had been locked up for five years; how long could bacteria keep? But she'd kept those thoughts to herself. Something didn't add up. Until now, Glash had been so careful. It seemed unlikely he'd make such an amateurish mistake. Was he deliberately misleading her? And if so, why?

On the opposite side of the nursing station she watched as he abruptly stripped out of his guard's uniform. He was completely naked, no sense of modesty, his genitals and bare buttocks clearly visible above the counter. That same lack of social appropriateness she'd observed when he'd taken her or Carla for their bathroom visits. It was clinical ... but maybe that wasn't the word. It just didn't register with him that people weren't supposed to strip naked in front of strangers. Or that there was something odd in taking down a woman's pants so she could pee.

As she watched, she noticed that for a man in his forties he had an outstanding physique, no trace of fat, or middle-age spread around the middle. Once naked, he began to pull out newly purchased clothing from plastic bags he'd deposited out of view.

'Do I look nice?' he asked, coming to stand in front of the window.

She stared at the tall man, now in Levi's, sneakers and a button-down shirt. At his side was the metal box he'd retrieved from Albert's property. 'Yes,' she replied honestly. 'You look very nice.' He'd even combed down his thick shock of black hair. She wanted to add, *You can almost pass for normal.*

'Where are you going?'

'To see my girlfriend.' A muscle in his cheek

fluttered.

She glimpsed the hint of a blush creeping up the sides of his face. Gently she tested the water, knowing that the slightest wrong step would set him off. 'What's her name?'

'Mary.'

Barrett shuddered. The only Mary she knew connected to Glash was the woman he'd twice tried to kill. Would this be the third time? 'Does she know you're coming?'

'Yes.'

Was this the accomplice? she wondered. 'Is that who you've been talking to on the phone?'

'You're trying to trick me.'

'I'm not,' she said, afraid to move. 'It's called small talk. Are you nervous?'

He paused and blinked. He said nothing as seconds stretched. 'I am,' he finally said.

She wanted to know what he intended for Mary. Was there any way he could be stopped, or she could be warned? Then again, he hadn't gotten dressed up for any of the other murders. 'What are you planning to do with her?' she had to ask.

'I told you already. I'm going to ask her to marry me.' He patted his breast pocket and pulled out Lucinda Peter's diamond engagement ring. 'I'm forty-two years old; I should have a wife. There's a ninety percent probability that I will not be alive in three days. I'll tell her that. But there's a ten percent chance I *will* be alive.'

'What if she doesn't say yes?' Barrett asked,

and immediately wished that she hadn't.

Glash's face contorted, his nose flattened and his jaw tensed as his fist came down hard on the glass wall that separated them. '*Shut up!*'

'I'm sorry,' Barrett said, jumping back.

Carla's eyes, both badly bruised, opened in slits. 'What's happening?'

'She has to say yes.' Glash shouted, and droplets of spittle landed on the window. 'I'll make her say yes. I'm forty-two years old; I should be married. She will say yes.'

He put the ring back in his pocket. He was breathing heavily and he glared at Barrett. He shook his head. 'You shouldn't make me angry.' He turned to leave, and then he stopped with his back to the two women. 'I'll kill her if she doesn't say yes. Then again, she might die anyway from the plague.'

'What have you done with it? With Albert's plague?' Barrett asked, pushing through her fear, wondering if it were already too late. She pictured her sister, her mother ... her unborn child.

He turned. 'I'm surprised, Dr Conyors. Didn't you take microbiology?'

'Yes.'

'Then you should know that the bacteria were frozen and in a suspended state. I'm waking them up and feeding them with enriched agar; I should have enough within twenty-four hours. Although I plan to test them first.' He hoisted up the box and opened the lid to reveal two quart-sized glass milk bottles filled with a swirling, coco-brown murk.

'Don't you want to protect Mary?' she asked, staring at the deadly brew, stunned to realize that the bacteria were quite alive. 'Don't you love her?'

'I love Mary,' he said, 'she's going to say yes. And either I survive or I don't. She survives or she doesn't. "A" and "B", "A" and "B".'

He walked away. Barrett stared down the hall, her eyes fixed on the metal box that dangled at his side. She heard the door to the ward bang open and then closed.

'Is he gone?' Carla asked, rolling on to her back. Her face was a puffy confluence of bruises, and unlike Barrett, he'd left her fully restrained with thick bands of duct tape across her thighs and her ankles.

'Yes,' Barrett said, barely able to speak. Her thoughts were racing – the bacteria were alive, this was all possible, horribly, undeniably possible. End of the world, end of everyone she loved.

'Check the door,' Carla said. 'I didn't hear him lock it when he brought you back last night.'

At first Barrett couldn't hear her, was too distracted and too frightened.

'Try the door,' Carla said again.

'Right.' She positioned her cuffed wrists around the steel handle. She pressed down, and with a start she felt it give. She glanced down the hall to make sure Glash hadn't returned, and then gently pushed. 'It's open.'

'Go for help. Please go quickly!' Carla pleaded. 'He's got to be stopped.'

Barrett glanced down at her fellow prisoner.

'No,' Carla said, 'don't waste any time on me. Get out of here. He could come back at any time. Please hurry!'

Feeling horribly exposed, Barrett stepped out into the corridor and glanced at the television sets that had been running non-stop. Glash had alerted the press to his every move. He was taunting the authorities, and now he'd started a panic with the threat of an anthrax attack. News shows were interviewing physicians at hospitals already overwhelmed with terrified citizens. People were barricading themselves in their houses and apartments. If they knew what he really intended, she thought, it would be even worse.

With her hands still restrained and in front of her, she ran awkwardly toward the steel door. She turned the knob. 'Shit!' He'd forgotten their cell door, but not this one. 'It's locked,' she shouted back to Carla.

She doubled back to the nurses' station and hunted for the release switch. After crawling under the counter and frantically feeling in the dark she found the button and pressed. She heard a buzz and the door clicked. She got up and raced for it. Halfway there it clicked again. 'No!' she screamed, as tears of frustration welled. It was on a short timer. Just a couple of seconds; no way could she press the button and make it down the hall.

'You're going to have to help me.' She ran

back to Carla. 'I need you to hold the button while I get the door.'

Carla nodded. 'Can you undo my legs?'

Barrett, her hands bound, struggled to pull back the duct tape he'd wrapped in thick bands around Carla's legs. Every millisecond she wondered if he'd returned. What would he do to them if he found them like this?

'It's taking too long,' Carla said, as Barrett's fingers struggled to get a firm hold. 'Can you just drag me?'

'I'll try.' And she grabbed Carla by her bare feet and clumsily started to pull. Carla's dead weight against the padded rubber floor made every inch a small victory. Sweat ran down Barrett's back and slicked up her hands. Carla tried to help, but every time she'd twist the wrong way, she'd slip from Barrett's grasp and her legs would thump heavily to the floor.

'I am so scared,' Carla said. 'If he comes back and finds us...'

'I know,' Barrett said, struggling to drag Carla off the rubber surface of their room and on to the scuffed linoleum squares in the hall. Less resistance now, but an entire news show, then a second, third, fourth ... they lost count as broadcasters came and went. Finally, she got Carla positioned next to the door-release button.

Exhausted, Barrett ran to the unit door. 'Do it now!' she shouted.

It buzzed and the latch clicked. She pressed down on the handle and pushed the door with her hip. 'It's open.'

'Barrett, wait!' Carla shouted.

'What?' Barrett asked, itching to get out.

'Please, call my ex and have him get April out of the city. He's got her in summer camp, and if I knew she was out...'

'You got it.' And Barrett bolted down the hall to the main lobby. But what would happen now if she encountered other locked doors? She tried to figure how long Glash had been gone. Had to be three hours, possibly more.

Her pulse pounded in her ears as she ran down the stairs and into the central foyer. The front door was chained and locked, so she turned toward the rear service entrance where Glash had brought them in. Her breath caught at the sound of a car pulling up. He was back. Panicked, she looked around and darted into a deserted office and hid behind the door. She thought about trying to ambush him. But though an accomplished martial artist, with her hands still in the plastic restraints she wouldn't stand a chance. The engine cut off and then she heard his footsteps in the new work boots he'd purchased for his date. She held her breath as he passed by the open door and headed up the stairs. She'd have almost no time before he discovered she'd escaped. She counted to ten, prayed that she was out of his visual field, and then scurried toward the service entrance.

Eighteen

It had taken over an hour, with the unmarked Crown Vic barreling down I-684 at over a hundred miles an hour, to get from the Lower East Side of Manhattan to the imposing iron gates of Albomar State Mental Hospital, north of Poughkeepsie. With the blue light on the dash flashing and the siren screaming, it had been a tense ride. Hobbs was still fuming over the interaction with Peter Glash – he knew something, probably quite a bit – when they caught a radio report of the murder and theft at Bioforward. That was quickly followed by a breathless phone call from the cryptologist, Geri Atwell.

'I can't believe this went unnoticed for five years!' Geri had fumed, referring to the rambling dissertation that Albert had insisted run in *The Times* as a condition of his surrender. 'It's the fucking end of the world!'

'Great,' Hobbs had replied, edging the speedometer to 120, and turning off the siren so he could hear. 'So what do we think Richard Glash just got his hands on?'

'It's plague,' Atwell started, 'but not just any plague. Albert had been working on this for years, systematically strengthening the strain to make it resistant to all known antibiotics.'

Hobbs listened in horror, feeling the blood drain from his face.

'It gets worse. Albert believed that he had strengthened the cell wall to where it would no longer require animal vectors.'

'Rats and fleas,' Houssman whispered.

'What?' Hobbs asked.

'That's how bubonic was spread. Still shows up occasionally, a few people die every year in the Midwest – prairie dogs can carry it – mostly the elderly or someone with a compromised immune system, but everyone else gets better with antibiotics.'

Atwell had then given them the rest of what he'd decoded. 'There's still another half to get through,' he said. 'The encryption is infuriating, but not impossible; the actual wording is twisted and pseudo biblical. The last bit seems significant.'

'Let's hear it,' Hobbs said, his eyes fixed on the road, occasionally laying on the horn to clear the passing lane.

'If I've got it right, he left his bacteria at Bioforward as a kind of time bomb.'

'I don't get it,' Hobbs said, swearing at some moron who wasn't getting out of his way fast enough.

'It's sketchy; I'll read you what I've got: "If mankind does not alter its course then the plague that visited Egypt will be brought forth by a great destroyer and savior – the new messiah. For years this plague will remain dormant, but the wickedness of man shall open the gates of hell and plague will flow. Only the just, and the persecuted, locked away by the wicked, shall remain. They, and not the meek, will inherit the earth.'"

'What a bunch of crap!' Hobbs exclaimed.

'Hey, I didn't say it was Shakespeare,' Atwell came back. 'So who else needs to know this?'

'The Feds,' Hobbs said, 'and of course Homeland Security.' He'd then given Atwell Cosway's number, as he cut across three lanes and shot toward the exit ramp.

Now, at the entrance to the sprawling and deserted grounds of the State Hospital, which included the Albomar youth facility, Hobbs faced a dilemma. His gut told him to barrel ahead, but between roughing up Peter Glash and partaking in the destruction of the crime scene at Albert's, a warning – honed through years on the force – told him that his emotions were way too involved. 'Don't be a cowboy,' he whispered under his breath.

'Good advice,' Houssman said as they drove through the gates.

'This place is massive.'

'You going to call him?' Houssman asked, understanding part of Hobbs's dilemma.

'I supposed I'd better.'

'Yes,' Houssman agreed, 'don't be a cowboy.'

Hobbs punched in Cosway's cell number. 'Where are you?' the Homeland agent demanded. 'I just got off the phone with Atwell. What the hell do you think you're doing?'

Hobbs held his breath. 'Which would you like answered first?'

'Don't pull this shit, Hobbs. Where the fuck are you?'

'Albomar. There's a good chance this is what Glash calls home.'

'Based on what?'

With the Ford slowly moving over the grounds, Hobbs gave Cosway an abbreviated version of their meeting with Peter Glash.

'Sounds like another of your fucking goose chases,' Cosway said.

Hobbs felt panic, seeing just how massive Albomar was. Thousands of rolling acres, the one-time state residential hospital had been its own city nestled in the foothills of the Catskills, housing 7,000 patients, and even the doctors and nurses had had tidy brick homes that now had holes in their roofs and were slowly crumbling.

Houssman stiffened in his seat, he grabbed the binoculars from under the dash.

Hobbs slowed the car.

'That's him,' Houssman pointed. 'See, he's going into the old youth facility. That's where he used to live.'

'What's going on?' Cosway asked.

Hobbs tensed. 'We just found our goose.'

'Do not approach him,' Cosway ordered. 'Stay where you are and keep him under surveillance. I'll be there in fifteen minutes. Do not approach; that's a direct order, Hobbs. Do you hear me?'

'Yes, sir,' Hobbs said, the scarred half of his

face starting to tingle. He knew she was close. Cosway viewed Barrett and Carla Phelps as expendable pawns. Hell, he'd done his duty and called the guy.

Houssman, still peering through the binoculars, said, 'He's gone inside. I know that building fairly well. He'll be up on the second-floor ward where they housed violent youths.'

Hobbs eased the Ford behind a thick privet hedge. The youth facility was less than a hundred yards away. He quietly opened the car door.

Houssman looked across at him. 'You have fourteen minutes before Cosway gets here. Go get her.'

Nineteen

Glash can't pull his thoughts off Mary as he drives into the loading dock. She said yes. He'd told her that there was a ninety percent probability that he would die. She'd said, 'Yes. I will marry you. If you survive, I will marry you.' He'd told her how much he liked her wig – blonde and soft; she'd said it was human hair – and that he no longer needed to kill her. He'd told her that he loved her. He'd never understood what the word meant, but something inside of him knew that his decades-long attraction to Mary, and the fact that he'd not killed her, had to be love. He had asked her to marry him. She had cried. He had asked her a second time. Still sobbing, she had said yes. She was a year younger than he, and as he drove back he calculated the likelihood of her being able to conceive. 'I'm forty-two years old,' he said aloud as he drove. 'I should have a wife. I should have children.' The probability of both those things happening was tiny. But she had said yes.

He gets out of the van and picks up Albert's metal box. This is his plan A; Mary and a family is plan B. He told her how soon he was going to be very famous. He predicted she would be impressed. Women like famous men.

He walks up the stairs, and knows that the bacteria are ready; it's time to clear one final hurdle. Was Albert telling the truth? Are the bacteria as virulent as he claimed? He will test them on Carla Phelps; this is his reason for a second hostage. Dr Conyors will record for posterity and write a book and Carla Phelps is a guinea pig.

He stops at the outer door to the ward. He'd left it locked; it is now unlatched. High probability that one or both of his hostages have fled. His mind races through the possibilities. How much time had elapsed? Is he walking into a trap?

Standing still, he hears a woman's footsteps and the unmistakable sound of the outside door creaking open.

He'd left Dr Conyors with her feet unbound – a mistake. But Carla can't run. He predicts that she's still inside. He pulls out his gun and pushes the door open. He runs into the ward and spots Phelps trying to hide under the nurses' station.

'Stay away from me,' she screams, and curls her limbs into a tight ball.

He pockets the gun and grabs her by her taped ankles.

'Don't hurt me,' she sobs.

He hoists her over his shoulder in a fireman's lift. He imagines that Dr Conyors is now running to find help. The grounds of Albomar are vast. She must go a quarter-mile in any direction to get off the property. If he gets to her first, he'll shoot her. A shame, because she is a good writer.

He glances at the television sets and sees blurred footage of Martin Cosway surrounded by reporters telling them that the break-in at Bioforward was unrelated to the string of murders. 'Regardless,' Cosway adds, 'the prudent next step is to raise the security level from yellow to orange.' Glash wants to watch. Another set has his mugshot, and a third runs grainy footage of Justin Green. He is getting to be very famous.

With Carla over his shoulder, he retrieves the laptop from the nurses' station, tucks it under his arm, and with Albert's box filled with plague dangling from his hand, he retraces his steps. It's time to leave this place. He needs a new hostage, and if he's lucky, he'll kill Dr Conyors, even though she had helped him dress for Mary – she said he looked very nice – but she just ran away from him; he's warned her repeatedly not to do that. He will kill her.

Even burdened, he moves quickly back down the stairs and to the van. Dr Conyors has a one minute and ten seconds lead on him. But she is on foot. He tosses Carla into the back, and checks to be certain that Dr Conyors isn't hiding under the vehicle to ambush him. He scans in all directions, hoping to spot her. She has either concealed herself or is too far away.

He turns over the engine and backs out. A

motion in the rear-view mirror grabs his attention. It's Dr Conyors, running barefoot toward an approaching tan sedan. She is slow and awkward, her bound hands impeding her stride.

He throws the van into drive. But to get to the hospital's main gate he'll be forced to pass this oncoming car.

There is great risk and unknown variables: who is driving the vehicle? Are they armed? He wants to kill Dr Conyors, but whoever is in that car will likely try to kill him.

He picks up speed and notes how the tan car is now heading toward Dr Conyors and not him. She looks back at him. He sees the fear in her face and the blood on her feet.

Yes, he'd taken off her shoes the first time she'd had to use the bathroom. Easier that way to get her pants on and off. But now he observes it slows her escape. He reaches into his pocket for the gun. He will kill her now.

He sees two men in the tan vehicle. Less than fifty yards away.

A queer emotion, like a stab of light to his brain, makes him stare. He sees the old man with the hat and in a split second his plan changes. He turns the wheel hard to the right, and aims the vehicle for Dr Conyors. He will run her down. He will take a new hostage.

She looks back and sprints toward an ancient oak.

The tan Ford swerves in front of her, placing itself between her and Glash's van. The rear tires skid out and its front end collides

198

with the tree.

He hears Dr Conyors scream and sees the airbags cushion the heads of the two men inside. He labels them 'A' and 'B'.

He scans the horizon for other vehicles, and gripping the gun, opens the van door.

Twenty

Hobbs felt the tires slide out on the gravel, as he slammed on the brakes. He saw Barrett dive behind the tree and felt panic – had he just miscalculated? Glash was about to run her over. Was he about to do it instead? He was going too fast.

He braced for the impact and threw his right hand back to protect Houssman. They hit the tree hard, and as the airbags deployed his thoughts skittered back to another car. That one had exploded with him inside. He pictured Barrett and then his ex-wife and his two daughters. His vision dimmed; it grew hazy like an old-fashioned television getting turned off. He struggled to not lose consciousness. He heard a banging noise.

'Hobbs!'

'Barrett!' His eyes shot open. She was pulling on the door trying to get it open.

'He's coming!' she screamed. 'Get out of the car!'

He turned to see Houssman, also stunned – his hat gone, his glasses hanging off his ear. 'Shit!' Adrenalin pushed through the haze as he caught sight of Glash bearing down on them with a gun pointed at Houssman's head.

'Shit!' He yanked the door handle, pushed it open and rolled to the ground. 'Get down,' he told Barrett, as he freed his Glock from its holster.

'I've got a gun to Dr George Houssman's head,' Glash yelled. 'Try anything and he's dead.'

They heard the passenger door being yanked open, and Glash breathing hard. From under the Ford they could see his boot-clad feet. Hobbs aimed the Glock, but before he could get a shot, Glash grabbed Houssman and dragged him from the car.

Barrett gasped as she saw her dear mentor, barely awake, an open gash on the side of his head, being used as a human shield by Glash. He gripped Houssman's bird-thin body in a one-armed embrace as he backed his way to the van.

'Try anything and I'll kill him. I'll kill them both.'

Hobbs, still on his belly, snaked toward the rear of the Ford.

'He doesn't care if he dies,' Barrett said. 'He's got to be stopped.'

'I know.'

They watched helplessly as Glash, with his gun pressed to George's temple, shoved him through the driver's side door.

And then they heard the sirens, dozens of them, shrieking in the distance and coming fast. Over the crest they saw Cosway's Town Car in the lead followed by FBI vehicles and state police cruisers.

Glash threw the maroon van into drive and roared toward Cosway's car.

'What's he doing?' Hobbs groaned. 'He's heading straight toward them!'

Barrett couldn't pull her eyes from the horror as the van's engine raced. 'George ... *no!*' she screamed as Glash rammed Cosway's black Lincoln. Tears welled as she saw Houssman's head yank forward on impact.

Hobbs was running toward them. But Glash was faster; he'd jumped from the van and pumped two bullets, execution-style, into Cosway's driver. Then, just as he'd done with Houssman, he put a gun to Cosway's head and ordered the stunned man out. Cosway was trying to say something. But Glash drew back his arm and viciously slammed the gun against the side of his head. Cosway slumped. Glash grabbed him before he could fall and threw him into the back of the van. As he did, Barrett could see that something, or someone, was dumped out of the back and on to the ground. Ed was closing on them. 'No,' she sobbed, too frightened to move.

It happened in seconds. By the time Hobbs was close enough to fire, Glash was back in the driver's seat. She wondered if the van might be too damaged too drive – Glash always had a plan B. What would he do? Who would he kill? With its headlights smashed and the hood crumpled she heard the van's engine come to life, and leaving deep ruts in the grass, it raced away from the oncoming cavalcade of law enforcement.

'We have to go after him,' Barrett shouted, looking around as marked and unmarked vehicles swarmed past them in pursuit of Glash. Overhead, a helicopter roared over the crest and dove in the direction of Glash's fleeing vehicle. Clouds of dust swirled around them. Sirens blared.

Barrett caught sight of Carla Phelps lying on the ground, curled in the fetal position, her arms and legs still bound; she wasn't moving, and as the armada of vehicles raced over the grounds all she could think was that they couldn't see Carla.

'Oh, Christ,' she murmured, hobbling up the sloping hill toward her, praying she would not get hit herself.

'Barrett, wait!' Hobbs shouted. 'You're going to get yourself killed.' He swallowed dust and coughed as he ran after her. He saw the blood on her shoulder. 'You're injured.'

'It's nothing,' she said, as they came to Carla's body.

Hobbs bent down.

'Is she dead?' Barrett asked.

Hobbs put a finger to her carotid; as he did she coughed, her body convulsed and she opened her bruised eyes to stare up at Hobbs and then Barrett.

'Thank God.' Barrett sank to her knees.

'Did they get him?' Carla asked, through hooded eyes. 'Did they kill the bastard?'

'No,' Barrett said, 'he got away ... he's taken hostages. He took George Houssman.' She stared off in the direction of the fleeing vehicles. The helicopter still barely visible. 'There's no way he'll get away. I just hope...'

Hobbs pulled out a pocketknife and cut through the plastic restraints, freeing Barrett's hands and then Carla's. 'What happened to your shoulder?' he asked Barrett.

'It was bad,' she admitted, 'but the bleeding stopped.' She rubbed her red-ringed wrists, and then looked at Hobbs. If it wasn't for him, she'd probably be dead right now. 'Thank you,' she said, looking at his scarred face. He'd once again put himself in harm's way to save her. He was good, a man who'd literally walk through fire for her, so why didn't she feel the same? She kept her thoughts to herself as she and Hobbs worked away at the dense mass of duct tape around Carla's legs.

'Now what?' Hobbs asked, as a black Taurus stopped next to his smashed-up Crown Vic.

'We should go after him,' Barrett said. 'This isn't going to end well. Maybe I could reason with him.'

He shook his head. 'He's got two hostages and a couple dozen vehicles with air support in pursuit. Unless we can bring something special to that party, we'd just make things worse.'

'George...' she said, hearing the sirens fading in the distance.

'He's tough,' Hobbs said, helping Carla to stand. 'I saw a couple teams of FBI negotiators who just went by. They're not bad ... at least, they're competent.'

'He was Glash's foster father for a brief time,' Barrett said. 'Glash hates him for not having kept him.'

'He told me,' Hobbs said, as the trio hobbled back toward their car and the parked Taurus. The driver's door clicked open and the sole black-suited occupant got out.

'Great!' Hobbs muttered as Cosway's second in command – Corbin Zane – approached; he was carrying a cell, and had a small speaker hooked to his right ear.

'Shouldn't you be off trying to rescue your boss?' Hobbs called out, as Zane approached.

'I can hear everything that's going on.' The ex-linebacker was sweating buckets. 'Dr Conyors,' he said, his tone polite, 'I'm glad to see you're safe.'

'Thank you,' she said.

'And you too, Ms Phelps,' he said, looking at the attorney.

Zane suddenly tensed, put a hand to the receiver in his ear. 'You've got to be shitting me! So where is he?' His face turned bright red. 'Yes, get dogs, get more air support.'

Hobbs's jaw dropped, he looked up at Zane. 'He got away!'

'They found the van,' Zane said, 'and another body.'

'Oh no,' Barrett said. 'Please tell me it wasn't Dr Houssman.'

'No. It was a woman in her thirties, her ID is gone. She was getting gas. He slit her throat, grabbed her purse and keys, took her car.'

'No one saw?' Hobbs sputtered. 'What about the hostages?'

'Gone,' Zane said, clearly shaken. 'The gas station has security video; they're checking it now.' He looked at Barrett. 'He just killed somebody as though it were nothing.'

'Listen,' Barrett said, desperate that he'd gotten away again, 'you need to know that he's carrying around quarts of what he believes to be deadly plague bacteria. He said he's going to contaminate the Ashokan Reservoir.'

'He told you this?' Zane asked.

'Yes, for the last forty-eight hours he's been telling me his life story. He wants me to write a book about him. He wants to be famous. That's why he didn't kill me. I was of use to him.' She pictured George Houssman and prayed that Glash had some use for him. If not, she knew he was as good as dead.

'The bacteria; you saw them?'

'I saw something in two big glass bottles. I also saw the vials he took from Bioforward.'

Zane stared at her. 'You've got to be shitting me. They said nothing was taken.'

'I don't think Glash lied to me. I was tied up in the van when he broke into Bioforward. He showed me two small glass ampoules. I have no way of knowing what was in them, but they were covered with frost, like they'd just been taken from some freezer. It had to have been eighty degrees that night – that ice came from somewhere.'

'Holy shit!' Zane exclaimed. 'Ashokan is the major water supply to New York City.' He pulled out his cell and dialed, he stepped away from Barrett and Hobbs, but they could easily overhear. 'We've got a worst-case scenario on our hands,' he said excitedly. 'Yes ... I don't know. Yes, we have confirmation that he believes he is in possession of resistant plague ... Yes, I realize that the Bioforward Corporation has stated that nothing was missing. But they lied! I'm telling you we have confirmation that something was in fact taken. This is not a drill. I repeat – this is not a drill.'

Twenty-One

Glash keeps the speedometer at eight miles above the speed limit in his newest vehicle – a gold Volkswagen Passat. He killed its previous owner and took her purse. Before he slit her throat he ripped a gold locket from her neck – Mary will like that. She liked the ring; men should give women jewelry. Now, he has a little time; he assumes the gas station had Closed Circuit TV, but all he needs is twenty-two minutes. He must remember to wipe off the blood from the chain before giving Mary the necklace.

He glances at George Houssman curled in the seat to his left, his hands tied with a black nylon restraint. He's too old now, he thinks. He sees the bruises on Houssman's face and wonders at the extent of his wounds from the Ford crashing into the tree. 'Why do you wear an overcoat in August?' Glash asks, noting that Houssman's eyelids just fluttered.

'I'm cold,' Houssman replies. 'Where are you taking me?'

'To the Ashokan Reservoir; we'll arrive in approximately eight minutes and thirty-seven ... *six* seconds.'

'What do you intend to do there?'

'I'm going to make people believe that I've contaminated the water with plague.'

'But you're planning something else,' Houssman says.

'Yes. The water is too cold and the culture would become too dilute. The probability of infecting a single person or animal in that manner approaches zero.'

'Agreed.' Houssman glances through the windshield. 'What happened to the other man?'

'He's in the trunk,' Glash says. 'He's unconscious; it's better that way. His chances of playing tricks on me are greatly diminished.'

'I'm awake,' Houssman says, testing Glash's reasoning.

'You're old,' Glash replies. 'I can kill you easily. If I hit you too hard you'll die.'

'That's probably right.' Houssman shudders and sinks into the warmth of his coat.

'If you played a trick and tried to escape, I'd kill you whether I intended to or not.'

'What do you intend?' Houssman asks. 'What do you want from me?'

'You're to take Dr Conyors' place. You'll write everything down. You will write a book about me. I like your books. I've read them all. You'll illustrate it with my pictures. You can decide which ones to include.' He turns to look at Houssman. 'I draw very well. I remember you told me that when I was a little boy.'

Houssman's breath is shallow. 'Why would I write a book about this?'

Glash turns back to face the road. 'Do not make me mad. You will do as you're instructed.' He silently mouths the minutes and seconds remaining. 'Shut up now.'

As frightened as he was, George couldn't help but search for traces of the little boy he and Delia had taken in thirty-eight years ago. Glash had lived with them for over two months before the horrific incident with the girl next door. He remembered how his daughters had been traumatized, not that they'd witnessed what had happened, but he and Delia had had to explain repeatedly how their new little brother would not be living with them after all. He'd sat on the edge of Alice's bed, feeling her little body convulse as she cried, frightened that she too might do something which would make her lose her family. They'd begged him to bring back Richard. Stephanie, his oldest, had pleaded through a wall of tears, 'I'll make sure he does not do anything bad. I promise. Please bring him back, Daddy. Please. Please.' It had ripped them apart. He and Delia had explained how what Richard had done made it impossible for him to remain; he was too dangerous. It was a cruel lesson from which none of them ever recovered. He knew, on that day, his two little girls learned that love – even a parent's love – is not unconditional.

Glancing at Glash he shuddered, and wondered what part he might have played in the man he'd become. *Could this have been changed? Should we have tried harder?* His daughters' pleas were still clear, their faces raw with unbearable grief. 'Bring him back. Daddy, please bring him back.'

Glash looked at him. 'I'm angry with you,' he said.

'I know,' Houssman replied, and gently pressed, 'I'm sorry.'

'You were supposed to be my new family. You were supposed to be my new father.'

'Yes.'

'You sent me away ... you never came back for me.'

'I tried to visit,' Houssman said, feeling the old regrets.

'I begged you to take me out of that place. I told you I'd never do that again. You left me there!' Tears rolled down Glash's cheek.

'I know,' Houssman said, struck at the odd disconnection between Glash's flat voice and stony face and the steady stream of tears that tracked down his cheek. His throat choked up as he remembered those horrible visits to Albomar, the children's facility where Glash had been taken – initially to be evaluated and then later where he would be held for the next fourteen years of his life. Delia had come with him for the first visit only; she never returned. Glash had shrieked and screamed from the moment he saw them. His tantrums brought the guards, as the little boy hurled himself at Houssman. When he'd been told that he couldn't return he'd flailed and kicked, demanding that he be taken home. He'd screamed to the point of exhaustion, shouting that Houssman was supposed to be his new father. At the last visit Glash had kicked him viciously and then clung desperately to his bleeding and bruised legs as he'd tried to leave. It had taken a team of nurses and aides to finally pry the little boy off him. After that, Glash's psychiatrist had recommended that Houssman no longer visit. 'He'll never leave Albomar,' is what he'd said, the words seared deep into George's brain. 'It's for the best that he tries to forget you and your family.'

'You said you'd try to take me home,' Glash stated. 'You never did. You lied to me.'

Houssman said nothing, his thoughts filled with ghosts of old dreams. The son he'd always wanted; Delia ... thinking of her now, how he missed her. Those long-ago excited evenings anticipating the perfect little boy to complete their family. And he had been beautiful ... at least at first. Houssman snuck a glance at the intense man who would likely kill him before this was over. He could see traces of that odd little boy, with his magical drawings and stilted speech. That first day he'd taken him home, dressed by some social worker in a navy blazer and corduroys. It was all so clear; Delia and he had dismissed the odd behavior, the lack of emotion. They'd assumed he was in shock; he'd just lost both his mother and father. As Houssman replayed the old memories the first basin of the reservoir came into view. Tall pines, sugar maples and ancient oaks surrounded the calm water, as picnicking families and small groups of hikers took advantage of the shade and the relative cool. He caught the smell of grilling meat and somewhere in the distance heard children shouting and laughing as they played.

'This is the Ashokan Reservoir,' Glash said dully. 'It was completed in 1917 and involved the flooding of nine villages: West Hurley, Ashton, Glenford, Olive Bridge, Shokan, West Shokan...'

George stayed silent as Richard lectured and drove to the far end of a mostly deserted dirt parking lot.

'...It was completed a year ahead of schedule and was considered the second most important feat of engineering of its time – the Panama Canal being the first. Eight hundred skeletons had to be removed from existing cemeteries, and the construction included a hundred and twenty-six miles of aqueducts to bring potable water to New York City.'

George looked through the windshield at a steep gorge hundreds of feet deep that was bordered on one side by a massive cement dam and High Point Mountain. A sluiceway from the reservoir created a bucolic scene at the base of the ravine, where a stream rolled over massive boulders into the distance, its waters swollen from the summer's unusually heavy rains.

Houssman wondered at this choice of location and watched as Glash backed in and parked next to a black panel van, the only other vehicle in the lot.

He stayed silent as Richard got out and reached under the van's left front bumper. He heard the jangle of keys as he unlocked the driver's side. Then Glash went to the back of the van, unlocked those doors and opened the trunk of the Passat.

Houssman watched through the rear-view mirror. It was difficult to see. The trunk door obscured most of what Glash was doing. Houssman assumed that Glash had transferred Cosway to the back of the van when those doors slammed shut. Minutes passed. He could hear Glash doing something from inside the van. Then he reappeared, carrying what at first appeared to be Cosway's unconscious body in a white shirt and slacks. Houssman strained for a better look and saw that the body had different hair from Cosway – it was red. But he could have sworn the clothes belonged to the Homeland agent. Glash crammed the body into the trunk of the Passat. He then yanked open the driver's side door. He was lugging a second body – it reeked of death. This one was tall and dressed – exactly as Glash was – in khakis and a button-down shirt. The body had dark hair, but must have been dead a couple of days. Translucent yellow maggots had nested in the decaying flesh of his mouth, eyes and nose.

Houssman gagged, and nearly vomited. Glash came around to his side, opened the door and roughly lifted him out, then carried him into the back of the van. Continuing his dissertation on the reservoir, he dropped him next to Cosway's naked body and proceeded to snip off his wrist restraints. 'Sixty-four miles of highway had to be discontinued, and eleven miles of the Ulster and Delaware train track had to be rerouted...' He yanked off George's coat and told him, 'Take off all of your clothes.'

Shocked, and overcome by the reek of death that permeated the van, Houssman couldn't move.

Glash reached over to his one-time foster father and roughly undressed him. 'Most of the displaced residents stayed in the area and established three new villages, West Hurley, Ashokan and Tongore.' He then cinched on a fresh pair of wrist restraints and looked at Houssman. George shivered, as Glash gathered up his clothes. 'Here,' he said, and he pulled back a blue plastic tarp to reveal a tall woman's dead and naked body. With an almost tender touch, Glash wrapped George in the crinkly tarp. 'It should keep you warm,' he said. He quickly dressed the woman in George's clothes. When he'd finished he dragged her by the arms out of the van.

Gooseflesh popped on George's arms and legs as he heard car doors opening and closing. He startled as Glash returned, reached into the back of the van and retrieved two five-gallon plastic gas cans. The doors slammed again, and over the smell of death came a strong odor of gas. George heard the liquid being poured out, more doors opening and closing...

Houssman struggled to get his breathing under control, the smell of the three unknown bodies that had been baking in the hot van was overpowering. Houssman's thoughts tumbled: Who were these people? How long had they been there? And most importantly, who had killed them? If not Richard, who was out there doing these things for him? What suddenly became clear was *why* he was doing this. Glash was about to fake all of their deaths.

Glash returned. Reeking of gasoline, his lips were moving silently as he retrieved Clarence Albert's metal box from the back and removed a glass bottle filled with a murky, yeast-colored liquid.

He reached under his seat and removed a small white first aid kit, and an empty glass bottle identical to the other two. He took out a HEPA mask and hunching down he walked into the back. He knelt next to George and fitted the mask over his face. 'Do not take this off without being told to do so.'

Glash looked at Cosway. He stared at his chest and put a finger to his neck. 'Good,' he said and then turned to George. 'Watch this.' He put on a HEPA mask and snapped on a pair of tan vinyl gloves. Carrying one of the two full bottles and the matching empty one he leaned over Cosway. He looked back to make certain George was paying attention. 'Watch me.'

'Don't do this, Richard.'

'You're not my father.' He cracked open the lid of the full bottle.

Horrified, Houssman heard a hiss as the seal broke and Glash propped up Cosway's head and proceeded to inoculate him with the deadly fluid. It was precise and clinical as Glash dipped a cotton swab into the bottle and wiped it on the mucous membranes of Cosway's nostrils and mouth. He recapped the bottle, and placing the contaminated swab in the palm of his left glove he removed the gloves and dropped them into a sealable plastic bag. He lowered Cosway back to the floor. 'I'll be right back ... Dad.'

Houssman frantically kicked at the rear doors – they were locked and secure. He looked toward the front of the van, and attempted to wedge his body through the opening between the two captain's chairs. He heard the sound of glass breaking not forty feet away, and made a desperate attempt to grab for the driver's side handle with his restrained hands.

Glash returned, and caught him as the door clicked open.

He said nothing as he shoved Houssman back. George landed with a thump. Winded, he coughed on the thick fumes of gas coming from the Passat. He looked up and tried to stand, he could see Glash opening the door of the small gold car. He heard an engine start, and for the briefest instant hope surged. Had someone spotted them? His head whipped to the left as the Passat shot through the underbrush. There were long seconds of silence as it flew over the edge of the gorge. Then came the jagged crash of metal on rock, a popping sound and an explosion that shook the van.

'Time to go home,' Glash said. He turned over the engine and popped open the glove compartment. He retrieved a cell phone and dialed. 'This is Richard Glash. I'm at the Ashokan dam; it's started.' And then he sang. *'Ring around the rosy, a pocket full of posy. Ashes, ashes, we'll all fall down.* You couldn't catch me, and now I'm dead ... then again, so are you.' He tossed the phone on to the ground where the Passat had been. He threw the van into drive, and glancing back at Houssman said, 'Time to go home.'

Twenty-Two

Barrett struggled to focus as Hobbs floored the damaged Crown Vic, with its dangling front bumper and crumpled hood. Carla was in the back on Hobbs's cell leaving desperate messages on her ex-husband's answering machine, as the radio and scanner kept up a steady stream of speculation, fear and urgency. Albomar was just twenty minutes from the Ashokan Reservoir, and at any other point in her life she might have appreciated the vibrant green foliage and quaint, twisty roads of the Catskills. Now as they raced through small towns with too many antiques shops, stop signs, artist collectives and deliberately homey diners with names like 'Dottie's Place' and the 'Come on Inn', she longed for a multi-lane highway.

'How could they lose him?' she muttered, staring out the window, wondering at the grinding clash of metal that came from the front right tire. She thought of George and the rage that Glash held for him. Was he still alive?

Hobbs turned down the radio and upped the scanner. He switched frequencies. A weird, high-pitched noise blasted through the speaker. 'They've scrambled it.'

Before she could ask for details he'd jammed on the brakes and taken a hard left. The car shuddered as bare metal hit rock and he turned down the gravel road toward the Ashokan Reservoir.

'Shit,' said Carla from the back, as they were surrounded on all sides by the sounds of sirens and a cavalcade of emergency response vehicles – cops, feds, large white trailers emblazoned with the Homeland Security crest, one with *Mobile Decontamination* emblazoned on the side.

'Come on.' Hobbs pounded the dash as the wheel on the Crown Vic nearly lurched from his hands, sending them off into a ditch. The rear tires skidded back to the right.

Barrett held her breath as he steadied the car and made a beeline for a black Taurus in the dirt parking lot. It was a scene of pandemonium, the sirens – everywhere and every type – emergency personnel unloading equipment and suiting up in white, blue or orange hazmat suits, all set against the breathtaking beauty of the clear blue waters and sloping mountains that surrounded the man-made reservoir's two massive basins.

Hobbs brought the Vic to a lurching halt. He looked at Barrett. He was unshaven and covered with dust; she noticed the blood and bruises on his knuckles. 'Any chance you two would stay in the car?' he asked.

'Nice try,' Barrett said, her hand already on the handle.

The three got out. Even in the shade it was over ninety; sweat popped on her back and between her breasts as she stuck close to Hobbs. They headed toward Corbin Zane, who was in the process of suiting up in a powder-blue hazmat suit while simultaneously attempting to speak into a voice-activated field phone strapped to his ear. Next to him was his driver, Pete Griffin – an eager ex-cop with less than a year in the agency – who was trying to steady him.

Zane shouted into the receiver and seemed to be having problems with the suit as he hopped unsteadily on one foot.

'Here,' Barrett said, placing a hand on the stocky man's other shoulder. She could hear another man's directives through the headset. *'Answers, Zane, we need answers and solutions. Do you understand?'*

'Yes, sir,' Zane shot back as Carla joined in, squatting down to help Zane get his left foot secure in the suit.

'Don't think of cost,' his superior instructed.

'Yes, sir.'

Barrett felt a twinge of sympathy for this sweaty man who had the desperate look of somebody in way over his head, and then she caught the smell – like burning meat, rubber and gasoline. Her head whipped around to find the source: a billowing plume of dark-gray smoke rose over a dense stand of pines.

'Thanks,' Zane said, as he looked at the hood and rebreather apparatus. 'I hate those things,' he said.

'What have they found?' Hobbs asked, as several large, covered military personnel carriers appeared in the parking lot. Armed National Guardsmen in white hazmat suits sprang from the trucks and proceeded to jog off in all directions.

In the distance Barrett caught a similar scene at the narrow aqueduct that divided the two basins. Families and hikers were being rounded up as more sirens, more trucks continued to fill the lot.

'Oh, crap,' Zane said, and watched a news vehicle from Channel Eight turn the camera in their direction. 'Get them suits,' he barked to his driver. 'The last thing I need is reporters.' And then under his breath, 'Course, they were the first to get here.'

'What did they find?' Hobbs repeated.

Zane looked at Hobbs as though seeing him for the first time, and then at Barrett and Carla. 'Get on suits and I'll show you.' Griffin ran back carrying four orange suits, just as a well-known Asian-American reporter began walking quickly in their direction, a cameraman at her side.

Barrett, having taken part in multiple disaster drills, braced against the Taurus and yanked up her suit. She zipped the front, popped on the hood and tested her rebreather.

Zane looked at the rapidly approaching reporter. 'Time to shit or get off the pot,' he muttered inside his sweltering suit, and then told Griffin, 'Get that bitch out of here.'

The news lady had picked up her pace and

was running in high heels. 'Dr Conyors, can you comment on Richard Glash's motive?'

'How do you want me to do it, boss?' the newly deputized young man asked.

'Get a bunch of Guardsmen and quarantine them. Be polite, because they're going to raise bloody hell, just get them out of my face.'

'Dr Conyors,' the reporter continued, less than thirty feet away, 'what does Richard Glash intend to do?'

Barrett said nothing as the reporter thrust a microphone in her direction. She looked through her face shield as armed Guardsmen surrounded them.

'What are you doing?' the reporter shouted, as they closed around her and her cameraman.

'You'll need to be quarantined,' Zane said. 'It's for your own protection. Turn off the camera ... do it now.'

'You can't do this!' she shrieked.

A windowless National Guard van approached. 'Excuse me,' one of the Guardsmen said politely, as he forcibly took custody of the camera.

Zane smiled as she was directed, at gunpoint, to enter the van along with her colleague. The smile then vanished. 'Come on,' he said, leaving Griffin to oversee the handling of the news team. 'I need to show you something.'

As the four of them strode rapidly across the parking lot, his voice-activated field phone rang. Zane answered. 'Good ... yes.

Really, detergent? I'll make certain that it happens immediately.' He said, 'Griffin!' into the phone, and then waited for him to pick up. 'Pete, you're to deploy a Guard squadron immediately. There's a shipment of laundry detergent on its way. It's to be dumped into the reservoir at thirty-foot intervals around the perimeter. Then put some on boats and dump it everywhere. Do you understand?'

'Yes, sir.'

'Report back when it's completed.'

'You're going to sterilize the reservoir,' Barrett commented.

'Yes,' Zane said, not completely understanding the reason for the orders he'd just received and passed on.

'Sterilize how?' Hobbs asked.

Zane continued to lead them toward the reservoir's edge, but slowed to hear her answer.

'The cell walls of bacteria,' Barrett explained, 'are composed of fat and protein. Detergent dissolves the fat and breaks the cell apart. That's why the best way to prevent the spread of disease in hospitals, is through hand-washing with soap and water. It's a simple solution; if in fact the bacteria were hardy enough to survive the temperature of the reservoir, the detergent, in high enough concentration, should destroy them.'

'Excuse me,' Zane said, as he pulled out his cell. He called Griffin. 'Pete, however much detergent they send, have them come back with ten times more.'

'It can't hurt,' Barrett commented.

'Right,' Zane said. 'Better safe...' And he brought them into a clearing by the water's edge. 'This is what I wanted you to see.'

Barrett's heart pounded and the tears came. 'George,' she mouthed as she stared down the ravine at the incinerated remains of Glash's last getaway car. The smoke billowed thick and black, but it was the smell ... the unmistakable stench of cooking human flesh. Her mask fogged up as she tried to suppress the sobs. She felt a gloved hand on her back ... it was Hobbs. She pictured George – Zane told her that Glash and the two hostages had all perished.

'Oh, God!' Carla whispered, standing to her right. 'I'm so sorry, Barrett.'

'I wanted you to see this,' Zane shouted. He was a good forty feet from the spot where the car had zoomed over the gorge. He was on the dam wall looking back at them. 'Dr Conyors ... Ms Phelps, I need you to see this.'

Barrett felt numb and horribly alone, despite Hobbs's closeness and obvious concern. She walked over to Zane and looked down at a flat boulder strewn with broken glass. She recognized the bottle caps and the general shape of the bottlenecks. Without hesitation, she said, 'It looks staged.'

Hobbs nodded.

'What do you mean? Why would you say that?' Zane asked, clearly not happy with her answer.

'It looks like the bottles he showed us.' She turned to Carla.

'Yes,' Carla said, as her eyes darted around the perimeter of the reservoir, taking into account the white-suited Guardsman holding rifles at thirty-foot intervals.

'You said there were two bottles of plague,' Zane pressed. 'There are two broken bottles here. What I need to know is, are these them? Do I have confirmation?'

Barrett studied the glass shards and the screw tops. 'They might be,' she said.

'What's wrong?' Hobbs asked. 'You don't sound convinced.'

Barrett found it hard to think straight – too much grief, too tired – but something wasn't right. She kept seeing George's face, his concern, his love in the background.

Zane snorted. 'I think that's the understatement of the day. Are these the bottles or not?'

'Here,' she said, looking around. 'Glash is ... *was* ... not stupid. He wasn't working alone, and I can't imagine this is what Albert would have instructed him to do.'

'What?' Zane said. 'What are you talking about? Clarence Albert is locked away. Are you saying the two were in contact, and that Albert was feeding Glash information? That seems far-fetched.'

'No ... not exactly. He has somebody on the outside helping him. But just this piece ... dumping all of the bacteria into the reservoir ... something's not right here...' Barrett looked around, her eyes drawn back down the ravine. A crime team dressed in clumsy white suits was awkwardly working its way down the side of the gorge, using ropes and hooks, as the fire burned itself out. It would be hours before they'd be able to pull the three blackened bodies from the wreckage. Even from the distance, Barrett could just make out traces of the collar on George's overcoat. She thought of his daughters and his beloved granddaughter, Faye, who he made no pretence about spoiling with lavish outings to FAO Schwartz, and a totally out-of-character trip to Disney. What would she tell them? She strained to see Glash, his body slumped over the wheel of the burning wreck. He seemed so much smaller in death; his powerful physique somehow diminished by death and the fire.

'Dr Conyors?' Zane asked. 'Do you have something concrete, or is this all speculation? I don't mean to be rude, and I know you've been through a great deal ... but if these are the bottles then...'

'When I was with him,' Barrett said, not taking her eyes off the burning car, 'he was completely focused on being the most famous killer of all time. Everywhere he took us, he wanted me to watch and to record what he was doing, then he'd dial a television station and leave his cell phone as a kind of homing device.'

'Yes,' Zane said, 'in two of the crime scenes – three if you include this one – the media was there ahead of the authorities. What has that got to do with the bottles? You said they're the ones he showed you.'

'They do look like them,' Carla said, her eyes on Barrett.

'They're standard glass milk bottles,' Barrett commented, a voice screaming in her head that this was all wrong. 'How hard would it be to have more than two ... what if his showing them to us was deliberate? What if he knew that we'd be here now, saying, "Yes, you've got it all"? The truth is, you have three bodies at the bottom of a ravine. It looks like Glash' – her voice caught – 'George Houssman and I don't know who the third is ... but what if it's not them?' As the words came, a wave of hope washed through her. 'What if that's not them, but just three more dead people? Richard Glash has no concern for human life and—'

'Dr Conyors,' Zane said, cutting her off, 'we have half a dozen witnesses who say they saw the car go over the edge. It's pretty clear that Richard Glash and his hostages are dead. He even called the media to let them know.'

'No,' Barrett said, abruptly. 'You don't get it. Richard Glash always has two possible options. This doesn't fit. There's no plan B. This is just a diversion. What if that's not him?' And to herself she let the wish take shape: *What if that's not George? What if he's still alive?* 'Richard Glash wanted to – *wants* to – do something very big.'

Zane was clearly pissed. 'You don't think

this is big?'

'It's too easy,' Barrett said. 'I don't think he's done.' She stared at the bodies, and looked around for how she might be able to get down to them. 'He knew that he might die ... but not like this. He said there was a chance that he'd survive. How do you survive this? There's no chance.' She turned to Zane. 'You've got to go after him.'

'Richard Glash is dead,' Zane repeated.

'Have you gotten a positive ID?' Hobbs asked. He stared at the painfully slow descent of the crime-scene team. 'You haven't even had a chance to examine the bodies.'

'We have eye witnesses,' Zane said.

'Of a car going over a cliff,' Carla added.

'This could have been staged,' Hobbs said. 'You don't have a positive ID?'

'There is no doubt,' Zane said, almost shouting. 'Richard Glash and his two hostages are dead. I'm sorry if this is unpleasant news to you; but it's a fact. I appreciate your assistance, but unless you have anything concrete to add, I have quite a lot on my plate right now.'

'That's not Glash,' Barrett said, squinting through her mask. 'His upper body was more muscular. You can't stop looking for him.'

Zane's headset rang. 'It's the CDC,' he commented, as he stepped away.

Hobbs tapped Barrett on the back of her suit. 'Let's get out of here.'

'Yes,' she said, keeping her voice low. 'They have got this wrong.'

'Move fast,' he said, 'before they notice.'

With Carla Phelps following close, the trio shed their suits in a trailer marked 'decontamination' and assuring the young Guardsman posted at the entry to the parking lot that they had Zane's blessing to be on their way. They fled the scene in Hobbs's banged-up Crown Vic.

Corbin Zane wrapped up his conversation with a top governmental scientist working for the biohazard unit at the CDC. He then took a call from his agency's director and another from a member of the Chiefs of Staff. Despite the sweltering heat and the incredible pressure he was under Zane had never felt more alive. He'd reassured his supervisor that both bottles of bacteria had been dumped by Glash at the reservoir and were being rapidly neutralized. 'Glash is dead, thank God. And sadly,' he'd added, lowering his voice and lending it a touch of grief, 'Martin Cosway, my boss and a great man, a true patriot and asset to the Department of Homeland Security, along with Dr George Houssman, also perished.'

Zane swelled under the praise of his director. 'You're doing strong work in a tough situation, keep it up,' he'd said.

When he'd finished with the last half-dozen calls he stopped to look around for Dr Conyors, who'd try to shoot holes in his slam dunk ... probably not able to deal with the death of the old man; she'd seemed pretty choked up about that. He looked around for her and the other two. He was certain she was still there, but with everyone dressed the same it was hard to tell. He scanned the periphery, admiring the regimented placement of the Guardsmen around the reservoir, and pleased to see that large buckets of white powdered laundry detergent were being rapidly dumped into the crystal clear water. Small, motorized pontoon boots were getting lowered into the reservoir. He was handling things well, everything was under control. *Look like you know what you're doing*, he reminded himself. He lifted up the cell and said, 'Griffin?' It buzzed a couple of times before Pete answered. 'Give me a status report.'

He listened as his eager underling told him that his orders were being followed to the letter. As an afterthought, Zane asked, 'You seen that lady doctor and the other hostage ... they were with an NYPD detective?'

'Yeah,' Griffin said, 'they went back through the checkpoint. They got out of here a good fifteen, maybe twenty minutes ago.'

'What? Under whose orders?'

'Don't know,' Griffin said, 'but I'll find out ASAP.'

'Good man, we cannot have them running around.' He thought of what Barrett had said, that she didn't think Glash was dead, that he was in fact just warming up. Zane had a terrifying moment's doubt: *What if she was right? What if she went to the press?*

'Pete,' he said, making his voice strong and authoritative, 'this is a priority. Dr Conyors, Carla Phelps and Detective Ed Hobbs need to be tracked down and quarantined; they have been in contact with the plague virus. Do you understand? This is a top priority.'

'Yes, sir.'

'Good man. I'll want a progress report in thirty minutes. I repeat, they represent a significant risk for the spread of the virus. They must be tracked down, they must be quarantined ... if they resist, force may be used.'

There was a moment's hesitation, and then Griffin asked, 'How much force?'

'Whatever is necessary.'

Twenty-Three

Naked and huddled in the back of the van wrapped in blue plastic wrap and wearing a protective mask, George Houssman's mind raced. He felt desperate and vulnerable, knowing that Glash intended something so horrific that if he succeeded 9/11 would pale in comparison. His anxiety was red hot as Glash drove across the Whitestone Bridge – he pictured his granddaughter, Faye, and his daughter; this was too close – and down the West Side Highway to Glash's father's building in the Lower East Side. 'I've not been home,' Glash said, in a dull conversational tone, 'since the day my father killed my mother.'

'Who were those women?' Houssman finally asked, dreading the answer, but even more the proximity between his beloved family in SoHo and the Lower East Side candy store – not even a mile as the crow flies.

'Joggers,' Glash replied simply.

'Why did you kill them?' he asked, his eyes falling on Martin Cosway's unconscious body.

Glash glanced back at Houssman. 'I didn't. Stop asking questions.'

Houssman swallowed. 'If you want me to write this book, Richard, I'll need details.'

Glash paused and then nodded. 'Yes, I can see that. My father killed three joggers. I'd originally meant for them to match Carla Phelps, Dr Conyors and me.'

'That's why she had red hair,' Houssman said, his stomach churning.

'Yes, to be the double for Carla Phelps. I had to make a switch and there wasn't time to get new bodies.'

'So you dressed them like us.'

'Yes, is that enough information for the book?'

George found it hard to breathe, and it wasn't just the lingering stench from the dead bodies. 'Yes,' he whispered. There was a strange flutter in his chest and a dull ache that ran from his jaw to his shoulder. 'Wait, I have another question, something I don't understand.'

'Yes?'

'You drive very well, Richard. When did you learn?' he asked, taking slow, even breaths, telling himself that no matter what he could not have a heart attack.

'At Albomar,' he said, while timing the lights on the West Side Highway. A cab tried to edge him out at the 34th Street exit. Glash slowed to let him get in front and then floored the van just as the light turned yellow. 'It was another lie,' he said. 'They taught us to drive, saying we'd need that skill when we were released. They even had special cars

234

with two steering wheels and two sets of brakes. Lies upon lies. I practiced every day; I took the test and passed. I had a license. I like to drive. My father has a motorcycle; he promised that he'd teach me how to ride it.' Glash turned again. 'I don't think he's lying.'

'So that's how he did it,' Houssman commented, realizing Peter Glash had planted the van and the bodies at the reservoir and then ridden off on a motorcycle.

'Yes,' Glash said. 'That's how he did it.'

They took the right off Houston and headed three blocks down Orchard. George saw the candy store's front was locked and gated; the alley on the right was also gated. As they approached Houssman braced himself on shaky knees and could just make out Peter Glash's tall figure in the alley behind the gate.

The gate creaked open and the van drove through.

'Hello, son,' Peter said, as he put a HEPA filter mask over his mouth and nose.

'Hello, Father.'

Peter Glash stared at Houssman in the back. 'Good,' he said. 'I'll enjoy watching you die. You deserve it.' He went around to the rear of the van and opened it.

Cosway's eyes shot open. 'What the fuck do you—'

Before he could complete his sentence, Peter Glash took a pistol from his jacket pocket and pointed it at Cosway's head. 'Shut up,' he said, not raising his voice.

'There's no way you're going to get away

with this,' Cosway hissed, as he struggled to free his wrists from the nylon restraints. He then realized his clothes were gone and asked, 'Why am I naked? What did you freaks do to me?' Gooseflesh popped on his pale arms despite the ninety-degree heat.

'I needed them,' Richard Glash said, as he joined his father at the back of the van.

'Is this the one you infected?' Peter asked his son.

'Yes,' Richard said, and he snapped on vinyl gloves, gagged Cosway and then dragged his kicking body over the filthy, bloodstained carpet of the van.

'How long till we know?' Peter asked.

'Four hours for the fever to start, twelve for the respiratory phase to begin. I hope Albert wasn't lying. I'll be very angry.'

Richard disappeared into the house carrying Cosway. Peter stared in at Houssman. 'Get out,' he said, 'and don't try to run.'

'Peter,' Houssman said through his mask, 'don't let him do this. Think of how many innocent people will die. You can't let this happen.'

'Of course I can,' he said. 'It's what we want. It's payback. You took everything away from me – my life, my son, my livelihood. It's time to even things out. What you took away from us, we'll take away from you.'

'But what about everyone else?' Houssman whispered, pulling the plastic close as he tried to steady himself on wobbly knees.

'They don't really matter,' Peter said, poking the gun into Houssman's back while directing him to the open door. He leaned in to Houssman and whispered, 'Don't think I haven't seen your pretty daughter – Alice, isn't it? – and her little girl. They don't matter, George. Perhaps we'll keep you around to watch them die.'

Houssman gasped, his foot caught on a crack in the drive. He stumbled and glimpsed the street through the chain-link gate with steel bars slotted through it. He had to do something. From under his HEPA mask he opened his mouth and started to shout as loud as he could: *'Help me! Somebody—'* The butt of the gun landed hard on the back of his head; he stumbled and dropped the tarp. He saw the ground coming toward him, the flutter in his chest turned to pain, a vice crushing his ribs. He gasped once, his vision faded and before he hit ground, everything went black.

Twenty-Four

Hobbs, Barrett and Carla hurriedly ditched their spacey orange hazmat suits and ran from the Homeland Security checkpoint at the reservoir back to the smashed Crown Victoria in the gravel lot a hundred yards away. 'You can't leave me,' Carla said, as Hobbs and Barrett tried to persuade her not to come.

'You'll just be in the way,' Hobbs said, looking to Barrett to back him up.

'I need to go with you. You don't believe that Glash dumped the plague here. You have to let me help. I know people, just please don't leave me.'

'Look, Ms Phelps,' Hobbs said, 'I don't know what we're doing right now, but—'

'I have a little girl,' Carla pleaded, her hand on the car door. 'One day, if she lives ... she'll discover that her mother was the one who helped Richard Glash escape; I can't let that happen. You've got to let me help.'

'It's OK, Ed,' Barrett said. She glanced back in the direction of the checkpoint where they'd just lied to get away and not get carted along with the Channel Eight crew to some hastily established quarantine unit. 'Let's just get out of here. I've got a horrible feeling.'

'Tell me something new,' Hobbs quipped, realizing that even covered with dust and days' worth of grime and sweat, he would have done anything for her. He pressed the button for the car's automatic locks. It didn't work. He unlocked it manually and reached over to open the other door. He said a prayer as he put the key in the ignition. 'Thank you, Jesus,' he whispered as the engine turned over.

The women scrambled in, Barrett next to him, Carla in the back.

He threw the car into reverse and did a clumsy U-turn, the tires struggling for grab in the loose gravel. 'Zane does not get it,' he said, sneaking a glance at Barrett. 'He didn't even want to hear what you had to say about Glash – idiot! God, we were so fucking close. How did they let him get away? How could I let him go?'

'You didn't have a shot, Ed,' Barrett said. 'He was using George like a shield.'

'I know,' Hobbs said, laying heavy on the gas as they roared and clanked away. 'But I can't shake the feeling that if George were here he would have told me to take the shot, to go through him if necessary.' He missed Houssman and there was a stab of regret. If anything happened to the old guy...

'But he's not here,' Barrett said, 'and you've never been someone for whom the ends justified the means.'

'Yeah, but every once in a while...' He

reached for his cell and dialed. 'Anderson, it's Hobbs.' He put it on speaker.

'What did you do?' Anderson asked. 'We just got word – along with everyone else – that you and the two ladies are to be sent to quarantine. Do not pass go, do not continue to traipse around the state of New York looking for a maniac with a bottle of plague in his pocket and a song in his heart.'

'I don't know about the song,' Hobbs said, 'but what did you say about quarantine?'

'Apparently you done pissed someone off. I think DHS is more interested in finding you than Glash. Are you messing with somebody's spin control?'

'Could be,' Hobbs replied. 'But no one here is infected with anything ... nothing that I care to share with you. What's the status with Glash?'

Anderson's frustration came through loud and clear. 'We're being told in no uncertain terms that he's dead and at the bottom of a gulch. Are you saying something else?'

'They've not made a positive ID,' Ed said, choosing his words, needing to know that Anderson got the message. 'And one of the ladies in question has serious doubts that our boy offed himself.'

'Fuck! They're telling us he's dead. They basically ordered a shutdown of any manhunt activities. All available personnel have been shifted to work on containment,' Anderson said. 'If what you're saying is true, we are so fucked.'

'How could he have slipped through?' Hobbs asked, struggling to comprehend how Glash had managed to elude the dozens of pursuing vehicles with air support that had gone after him from Albomar.

'Don't go there,' Anderson said.

'I don't get it,' Hobbs said. 'It was like shooting fish in a barrel.'

'Look around,' Anderson said, a bitter edge to his voice. 'Way too many yahoos in the mix. My guess is we have over half a million in trashed vehicles, none of the damage caused directly by Glash. It's a miracle no one got killed ... except the poor woman who'd just stopped to gas up. He just keeps slipping through.'

'What about his accomplice?' Ed asked.

'We checked the father like you asked. Went back through every prison log to see if he ever visited ... nothing. We even paid the old guy a visit ... he doesn't remember you fondly, which judging by the black eye you gave him makes sense. Searched the place, not a damn thing. We're chewing through every person on that list who visited Glash even a single time while he was locked up.'

'It can't be that long a list,' Hobbs said, his desperation mounting as he turned on to 28, heading east. 'He's not exactly Mister Personality.'

'You'd be surprised,' Anderson said. 'Trouble is, they all seem to be either lawyers, writers, there's even a couple of art agents. We chatted with one creep who wanted to represent Glash and sell his paintings. He dropped that when I told him that the way the laws were constructed, Glash, or anyone helping him, couldn't make a dime from the sale of his artwork. But the writers were a different story. Seems Glash went on a letter-writing spree a dozen years ago, contacted just about everyone who'd written a true-crime book. He wanted to get his name in print. A couple bit, and came for a visit or two. According to his prison records, that stopped after he threw a tantrum and attacked one of the authors.'

'Why?' Hobbs asked.

'Our boy wanted the whole book to be about him and he got a bit upset when he learned he'd just get a paragraph or two.'

'There is someone helping him,' Hobbs said. 'But who and why?'

'There is someone...' Barrett said.

'Hey, doc,' Anderson greeted her.

'Agent Anderson,' Barrett said, talking fast, 'he's got a girlfriend named Mary, or at least he thinks he does,' and she gave them the highlights of her fashion tips to the love-struck Richard Glash.

'Mary,' Anderson repeated. 'Well, that certainly narrows it down.'

'Can you still access the visitors' logs?' Hobbs asked. 'There's got to be something we missed.'

'I'm pulling them up as we speak ... let's see. Here we go. I've got two Marys to pick from. I've got a Mary Sullivan that goes way

242

back and then more recently a Mary Fleming. She signed in as a social worker with the Department of Mental Health.'

'Oh God,' Carla muttered from the back. 'Oh God, that can't be true.'

Barrett turned back. 'What is it?'

'Mary Sullivan was the little girl Glash first tried to scalp. Why would she visit him?'

'You have an address?' Hobbs asked. 'Seems like we got a person of interest. Course, if he went after her twice...'

'Third time's a charm,' Anderson said grimly.

'Yeah.'

'I got a number here, and an address in Katonah for Mary Fleming, nothing for a Mary Sullivan. I'll give you the first call, and I'm sending a team out now. Christ, I should have picked this up sooner.'

'If I reach her,' Ed said, 'I'll get right back to you.'

'Based on our boy's track record, if he's been there, something tells me she won't be picking up.'

Ed hung up and with one hand on the wheel he dialed. The phone rang. No one picked up, but he let it keep ringing over the Crown Vic's speakers. Hobbs turned to Barrett and shook his head. He was about to hang up when a woman's voice answered.

'This is Detective Ed Hobbs with the NYPD. I'm calling for a Mary Fleming.'

'Yes,' the voice answered, then a long pause, 'this is she.'

'Ms Fleming, I'm calling regarding Richard Glash, an escaped prisoner. We have reason to believe he might be coming after you.' He listened intently as he edged the car on to I-87 south.

'You're too late,' she said. 'He's already been here.' She was crying.

'Is he there now?' Hobbs asked, mentally mapping the shortest route to Katonah, and frantic over the distance – even flooring it, over an hour. 'Is he there?' he repeated.

Her sobs grew louder and convulsive, like she was hyperventilating. They heard the phone drop to the floor and then Mary Fleming screamed.

Twenty-Five

Houssman felt his breath warm and damp against the gauzy fabric of the white mask that covered his lower face. The right lens of his glasses had shattered and the side of his head pounded where he'd been struck. He shivered, naked under the blue plastic tarp; he wrapped it tight around his shoulders. He didn't know how long he'd been unconscious; it must have been hours based on the changes that were already visible in Cosway. His physical pain and discomfort were nothing compared to the tortured thoughts of how close they were to his family.

He watched as Richard Glash adjusted a digital camcorder on a tripod. He saw it trained on a six-by-eight-by-four-foot steel dog kennel. Inside, illuminated by bright fluorescents, Martin Cosway, bruised, dirty and naked, lay curled on a bare mattress. The agent hugged his knees, and despite the beads of sweat that dotted his body, he shivered. 'What have you done to me?' he shouted, as tears squeezed from the corners of his eyes. He then tried to stand and pressed his back against the metal bars in an attempt to break out. Houssman could see the man was ill, the exhaustion, the beads of sweat despite the dry cool of their cellar prison. Something bad was happening here.

Glash peered at the camera's screen and pressed the button to zoom in. 'You're not a smart man,' he commented. 'I told you that seven and a half hours ago you were inoculated with a resistant strain of *Yersinia pesti*, also known as the bubonic plague or the black death. It killed one third of all people in Europe during the Middle Ages.'

'Let me out of here, you sick fuck!'

'No,' Glash replied, and he glanced back at Houssman – chained to a cot, and wearing only the blue plastic tarp – to insure that everything said was being recorded. 'You understand what I'm doing,' he commented to Houssman.

'Yes,' Houssman said, his naked arms exposed and with pen in hand he dutifully wrote down all that was being said and done on a legal-sized yellow pad.

'Then tell me,' Glash demanded, as though administering a pop quiz, 'what am I doing now?'

'You're testing the bacteria,' Houssman said. The words rang horribly in his mind. 'He's your guinea pig.'

'That is correct.'

Houssman, who'd spent his career studying criminals and the workings of their minds, found Glash's actions sickeningly interesting. He wanted what many wanted – fame, recognition ... even a family, it seemed. It made a

246

kind of sense, but it had all been twisted inside a brain that couldn't really feel human emotion.

'It has to be perfect,' Glash said, as the camcorder's light flicked red to show that it was recording. 'Sometimes things don't go as planned. That's why you have to have a back-up plan. There's an "A" and there's a "B"; you have to be able to switch when the probability of success with either one goes up or down. Sometimes you can do both the "A" and the "B"; sometimes you have to switch.'

'Like taking two hostages.' In spite of his paralyzing fear, George couldn't help but fall into the practice that had been such a part of his life for the past fifty years. He desperately wanted to know why Glash was doing these things. But then he pictured Stephanie – his oldest – a leading Manhattan interior design-er just blocks away in SoHo with her hus-band, Mark, their two teenage daughters and Faye, just ten years old ... he would never say it out loud, but she was his favorite; the child that Stephanie and Mark hadn't planned, the one with Delia's eyes and that quirky turn of expression as though she'd been born in the body of a child with the mind of an adult. If only Ed had gone ahead and shot Glash when he'd had the chance, even if it had meant his getting injured ... or even killed. He had no death wish, but he would gladly give his own life to end this nightmare. He glanced at Cosway, who'd now sunk back, exhausted, on the mattress. He was sobbing, the vertebrae of his spine seemed oddly sharp, as if they might poke through his pale white skin.

'Yes, two hostages provides both an "A" and a "B",' Glash said.

'How did you know to get the bacteria?'

'That is a good question,' Glash replied, hooking the camcorder to a flat-screen monitor. 'Dr Albert is a brilliant man. I admire him greatly. Do you think he's a genius?'

'Yes,' Houssman replied.

'Am I a genius?'

Houssman paused, knowing he had to find the right tone, to stroke Glash's ego without being obvious. 'You know that your IQ is well in the genius range.'

'But not in all areas,' Glash replied.

'Correct.'

'I've read my chart from when I was at Albomar. I've read everything, even Dr Conyors' recent evaluations. She's a genius, too.'

'Yes.'

'Do you think her IQ is higher than yours?'

'I don't know,' George replied, thinking of Barrett – like a third daughter, it caused his breath to catch. He wondered at this line of interest ... Glad to be here in her place. At least she was OK ... at least for now. He thought of Hobbs, too, so obviously in love with her ... would any of that matter?

'Is it higher than mine?'

'I don't know,' George said, deliberately keeping his answers and questions as clear as possible. 'Why are you asking?'

'It's just that the probability of her stopping

me goes up if she's smarter than I am. She doesn't seem so smart in some ways, although she did help me pick out clothing. I'm not smart that way.' He turned on the monitor.

Houssman watched as the screen lit up.

'She's pregnant,' Glash said.

'Yes,' Houssman answered. 'She told you?'

'I asked her; she throws up in the mornings. I asked her why a pregnant woman would risk her life; that doesn't seem intelligent.'

Houssman found it difficult to breathe. 'What did she say?'

'She wouldn't answer. I asked her if it was Jimmy Martin's baby. I wanted to meet him. He's at the hospital where they were taking me – it was my plan B, in case I didn't escape. Dr Conyors said the baby is her dead husband's. A trombonist, he played with the Philharmonic. He was killed by Jimmy Martin. Do you think she's telling the truth?' He looked directly at Houssman.

George paused. 'Yes, that's true.' He wondered at Barrett's lie. Then again, what business of Glash's was it to know that she was carrying the fetus of a criminally insane killer?

'Jimmy Martin and his sister wanted a baby,' Glash started to speak, his tone bland, like a third-grader giving a book report to the class. 'It was in all of the papers. They kidnapped Dr Conyors and her sister, Justine Conyors. See, an "A" and a "B". Dr Conyors' husband was killed and she killed Ellen

Martin. Now she's pregnant and her husband is dead. I believe that there's a probability that the baby is Jimmy Martin's. But she said "no". There's a high probability that she lied. Her sister is a surgeon. Her name is Justine Conyors,' he continued to lecture on the topic of Barrett and her family. 'She is a fellow at University Hospital. That is the same hospital where I was taken, after I had first tried to scalp Mary Sullivan, who got married and changed her name to Fleming; she didn't change it back after she got divorced.'

'Yes,' Houssman whispered, sick to his stomach at all of the details Glash knew about Barrett and her family. This wasn't a coincidence; he had done a great deal of study, and Houssman knew it was with reason.

'Do you remember that day?' Glash asked.

'Of course I do.'

'You were supposed to be my father and to protect me and to love me.'

Houssman said nothing, as a wave of gooseflesh spread across his naked arms.

'They locked me up. You visited me for a total of three times after that. You never answered my letters. You lied to me. Dr Conyors lies. My mother lied to my father. She was having sex with Mr Barker. He killed her with a seven-pound hammer. That was the right thing to do. Do you agree?'

'No,' Houssman said, 'killing was too much. He could have divorced her.'

'No. You're wrong,' Richard spat back. 'Even the Bible says so. A woman must be faithful to her husband. If I survive, my wife will be faithful to me. She will love me. We might have children. If Dr Conyors is having Jimmy Martin's baby, then she was unfaithful to her husband. It's backwards that she's alive and he's dead. He should have killed her.'

'I wanted to know, and it's important for your story,' Houssman said, trying to shift Glash's attention away from Barrett, 'that you tell your reader how you came upon the bacteria. You were going to tell me about your relationship with Dr Albert.'

Glash looked back at George. 'Thank you,' he said, 'this is important.' And apparently satisfied that the camera was correctly positioned, Glash picked up a sketchpad and a charcoal and sat down beside Cosway's cage. As he rapidly sketched, flipping pages at three- to five-minute intervals, he kept up a steady narrative with Houssman, who occasionally asked for clarification.

'So,' Houssman said, about to take a calculated risk of tripping Glash's fury. 'What you've just told me changes your story a great deal.' He held his breath, knowing to tread lightly.

'I don't understand,' Glash replied, not looking up from his latest drawing.

'You just told me that Dr Albert was waiting for you, or someone like you, to activate his bacteria.'

'That is correct.'

'He led you to the security codes for Bio-forward. He gave you the instructions for rapidly culturing the bacteria.'

'Yes. This is all correct.'

'So it's *his* plan, not yours,' Houssman stated, applying pressure on Glash's fragile ego.

Glash looked up. 'No. It is mine.'

'Are you certain? Or will history view you as a pawn of the brilliant Dr Albert?' Houssman trod carefully; he wanted to see what would happen if Glash were pressed. 'It's his bacteria. It's his name that will be attached to it, and to whatever happens.'

'No,' Glash said, looking at Houssman, 'you're trying to upset me, aren't you?'

George didn't let up. 'I'm stating facts,' he replied coldly, attempting to match Richard's tone. 'You are the instrument of Clarence Albert's plans. You've just said so. He left the bacteria for someone else to find. He knew that it was so deadly, that the safest place to ride out the death and the destruction would be in prison. His plan is brilliant. There is a high probability that you will not survive. There is a high probability that he will.'

'I'm not stupid,' Glash spat back. 'There is a ninety percent chance that I will die.'

Houssman startled at the sound of a door opening overhead. A shaft of light spilled into the gloomy cellar and footsteps descended.

Peter Glash entered with a wooden breakfast tray that held a plate with neatly arranged sandwiches and a large pitcher of iced tea with four glasses.

The elder Glash looked at his son. 'What's the matter, Richard?'

'He's trying to upset me. He's saying that Dr Albert will get the credit for the plague.'

Peter Glash put down the tray and poured tea, the ice clinked as he methodically filled each tumbler to within an inch of the top. 'He will get some credit,' he finally commented. 'But whatever happens in the next two days will be your doing.'

'You helped me,' Richard said, looking at his father.

'Yes, son.'

Houssman watched the two of them from his perch on the cot. He stiffened as Peter Glash sat next to him and carefully removed his mask. He handed him a sandwich and glass of iced tea. 'Eat this.'

Houssman worried if the meal might be drugged, but observed Richard devouring one crustless sandwich square after the next. And in spite of the situation, the food – chicken salad sandwiches with crisp lettuce and tomato – tasted good and the cool beverage with the tartness of lemon and not too much sugar carried the off-kilter whiff of Alice's tea party with the March Hare and the Mad Hatter.

'Have you had enough?' Peter Glash asked Houssman.

'Yes, thank you.'

'You're welcome.'

George tensed as Peter Glash rearranged

his mask. The proximity caused him to shrink back. The man's eyes were dull and expressionless. He caught George looking at him. 'I'm going to win,' he said, 'you're going to lose everything. You're going to know what you did to me and to my son. An eye for an eye.'

He then got up and walked by Cosway, who coughed a single time, and like a spark landing on gasoline, the agent doubled over in an uncontrollable paroxysm of coughing.

Richard put down his sandwich and looked across at his father. 'It's been just eight hours,' he said. 'It's four hours faster than we thought.'

'Are you certain, Richard?' Peter asked. 'There might be another way.'

'I know,' Richard replied, 'but the probability for success goes down.' He walked across to Cosway's cage and unlocked it.

'Are you certain, Richard?' Peter repeated. 'I would try to help you find another way.'

'I'm certain,' and Richard looked back at his father. 'Thank you.' The two men looked at each other across the brightly-lit basement. 'Thank you for everything.'

Peter Glash nodded. 'You're welcome, son.'

Richard said, 'It's time, then. The clock starts.' He opened Cosway's cage. The naked and shivering bureaucrat looked up, as Glash roughly forced him back against the hard metal bars.

Horrified, Houssman watched the enlarged image on the monitor in front of him. With the taste of chicken salad and iced tea still in his mouth, he saw Richard press his mouth hard over Martin Cosway's. The agent's eyes bugged wide as Glash forced his tongue into his mouth.

Houssman couldn't breathe or tear his eyes away; he scrambled blindly for his pen and yellow pad. In a shaky hand he scribbled *Kiss of death*, and next he recorded the time, which ticked off in red block letters at the bottom of the screen: it was 8:04 p.m. on Thursday.

Twenty-Six

Barrett's anxiety flared as Hobbs floored the accelerator and they raced from the mansions of Katonah toward Manhattan; it was dusk. She glanced at the clock on the dash – it felt like days had passed, but it had been only four hours since they'd fled the reservoir.

Carla was in the back. She had her head in her hands. 'Oh, my God, what if we're wrong? What if she misunderstood? What if she got it wrong?'

'We're not wrong,' Hobbs said. 'It's the only possibility, the only thing that makes sense. I should have locked the bastard up when I had the chance.'

Barrett thought back through the last forty minutes spent with a shell-shocked Mary Fleming. Throughout it, her eyes hand wandered to the short blonde wig the woman, who had twice been attacked by Richard Glash, wore.

Mary had caught her at it, and with a single motion removed it, to reveal two vivid scars that scanned the dome of her scalp, one a faded soft pink and the other more jagged.

To Barrett, what had followed revealed a side of Glash she'd barely glimpsed.

'He told me that he loved me,' Mary said, leading them to a sprawling back deck where a day earlier Richard Glash had stood.

Barrett took in the pricey views that stretched down to the Hudson River a few hundred feet below, and the neatly arranged wicker furniture and umbrellas. Mary Fleming had money and taste.

'Strange way to show it,' Hobbs remarked.

'I always knew that if he ever got free, he would come for me. I knew that he'd kill me, so that's why I did it. It was the only way.' Mary sat on a white wicker chair and let her eyes drift to the river that meandered below her hillside house.

'Did what?' Barrett asked, trying to capture her attention as Mary gazed off. 'What did you do, Mary?'

Still staring into the distance with her wig in her lap, she replied, 'Isn't that how you found me?'

'Yes,' Hobbs said, 'your name came up on the prison visitors' log. It came up as both Sullivan and Fleming.'

'I was married,' she explained. 'I suppose it's a good thing we're divorced. I don't know what Richard would have done if John had been here. Killed him, I imagine. I thought he'd come to kill me.'

'What happened?' Barrett urged.

'I still can't believe that I'm alive,' she said. 'I'd been watching the news. I knew Richard was out. I didn't think he had my address, but he's a genius. I knew he'd find me. I didn't

257

know what to do. In the end I did nothing. I sat here ... waiting, and then he came. Just like you're here now, he showed up.' She'd pointed with a trembling finger at an arrangement of daisies and black-eyed Susans in a chunky crystal vase. 'He brought me those flowers and candy.' She hiccoughed. 'He told me that he loved me.'

'And then?' Barrett urged, noting how Mary seemed to be disconnected, in shock.

'I asked him if he was going to kill me. In a way, I'd been waiting for him all of my life. That's why I did it.' She glanced up at Hobbs. 'I didn't finish telling you...' She shook her head, seemingly frozen. 'What was I saying?'

'You were telling us about his visit,' Barrett prompted softly.

'I was ready to die,' Mary said, 'almost a relief, knowing that he'd one day come for me. He said, "I don't have to kill you anymore." He said he'd taken care of it. He told me that he loved me and that he wanted to marry me. He said that he was going to do something that would make him very famous, that he'd make a good husband, that he'd be faithful and that we could have children. He got down on one knee – right there between the begonias – and asked me if I would marry him.' She looked down at the human-hair wig she was gripping and twisting.

And then Barrett caught the glimmer of the diamond.

Mary held up her hand. 'He'd even brought a ring.'

Carla gasped, looking at the small, emerald-shaped diamond in platinum. 'That was Lucinda's. Oh my God!'

Mary turned, as though just noticing her. 'Who's Lucinda?'

And while Barrett didn't say it, what she thought was, *Lucinda Peters got the murder Richard Glash had intended for you.* 'It doesn't matter,' she said, and looked at Hobbs. 'Mary, Richard Glash is attempting to do something so horrible that if he succeeds thousands of people – maybe more – will die. He's not working alone, someone has been helping him.'

The bald woman with her scarred scalp just stared across the Hudson River Valley.

'Mary,' Barrett persisted, 'is it you? Have you been helping him?'

'No,' she said, and then stopped. She looked up at Barrett and then at Hobbs on her other side. 'I don't think so. How could I?'

'Did you leave a pickup truck for him in the parking lot of the Croton Forensic Hospital?' Hobbs asked. 'It's not far from here,'

'I know where it is,' she said. 'And no, of course not.'

Barrett's frustration mounted with each passing second. They'd been wrong, Mary hadn't been the accomplice – or was she lying? She felt for the woman who'd been so badly traumatized by Glash, but at the same time had the gut sense there was more. 'Why did you visit Richard Glash in prison?' she asked. 'Not just once, but you were going at

259

least monthly ... for years.'

'Because I knew eventually he'd get out,' she said. 'No matter what anyone says, one day he would have been let go, and that would be the day he'd come for me. Richard Glash never lets go. I know that better than anyone.'

'Of course,' Barrett said, 'but why the visits?'

'When I was a little girl, I lived next door to him. What he did to me was horrible, but before that, for a little while, although in my mind it seems longer, he and I were friends. For the couple months that he lived there we played together every day. I don't remember much; just that he was my friend, and then one day he tried to kill me. Years later, he tried again. He wasn't angry or mad, and I think the reason he didn't succeed when we were teenagers is that somewhere buried inside him, he was still my friend. He could easily have killed me then. I begged him not to. I don't remember much of it, just that he told me he'd try not to kill me, but that he needed to remove my scalp, and because the vessels in the head bleed so much; "there was a high probability that I would die from the blood loss".' She shivered in her chair, despite the ninety-plus degree heat. 'That's why I visited him in prison. He could have killed me that afternoon, but he stayed for hours doing ... no, I can't talk about what he did to me that day. But he stayed so long they caught him. In a sense I owe him my life, the only thing that saved me then ... and now ... is that I may be his only friend.'

'You visited him to keep the friendship?' Barrett asked.

'Yes.'

'And you didn't help with the escape or buy him prepaid cell phones?' Hobbs interjected.

'Of course not. I never wanted to see him out. I just knew it would happen.'

'Then who's been helping him?' Hobbs asked.

'You say someone left a truck for him?' Mary asked.

'Yes.'

'Was it black?'

'Yes, why?' Hobbs asked.

'Richard would talk about his dreams when I'd visit him. He had two sets. One very normal and the other to go on a killing spree that would make him famous. He'd show me pictures he'd drawn of the two possibilities. In both, whether it was the wife and kids or the murder spree, there was always a black pick-up truck. I can even see the logo on the back – a Ford, I think.'

Barrett nodded. 'Who would know that he wanted a black truck?'

'The only person I can think would be his father.'

'What?' Hobbs spat out.

Mary turned and looked back at him. 'Peter Glash ... his father. He has some sort of store or warehouse in the city.'

'I know,' Hobbs said, crouching beside her

chair. 'What makes you think the two men were in contact? His name never appeared on the visitors' log.'

'I'd forgotten that,' she said.

'What?' Hobbs persisted.

'He wouldn't visit Richard. He'd visit another prisoner. I'm trying to remember his name.'

'Clarence Albert?' Barrett offered.

'Yes,' Mary said, twisting to face her. 'That's right. And then Mr Albert would let Richard know what his father had to say. It was very odd ... of course, with Richard one doesn't expect anything different...'

They'd left Katonah and Mary twenty minutes ago. Now, with his jaw set tight, Hobbs kept flooring the banged-up Crown Vic. As they turned off 684 and on to the Hutchinson they hit traffic. Though mid-afternoon, they had to slow to a stop-and-start crawl.

'What's going on?' Hobbs muttered, looking at the jam that seemed to stretch for miles ahead of them.

Barrett flicked on the radio. Every station was emphatically announcing that the Department of Homeland Security had raised the alert level to red for Manhattan and the New York City boroughs. People were being urged not to panic – *This is only a precaution* – and they were being reassured that a major act of bioterrorism had been averted by the Department of Homeland Security working in collaboration with local, state and federal authorities.

As they listened Hobbs's cell went off. He glanced at the readout – his boss. 'It's Felix.'

'You going to pick up?' Barrett asked.

'What the hell.' He flipped it open. 'What's up, Felix?'

'Where are you, Hobbs? I've got those morons from Homeland Security calling every five minutes asking why you and Glash's two hostages haven't reported to a quarantine facility. Who'd you piss off?'

'Jesus! You'd think they'd have more important concerns. Like finding Glash.'

Felix Schmitt paused; he and Hobbs went way back. 'I take it that getting to quarantine isn't your top priority; what is?'

'Getting Glash before he infects Manhattan with bubonic plague.'

'You working with a different script than the DHS? They say all of the plague was dumped in the reservoir, that it's been neutralized – that the manhunt for Glash is over. They're saying he and his last two hostages are dead.'

Hobbs asked, 'Yeah, but do they say they have positive ID?'

'Yes, why?'

'Because they're lying bags of shit! Look, Felix, we were at the reservoir. Somehow Glash drove a Volkswagen with some stiffs in it over an impossible-to-reach ditch. As of two, three hours ago, no one had even made it all the way down to the bottom to ID the bodies.'

Felix again paused. 'Hobbs, you're in such deep shit right now. In fact, getting you and your two lady friends tucked away into quarantine is like their number one priority. Right now, it's you, and not Glash, who's the threat of contagion. They're saying if we can't haul your asses in we might be looking at a large-scale quarantine – location determined by all the places you've been.'

Hobbs's jaw twitched and his knuckles turned white as they gripped the wheel. 'Felix, this is a bunch of cover-your-ass spin. None of us are infected; we're feeling just fine, thanks.' He looked up at the sign for the Whitestone Bridge and the West Side Highway.

'Ed,' Carla said, 'behind us.'

Barrett turned and Hobbs looked in the rear-view. Two patrol cars were plowing through the traffic, with lights and no sirens. Ed looked at the cell in his hand. 'Felix, you're a total shit!'

'Sorry, Hobbs. Just following orders.'

Hobbs rolled down the window and hurled his phone out. 'Hold on,' he said, as he turned on his siren and, clipping a limousine on their right, shot across three lanes and then accelerated toward an off ramp into the Bronx.

The patrol cars gave pursuit; their sirens wailed and were joined by two more unmarked vehicles.

Ed flew through the quiet residential streets. Small children looked up agape; one woman jumped back from her mailbox; a collie tied up in its front yard howled.

'Hobbs,' Barrett said, 'they've got it all wrong.'

'I know,' he said, turning off the flashing light and siren. 'I could kill Felix. It's one thing to rat me out. He could have at least listened to me. But I shouldn't have thrown that phone out.'

'They were using it to trace us,' Barrett said, as Hobbs took a hard right toward the tan-brick housing projects around Riverdale Park.

He glanced in the mirror; now a single squad car was chasing. 'Hold on to something,' he yelled.

Barrett and Carla braced as Hobbs slammed on the brakes, threw the car into reverse, then shot behind the squad car. He reversed directions with a jagged J turn and headed back toward Johnson Avenue. Glancing behind he could see he'd momentarily eluded their pursuers. He turned in to a residential street of two-story homes and spotted a garage that had been left open. He pulled in and shut off the motor.

He jumped out of the car, glanced down the street and rolled down the door.

'Hobbs,' Barrett said, 'we've got to get into the city and stop him.'

'I know,' he said, breathing heavily.

Through a row of small windows at the top of the garage door they spotted two black Cherokee helicopters flying noisily toward

Harlem.

'You don't think those are for us?' Barrett asked.

'I think they are,' Hobbs said. He looked around the garage and tried the door that led into the two-story brick home. It was locked. He knocked – no reply. He waited less then ten seconds and kicked it open. Inside, it was homey and warm. The smell of potpourri wafted up from terracotta dishes and the walls were covered with dozens of framed family photographs, many of them large montages of weddings and children's birthday parties.

Barrett let the smells and warmth of the cozy house wash over her. The normalcy of it brought tears to her eyes as she walked into the carpeted living room and switched on the large-screen television. The first image was Corbin Zane in his hazmat suit. He'd taken off the protective shield for the camera; behind him was the activity at the Ashokan Reservoir. At the bottom of the screen the rolling dialog was that the alert level had been raised to red for Manhattan and the five boroughs.

'We believe,' Zane said, 'with a high degree of confidence that the biological weapon has been isolated and neutralized. But based on the seriousness and the potential for devastating consequences we are taking all precautions until we have one hundred percent certainty that the virus has not been transmitted.'

'Bacteria, you moron,' Barrett muttered. Her frustration and fear were at boiling point. She pictured her mother, probably at work right now, her hair in a gingham kerchief over big plastic rollers, setting up the bar ... no way to get out of the city, and her sister who wouldn't leave even if it were an option. She knew that Justine would be at University Hospital getting prepared for the massive influx of worried Manhattanites. She looked at Hobbs, who was dialing the phone, hanging up and then dialing again.

He looked back at her and pressed the button to put the phone on speaker. 'I'm sorry,' a voice said, 'all circuits are currently busy. Please wait and try your number again. This is a recording.'

'Glash,' Carla said. 'We have to go and stop him. There's got to be a way into the city.'

They turned as flashing lights flooded through the lace-curtained windows. They heard sirens and saw one of the patrol cars that had been pursuing them head slowly down the tree-lined street. The siren was then turned off and a woman's voice blared through the car's loudspeaker.

'Detective Hobbs, you and your passengers are to surrender immediately. This is a direct order from the Department of Homeland Security.'

Ed glanced in the direction of the garage. 'Shit.'

'The police radio?' Barrett said. 'It has GPS too?'

'Yup.'

'What do we do?' she asked.

The cruiser stopped in front of the house. The voice again came loud and clear. 'Detective Hobbs, we are instructed to escort you and your passengers to the nearest quarantine facility. If you do not comply we have been instructed to use whatever force is necessary.'

'What are we going to do?' Carla was peering through the curtains, as the cops exited their vehicle and drew their weapons. Behind them two other cruisers and a National Guard personnel vehicle were pulling up as additional sirens wailed in the distance. Overhead the roar of a helicopter shook the house. A wedding photo fell from the wall; its glass shattered.

'We surrender,' Hobbs said.

'What?' Carla replied.

Barrett caught Hobbs's eye. 'Why, Ed? We can't give up. If we all took off in different directions, maybe...'

'For God's sake, Barrett, would you listen to yourself?' Hobbs blurted, struggling to be heard over the sirens and the roar of the chopper. 'These guys aren't fooling around. If Zane is anything like Cosway we're dealing with a shoot-first-ask-questions-later mentality. Now, listen to me,' he said. 'Since nine-eleven I've been in a dozen major disaster drills for the city.'

'And,' Barrett said, taken aback by Hobbs's vehemence; he seemed angry ... at her, 'I've

268

been in some too. What's the point?'

'We did a couple of city-wide drills with bioterrorism themes.'

'I still don't get it,' Barrett said.

'All the quarantine facilities were in Manhattan. It's our best shot right now. If we resist ... they'll level the house and everything – everyone – in it.'

'Ed,' Barrett started to protest, 'once they have got us—'

'Barrett' – he grabbed her by the shoulders. She startled, torn between breaking free and wondering why he was so angry with her – 'please do this for me. I can't take the thought of anything happening to you. Please...'

'OK.' She realized it wasn't anger, and his hands felt strong on her shoulders. She stared into his eyes, and wondered if he'd try to kiss her.

He gave a half-smile and let go. He walked toward the front door, opened it slightly and shouted, 'Don't shoot. We're coming out.' He put his hands on his head.

Barrett looked at Carla, shrugged her shoulders, and followed him out.

Twenty-Seven

Night had fallen as Barrett, Hobbs and Carla huddled in the back of the locked police van. Hobbs had been correct about the quarantine sites – all in Manhattan. He'd grimly commented, 'Probably because it's an island.'

'So are Staten and Riker's, for that matter,' Carla responded.

'Yeah,' Barrett said, 'so are Ellis and Roosevelt, but none of them have the medical facilities all set up and ready to go.'

Hobbs had convinced their NYPD escort to take them to the quarantine facility that had been established at University Hospital in the Village. It was the closest to the Lower East Side and it was where Barrett's sister worked.

As they drove across the Whitestone Bridge that connected Queens to the Bronx he again tried to reason with the hazmat-suited driver. 'Could I at least speak to my supervisor?' he asked, still fuming over Felix's betrayal, but maybe now that the heat was off and the three of them were in custody he'd listen.

'I'm sorry, sir,' she replied. 'I've been given direct orders to take the three of you straight to quarantine. Your supervisor is aware that you've been found and of where you are being taken.'

'I have vital information,' Hobbs persisted, 'that pertains to Richard Glash. He needs to know this.'

'Sir,' the driver replied, uncertainty in her voice, 'my orders come from very high up. I can't go against them.'

'You said your orders were to take us to quarantine. What does that have to do with my speaking to Captain Schmitt? Or if not to him I could give you the number for Agent Anderson with the FBI?'

The driver hedged, as the vehicle slowed at the tollbooth. Her male partner flashed a badge through the windshield and they were waved through. 'I'm sorry, sir, but my orders state you are to speak with no one. That you and the ladies are to be processed in quarantine and kept isolated.'

'Who would give such a bone-headed order? And why?'

'They're trying to spin this,' Barrett muttered. 'What do they think we're going to do, go the press? Look,' she said, pleading with the driver and her partner, 'Richard Glash did not dump all of the plague bacteria into the reservoir. I know because I was there. I was his hostage and I saw what he did. I also know that he's not dead. They're saying they've made a positive ID, but they haven't. We have vital information, and no one will listen to us.'

'I was there, too,' Carla said, backing up Barrett, and making certain the two hazmat-suited cops had their attention. 'He did not dump all the bacteria, but that's what he wanted people to believe. Even if he's dead, which he's not, there's more bacteria out there.'

'Listen,' Barrett said, 'as we speak he's somewhere in Manhattan, quite possibly at his father's place in the Lower East Side. He'll be figuring a way to infect the most people possible. The reservoir was just a ploy to buy time.'

'Guys, you've got to believe them,' Hobbs pleaded. 'Think of your families, your children, millions will die if he's not stopped.'

'I'm sorry, sir,' the driver repeated, her voice wavering. 'I have orders; you're to speak with no one. I was told that you'd try to get me to deviate from my orders. We cannot do that, sir.'

Hobbs felt like his head might explode; it was futile, but he couldn't let up. They pleaded and begged. Hobbs gave them the numbers for Schmitt and Anderson. He gave them the street address for Glash's father. It was met with a steady stream of 'We are to take you to quarantine. We are under strict orders.'

In the dim light of the van he saw Barrett lose it. 'Look, we're not in Nazi Germany. Can't you think for yourselves? Just imagine for half a second that the three of us aren't all psychotic. Maybe what we're saying is the truth. Even if it's a remote possibility don't you think you should follow it up?'

Hobbs felt for the driver and her partner, their hands tied by bureaucratic threats; if they deviated in the slightest they'd be brought up on insubordination. They were probably thinking of their families and their mortgages. Even so, he couldn't let up. 'Please, at least let me talk to Detective Schmitt.' He could see the man turn to the driver and shake his head. Neither one of them would say anything further as they drove down the West Side Highway across 14th Street and down Broadway to University Hospital. When they arrived they were ordered to put on HEPA masks and were escorted at gunpoint by Guardsmen in hazmat suits.

Barrett and Carla didn't stop as they stared into the frightened young faces through the visors of the suits. They continued to plead their case, rattling off the phone numbers and Peter Glash's address.

Barrett searched over their heads and between them, hoping to catch a glimpse of Justine among the doctors, nurses and aides gathered at the far end of the corridor. She knew that her sister would be there, even though she desperately wished that both Justine and her mother were far away from the city.

'Barrett!' Justine shouted over the wall of guards.

'Justine! You've got to get someone to listen. Richard Glash is in the city.' Before she could say more, three guards detached themselves and rushed away Justine and all of the other medical personnel who'd gathered.

'Somebody has got to listen to us,' Carla pleaded, attempting to make eye contact with the guard next to her. She saw her reflection in his visor. 'Why won't anyone listen? You're making a horrible mistake. Richard Glash is here, in the city. He has the bacteria. It didn't go into the reservoir.'

Nothing any of them said seemed to matter as they were led to a small reverse-airflow medical isolation room. To Barrett, the small, windowless room with its three beds seemed more a prison cell than a hospital room.

'Hobbs,' she said, 'somebody has got to believe us.'

A hazmat-suited sergeant leading the squadron of Guardsmen locked them in. 'Homeland Security has informed us that all of the bacteria was accounted for,' he said. 'It was all introduced at the Ashokan Reservoir. It's been isolated and what we're doing now is just a precaution.' His tone was meant to re-assure the trio. He'd been thoroughly briefed.

'That's not true,' Barrett said, trying to make eye contact through his mask.

'Of course it is,' he said. 'Why would they lie to us and put the entire city in jeopardy? That makes no sense. I understand the three of you have been through very traumatic events. That can confuse your thinking.'

'I'm a psychiatrist,' Barrett said, feeling like she wanted to scream. 'I know the effects of trauma. But you have three people who all

274

believe the same thing. Richard Glash intends to infect as many people as possible with bubonic plague. He doesn't care if he survives. You've got to believe us. And even if we're wrong, won't it have been better to be safe? To just have someone check out what we're telling you?'

The sergeant hesitated. He glanced behind him, and then in a low voice said, 'If you were going to call someone, who would it be and what would you tell them?'

Hobbs quickly rattled off Anderson's cell and the message, which included Peter Glash's address.

The sergeant nodded, and then closed the door behind him.

'He's not going to do anything,' Carla said.

Hobbs looked at her. 'You're probably right.'

'He just did that to humor us,' she added, 'to get us to go into our cell – excuse me, *hospital room* – without a fight.'

Barrett was frantically checking out the space – three small cots made up in white linen with folded hospital-issue pajamas in faded shades of brown, green and blue. There were three small end tables, a telephone and a fifteen-inch television bolted to a corner stand that jutted from the wall. Overhead, vents sucked up the air, sending it through a series of filters, while fresh air got pumped back through a second set in the floor.

Hobbs picked up the telephone receiver. 'Great!' he muttered.

'What?' Carla asked.

'This,' he said, punching the button to put it on speaker. A mechanical voice spilled out, *'This extension is equipped to receive only. If you wish to make an outgoing call please consult with your hospital courtesy coordinator. Thank you.'*

'They don't want us talking to anyone,' Barrett said, and the three of them spent the next four hours searching fruitlessly for a way out.

At midnight, the lights shut off without warning.

'I guess they're trying to tell us something,' Hobbs said.

'Yeah,' Barrett agreed, but as she lay back on the freshly-made bed, convinced that she would never fall asleep, she was out cold in minutes.

When she opened her eyes, the room was still dark. She heard Hobbs's snoring and as her eyes adjusted, she saw Carla curled up in the bed next to hers.

Easing out of the bed, she went to the small en-suite bathroom with a stall shower. She closed the door and tried the light; she was surprised that it worked.

She looked at the shower, and realizing it wasn't exactly the thing to do at the end of the world, she turned on the water and peeled off her torn navy slacks and once-white shirt. Blood had fixed the thin cotton of her blouse to the gash on her right shoulder. She slowly pried it back, trying not to rip the scab. Fresh blood oozed around the edges. She thought about how nice it would be to have fresh clothes – even if it were just hospital pajamas. She put a hand under the spray and adjusted the heat. She unwrapped a bar of white soap and stepped under the warm, cascading stream. It felt wonderful to stand there letting the warmth touch her skin, to let it melt away four days of sweat and grime. She smoothed the soap across her belly. Had it started to swell? She thought about the lie she'd told Glash, that the baby growing inside her was Ralph's. Who would ever know? 'Right,' she said aloud, knowing that three people would know – Justine, Hobbs and George. So what? she argued with herself. If they truly cared for her ... loved her ... and this is what she wanted ... She stopped herself as the fantasy took shape: her with a baby, holding him or her, realizing she actually had a preference – a girl. For the briefest of moments she let an old, cherished dream return. Her own little girl. Holding her, breastfeeding, changing diapers, buying pretty outfits, bringing her to her mother's apartment in the East Village for babysitting. The vision of her mother, Ruth, still young looking with her Country-Western auburn hair and loving eyes, caused her to gasp.

She startled at a knock at the bathroom door. It was Hobbs. 'Barrett, Justine's on the phone ... are you in the shower?'

'Hold on.' Still soapy, she turned off the water, grabbed the largest of the towels and wrapped it around her. She went out into the room where the lights had come back on and caught odd looks from Carla and Hobbs. 'It's not like we're going anywhere,' she said, taking the phone. 'Justine?'

'Barrett, you don't know the trouble I had finding your room number. What did you do?'

'Justine, let me talk. The so-called authorities have gotten everything wrong and you've got to get us out of here.' She quickly filled her sister in on the salient points.

'Barrett, I understand what you're saying, but if Glash has been walking around with this stuff, and you've been with him for the past few days, isn't it possible you've been exposed?'

'I don't think so, Justine. What time is it?'

'It's a little after seven.'

'In the morning?'

'Yuh.'

'Great! Look, it's been over a day since we were last in contact with Glash. He always kept it bottled up and away from us. If we'd been infected, we'd already ... be sick.'

'Jesus, Barrett!'

'You've got to get us out of here.'

'They've got that entire floor locked off,' Justine said. 'It used to be a psych floor.'

'Yes, I recognize it, even though everything's been changed ... there's got to be a way.' Barrett again looked around the room, taking in the neatly arranged furniture, the oxygen hook-ups, all its typical hospital-room features, minus a window and with a single locked door. Hobbs was standing on the mid-

278

dle bed poking at the ceiling tiles and shaking his head. The vents were bolted shut with the screws on the opposite side. Carla was sitting on the far bed watching Barrett intently and listening.

'People escape from psych wards all the time,' Carla said.

'That's true,' Barrett replied as Hobbs got down from the bed, having given up on the ceiling.

'How?' he asked.

Barrett quickly ran through every instance she could think of. 'Usually in the company of friends and family, or they attach themselves to visitors leaving the unit. You'd be amazed how visitors don't want to say anything even if they think it's weird that one of the patients – in pajamas – is following them off the unit.'

'Makes sense,' Hobbs said, 'herd mentality. Like this bullshit! Is that the only way?'

'Laundry carts and meal carts,' Carla added. 'They've got to feed us at some point.'

'I wonder if they've even thought that far,' Barrett said. 'From what little I saw, we're getting the luxury accommodation.'

'You have no idea how confused things are right now,' Justine said through the receiver. 'We've been told that no medical personnel can leave for any reason, and that until the all-clear is given, we have to be prepared to quarantine as many as twenty thousand people in a hospital with a twelve-hundred bed capacity.'

'Good,' Hobbs said. 'Chaos is good. What's bad is we seem to have pissed off people in high places.'

'Justine,' Barrett said, 'I'm going to ask you to do something that could get all of us into big trouble. I don't even know how big, but—'

'Stop right there,' Justine said. 'This could actually work. I've been issued a hazmat suit and I've got my hospital ID. I'm assuming this will be two for lunch?'

'I'm coming too,' Carla spat out.

Hobbs and Barrett exchanged glances.

'Look,' Carla said, 'you need every bit of help you can get. You don't know what we're going to find out there. I have friends in the DA's office, maybe I can get someone to listen to us.'

'What the hell,' Barrett said, grabbing the closest of the pajamas. 'Make it three, Justine. And please ... hurry.'

'I'll see what I can do.' And she hung up.

Barrett, with her hair wet, dripping suds and still dressed in a towel, felt something close to hope flutter in her chest.

'Do you think she'll be able to do it?' Carla asked.

'I don't know,' Barrett said, retreating to the bathroom, not wanting to change in front of Hobbs. 'She'd do anything for me. I think it's our only shot.' She closed the door and looked down at her ripped slacks. Her blouse reeked of sweat and blood. She pulled on the pajama top, her filthy slacks and rubber-soled hospital slippers. Her heart was pounding, and it wasn't just fear. There was something more. She sat on the bathroom floor and hugged her legs. She thought about Hobbs and about Justine and what they'd say if they knew what she was thinking. *But there it is*, she thought. *If I survive, I'm having this baby, and no one is going to talk me out of it.* And in spite of everything, she thought of Justine's bad joke when she was trying to get her to have the abortion; she grinned and whispered aloud, 'Call me Rosemary.'

Twenty-Eight

Chained to a cot and covered by only the blue plastic tarp, George Houssman shivered and stared at Cosway across the brightly lit and windowless basement. The mask on his face caused his broken glasses to steam; he had to keep pushing them up to let them vent so he could see. He squinted and checked the time at the bottom of the monitor that recorded Cosway's infection. It was 8 a.m. Friday morning and less than one day after being infected, he was clearly dying. The poor man lay on the sweat-stained mattress staring up at the ceiling, his face bloated, an effect of the angry pustules and weeping sores that covered his naked flesh. As a medical student decades ago, George had seen textbook photographs of bubonic plague; then it had been fascinating, now it was horrifying and cruel ... and real. His thoughts hammered away at him: Was all of this on some level his fault? Decades-old regret flooded him; he and Delia should have tried harder to save the boy. Tears of frustration clouded his vision as he watched Cosway's breath take on the odd, bellows-like quality of someone close to death; not yet the agonal rasps of the last hour, but that was near.

'Cosway,' Houssman called.

The sick man turned his head, the effort bringing on a fresh wave of coughing. 'I don't want to die,' he wheezed. Tears tracked into the open sores that had erupted on his cheeks and chin.

It was like Cosway was melting, his blood vessels, and even his cells, exploding out their contents. From what little Houssman recalled from med school, this was what should have happened eventually; but what Albert had developed looked far worse. Plague, he recalled, should take days or even weeks to get to this stage ... not twenty-four hours. Houssman couldn't stop shaking; he gathered the crinkly tarp tight around his shoulders. There was nothing he could do to comfort the dying man. He wondered if there was anything anyone could do. Or was it as Richard had said, that this was something that could not be treated with existing antibiotics?

He heard the cellar door open and looked up. Peter Glash descended, ducking his head to miss a low-hanging beam. His face, like George's, was covered with a protective mask; his eyes with shiny black and purple bruises from Hobbs's fist. He glanced at Cosway. 'It won't be long,' he commented. He looked at Houssman. 'Richard says he'll be dead within eight hours.'

Peter then checked the camcorder to insure it was still recording. He fished a fresh tape

283

from the breast pocket of his denim work shirt and inserted it into the machine.

Houssman tried to calm himself, to stop shaking. After fifty years of dealing with mentally-ill criminals he was not easily flustered. The difference now, he realized, was that he'd always been able to keep his children safe from his work. Their very real peril was eating away at him, making it hard to think straight. He thought of Barrett and the horrible risks she had taken; it's what most worried him about her. She'd not developed the skill, the distance that was so important to keep the work at arm's length. He hated to fault her, but she had jumped right into Glash's truck, and she was carrying the child of another killer and...

'Peter,' he said.

'What, George?' Glash's tone was sarcastic.

'Why don't you stop him? What he's intending is inhuman.'

'So?' Glash replied, and then settled in a folding metal chair across from Houssman. 'Richard wants me to tell you my story. He thinks it's important. Some of it you know. Pick up your pad. He's excited about the book you're going to write.' His tone was dull. 'Personally I'd just as soon see you dying in that cage.' He reached toward Houssman.

George recoiled as Glash took off his broken glasses, wiped the condensation off on his sleeve and then put them back on. George stared into cold blue eyes that held a deep hatred. The bruises on Peter's face were

284

like a second mask or some kind of circus make-up.

'He tells me that several of your others have been bestsellers. He wants me to read them. Perhaps I will one day ... if I survive.'

Houssman looked at the yellow pad, now over half-filled with his small, careful script. 'What if I refuse?'

Peter glared. 'You think my son is joking?'

Houssman tried to quiet his breathing; he didn't want Peter to see his fear, his weakness. 'No. I realize this is deadly serious.'

'Yes, many are about to die.'

'You could stop this,' Houssman said, keeping his voice low in case Richard should be trying to listen in.

'Of course I could; I choose not to.'

'Why?'

'Write, and I'll tell you. It's all connected, and part of what needs to happen is the recording of it. Should you choose not to do this he'll kill you ... or I will; I'd like that. Your purpose will be gone' – he paused, and then added – 'you did have another purpose for Richard. You failed him.'

'He wanted me to be his father.'

'Yes. But because Richard is special, you refused. You failed him.'

'I did,' Houssman admitted, finding it hard to catch his breath.

'Correct, you were given something precious – my son; you failed us both. Now I'm going to tell you my story. Either you write it down, or I'll tell him that you refused and he'll come down here and put a bullet in your very old head. It's your choice. You know, as I think about it, I could just tell my story on to a tape – anyone could write the book then.'

Houssman picked up the pad and the pen. The tarp gaped, exposing his thin chest to the damp basement air. 'I'll write.'

'Of course you will,' Peter Glash said. 'You're a smart man. I know what you're thinking, that as long you're alive there's still a chance. You're wondering if there's some way you could escape and stop this. I imagine there is some small chance ... while you're alive. That goes to zero if you're dead. Richard knows where your children live. He knows the names of your grandchildren and what school Faye attends on West Third Street.' Peter Glash smiled over rotted teeth. 'Shall we begin?'

'Yes.' Houssman seethed, his fear gone, replaced with surging adrenalin at the mention of his children ... of his granddaughter, Faye. She'd be arriving at school right now, lining up with her classmates outside the old brick building in Greenwich Village.

'Good. You think you know me,' Peter went on. 'You don't. You knew that I killed Dorothea; she was a whore. It's a husband's right to punish his wife. Richard understands that. That's why I made him watch.'

Houssman startled. 'What? I thought he came home after the event.'

'No,' Peter said, 'it was an important lesson. A boy needs to be taught what it is to be a man. Women need to know their place. I made Richard watch.'

Houssman shuddered, his hand shook on the page, imagining the horror of what a four-year-old Richard Glash had been made to witness – this man bludgeoning his wife to death. Tears came to his eyes, as he remembered the little boy and his ever-present sketchpad.

Peter Glash saw Houssman's revulsion. 'See, you think you know me, but you don't. I was born in this house. I was the sixth and last child.' He stood and looked down at the yellow pad to be certain Houssman was getting it all. 'Four of us are still alive; we don't talk much. My sister Bertha died of influenza when she was three. And only my brother Frank visited me while I was in prison. I paid him to do that. Frank is the only other one of us to marry and have children. Don't you find that odd?' he asked. 'Don't you want to ask me questions to clarify this point?'

Houssman's throat was dry; he struggled to find his voice. 'You said four of you are still alive, and you told me about a sister and your brother Frank. Who else died?' His heart pounded and raced in his chest, the dull, squeezing ache had returned to his jaw.

Glash smiled. 'Good, you're paying attention. I'll tell you about my brother Edward. He was three years older than I and mean. He'd play tricks on me and my sister Katie. He'd lock us in closets and hammer us up inside packing crates. He'd leave us for hours. One time we couldn't find Katie for over a day. She was down here in the cellar. He'd put her inside a packing crate with no food or water. He took her favorite doll and cut off its head, arms and legs and put it in with her. When we got her out she cried for days. She'd soiled herself and wouldn't let my mother throw away her doll.'

'What did your parents do? Did they punish Edward?'

'My father laughed,' Peter said. 'He thought Edward was funny. He thought the cruel tricks he played were amusing. Edward was his favorite. He was the oldest.'

'What about your mother?'

'She was weak. Women are naturally weaker than men. She bought Katie a new doll, but she couldn't stop Edward.'

Houssman, realizing there was more to this story, looked hard at Glash. 'But you're not a woman, and you're not weak. What did you do to your brother Edward?'

Peter cocked his head and met Houssman's gaze. 'You are a smart man, aren't you? A pity that you couldn't have taken care of Richard. Do you wonder about that? What if you could have figured this out and found a way to take care of him? You failed him, but if you hadn't' – he held up his hands – 'would any of this have happened? I think not. And, if that's true' – he cocked his head and now stared at a corner of the room – 'and I think it is, then this will all be because of you...' He turned and met George's steamed-up gaze. 'But let me tell you about Edward and how I killed him – although my father convinced the police it was an accident. He was fourteen. After that, I became my father's favorite. It's why he left the business to me. It's why my name is on the deed. You want to know what I did to my brother Edward?'

'Yes,' Houssman said.

'He deserved to die for what he did to Katie, just as Dorothea deserved to die for being a whore. Katie never recovered. Edward had done other things to her, terrible things ... sexual things. Incest is a grave sin. Don't you agree?'

'Yes ... What did you do?' Houssman asked, feeling like an archeologist delving back into prehistory. He'd evaluated Peter Glash decades ago, but none of this had ever come up.

'We had rats in the basement,' Peter began. 'We had to keep them out of the candy. They'd chew right through the crates. If they got in, my father would have to dump it. He'd get very mad, losing lots of money. So every day he'd come down here with Edward and they'd shoot the rats ... I asked to help. He gave me a gun and showed me how to use it. We practiced on the rats. When I was able to hit them every time, I came down here and shot Edward in the head. I wanted to be certain that he was dead. I needed to be certain that my father saw that I had killed his favorite son. He asked me why I shot Edward. I told him because of what he'd done to Katie. He deserved to die.'

'What did he do?' Houssman asked, as his eyes darted around the basement, now aware that this was a place where many horrible things had occurred.

Glash stared past Cosway toward a windowless corner of the cement-floored space. 'He said that he understood, and that no one must ever know. I'm only telling you now because it no longer matters. My father told me that we would tell the police it was an accident. He told me that I would have to cry and that I would have to tell everyone that I was very sorry for accidentally shooting my brother. He told me that if I did all of those things, and never told, not even my mother, not even Katie, then I would become his favorite son, and when I grew up he would give me the store. I did as he asked. I cried real tears; they weren't for Edward, but for what he did to Katie. She never recovered ... I love my sister Katie. Edward deserved to die.'

'How did you manage to keep this building?' Houssman asked. 'I'm surprised the state didn't take it, while you were incarcerated.'

'They tried,' Peter said, 'but my father had the foresight to leave it to me in a trust, just as I'll do with Richard – they couldn't touch it. And I always made sure the taxes were paid, and for a while Frank continued the business.'

More questions formed in Houssman's mind. He couldn't help but be fascinated by the multi-generational transmission of some variant of autism, with its rigid thought pattern and mathematical approach.

Peter Glash looked at Houssman. 'The question you really want answered is why I'm doing this. Why I am helping Richard?'

'Yes,' Houssman said, again pushing up his glasses so he could see.

'I was locked away for over ten years. My son was taken from me. He in turn was locked away far longer. How do you put a price on those things? Certain things are priceless ... aren't they?' He peered intently at Houssman. 'Aren't they?'

'Yes,' Houssman agreed.

'Time is priceless – we have just so much. The love of a child is priceless. Freedom is priceless. All taken from me and from Richard. We need to be paid for our time and for the love that was taken away. We are taking payment in kind.'

'You don't care that thousands could die?'

'I hope it's more,' he answered, getting up, 'for Richard's sake. He has the ambition to be the greatest killer of all time. As a father, it's important to support my child. Wouldn't you agree?'

'Don't you care that you'll both probably die?' Houssman replied. 'That your son will die?'

'No, because what we have is not a life.'

'But your son, don't you want to see him go

on with his life? To maybe have a family, a child of his own?'

Peter Glash shot across the space that separated them and slapped Houssman hard across the face.

His head jerked to the right. The sharp pain and the crack of flesh on flesh shocked him. His glasses caught in the band of his mask.

'I'm not a fool,' Peter said, glaring at Houssman. 'Those things are not possible for Richard. We both know that. He's being hunted down and they'll shoot to kill. My son is destined for greatness, and I'm doing everything possible to see that happen. I don't want just thousands to die,' he added, moving toward the stairs. He glanced back at Houssman and then at the monitor and Cosway. 'I want them all to die.'

Twenty-Nine

Richard Glash wakes in a bed-drenching sweat. Dream remnants float in his mind: a giant clock ticking, a river of blood and him running toward something. He stares at the cracked plaster ceiling of the bedroom that should always have been his. In the dream he'd known what he was racing toward, and that it kept stretching ahead, just beyond his reach. Now, as he listens to the beat of his heart pounding in his ears, he can't remember what was so important.

He sits up, and has to pause, noting a light-headedness. He holds still, thinking for a moment that he might pass out. He grabs the TV remote and examines his hand; it looks thinner, the flesh taut over clearly visible veins, tendons and arteries. He sees the pulsing of blood.

He flicks on the television. As he surfs, he stops to hear experts discussing him ... and then Clarence Albert – 'Both paranoid,' one dark-suited commentator remarks, 'but both with IQs in the genius range.'

He turns up the volume as a beefy man dressed in a white space suit with the hood and shield removed gives a press conference with the Ashokan Reservoir in the distance. At the bottom of the screen it reads: 'Last night's 9 p.m. press conference with Homeland Security Agent, Corbin Zane.'

'We've dodged a bullet,' Zane responds to a reporter's question.

'Mr Zane! Mr Zane!' Hands shoot up, as the Homeland Security agent points to a local correspondent.

'Mr Zane, what is the status of Richard Glash and his hostages? We've heard conflicting reports, including one stating that he's dead. Where is he?'

Zane pauses and stares into the nearest camera. 'I am now authorized to inform the public that Richard Glash, the man responsible for this heinous attack, is dead. It is also my unfortunate job to add that Martin Cosway, a dedicated American, a true patriot and my mentor in the Department of Homeland Security, also died along with the esteemed psychiatrist Dr George Houssman.' Zane takes a deep breath. 'Their deaths were not in vain. They made the ultimate sacrifice—'

Glash flicks the channel. He sees a photo of Martin Cosway and one of Houssman. His breath feels hot through his nostrils. He looks across at the dark mirror over the dresser that was once his mother's. Even from a distance, his face looks different. He turns on a bedside lamp and studies his reflection. Under his right eye he sees the cheek puffing out, a blister has popped up over his left brow and another tingles below the surface of his lip.

He takes a deep breath and as he lets it out, he feels a rasping inside his chest; it's almost time.

He pictures Albert, and remembers their many discussions, as they weighed the perfect point for spreading the disease.

'It needs to be in the lungs,' Albert had said. 'Then, when you start to cough you'll send millions of active bacteria through the air.'

Behind him another station reports on safety measures being taken around Manhattan and the five boroughs. 'At this point,' he hears the newscaster say, 'quarantine has been determined to be unnecessary. Scientists from the Centers for Disease Control have taken thousands of samples from the Ashokan – thus far there have been no detectible quantities of plague or any other infectious agent. We've received word from the Department of Homeland Security that there has not been a single reported case of plague. It's good news.' She smiles into the camera. 'We've been informed that the lethal bacteria that was introduced into the New York City water supply has been effectively neutralized.'

Glash feels a tickle in his throat. He thinks about Mary ... how pretty she had looked. He starts to cough. She'd told him that she would marry him. 'I'm going to be very famous,' he says aloud.

He catches his breath, stands up and waits for the dizziness to subside. He heads downstairs to the cool basement. It smells bad, like something died. It reminds him of dead rats.

His father sits across from Dr Houssman. He doesn't want to look at the old man; every time he does, the bad feelings come back. So he focuses on Cosway, who is barely conscious, his face and skin covered with open pustules, his breath just wheezes. 'He'll be dead soon,' he says.

'Yes, son. We don't have much time.'

'You've replaced the tapes?' Richard asks.

'Yes.'

Richard looks at the red light on the camcorder and then at the monitor that's relaying Cosway's demise – it's perfect.

He walks over and disconnects the camera. He carries it back to a workbench set up with a laptop. He plugs the camera into a USB port on the computer and clicks on the icon for his cinema player. Pressing the fast-forward his eyes scan on the rapidly moving images of Martin Cosway. His fingers move quickly over the keyboard, slicing small wave files and rapidly stringing them together. He presses save and then replays his home movie. It's about a minute long and he includes the red time stamp at the bottom of each frame. It shows the progression of the plague. In only twenty-four hours Martin Cosway has been brought close to death. 'He'll go within the hour,' he says.

His father answers, 'Yes.'

Richard plugs the high-speed Internet cable into the back of the laptop and composes an email. He then collects the addresses he's had his father collect for both the national and local news stations and programs, as well as for the video-posting website YouTube. He reviews his message:

To the media:
I am Richard Glash and I am alive. I faked my death at the Ashokan Reservoir.
Attached is evidence that the strain of bubonic plague developed by Dr Clarence Albert is viable. Minutes after you receive this, I will have begun to spread plague. I cannot be stopped and by the time this is over I predict that millions of people will be dead. Bubonic plague killed one third of Europe's population in the middle ages. The strain developed by Dr Albert cannot be treated with antibiotics. I predict one third of the world's population will die from it.
Ring around the rosy,
A pocket full of posy.
Ashes, ashes,
We'll all fall down.
Sincerely:
Richard Glash

He attaches his homemade movie of Martin Cosway. He looks at his father and hazards a glance at George Houssman, still wrapped in the blue tarp from the van. 'You're old,' Glash says to Houssman. 'Write this book quickly...' He presses the send button for his email.

'Father, it's time.'

'Yes, son,' Peter Glash says. 'I'll get the van.'

297

Thirty

Justine turned her plastic nametag backwards as she pushed the six-foot tall breakfast cart toward the heavily guarded quarantine ward. Her stomach cramped – this was taking a horrible risk and she'd only get one chance. She pulled down the thick gray plastic curtains – designed to keep the food warm. Dressed like everyone else in a hazmat suit, she struggled not to think about what could happen if she were stopped. The cart was mostly empty, but she'd managed to steal several fresh breakfast trays from the cafeteria.

She rang the buzzer for the ward's outer door.

'Yes?' a voice asked through the intercom.

'Breakfast.'

The door buzzed and she was in.

She passed three armed guards seated around a TV at the nurses' station dressed in hazmat suits, and thought how eerie this felt, more like a prison than the wing of a hospital. At the end of the hall was the room where Barrett was being held. As far as she could tell they were the only patients in the ward.

'Hey, you!' a guard called out.

Justine froze. 'Yes?'

'You got any extras? I'm starving.'

'Just the meals for the patients. Didn't they send you up anything?' she improvised.

'Hell no, and they've not relieved us since yesterday.'

'Let me deliver these and then I'll get some food for you guys. They're at the end of the hall, right?'

'Yup,' he said, and turned back to the TV.

Justine tried to steady her breath. No backing out now. But what if Barrett had everything wrong? As the thought passed through her, she knew her sister was solid. If Barrett said there was a problem, you'd better believe there was.

As she approached the guard outside the room she tried to make eye contact through the visor of his suit. 'I've got their breakfast. Is it safe for me to go in?' *This is not good,* she fretted, as the guard got to his feet. He walked over to the cart. 'God, I'm starved,' he said, poking the edge of the curtain with the tip of his M16.

'I hear you,' Justine said, and then trying the helpless female bit, added, 'I'm a little nervous. Can you come in with me?'

'Maybe,' he said. 'You got one for me too?' He unlocked the door. 'They haven't come by with anything since this morning. Not even a bottle of water. I'm starving.'

'That's terrible,' Justine said, pushing the cart through the opening. 'That's just what the guys at the nurses' station were saying.

Seems like somebody needs to be taking care of our men in uniform. You know,' she said in a conspiratorial tone, 'I didn't have enough for the guys down the hall, but I do have one extra tray.'

'God, I love you,' he said, holding the door as she passed.

Thank God this guy wasn't a regular hospital security man who'd know she wasn't supposed to bring the cart into the room – especially one where yellow and orange biohazard signs were clearly posted. She looked up and caught Barrett's eye, as she continued to chatter with the guard who'd followed her in. 'I can't promise you'll like what I've got, but if you don't I'll find something better in the kitchen. But let's see. OK, the choices are...' She parked the cart in the middle of the room and lifted the gray plastic flap in order to take stock of her offerings. 'We've got scrambled and bacon, some kind of breakfast sandwich thing ... this could be oatmeal, but it looks kind of nasty. Then we've got...' She heard a thump and turned to see Hobbs standing over the unconscious guard. 'Grab some sheets,' he said.

Barrett and Carla hurriedly ripped off the bed linen as Hobbs stripped the guard of his hazmat suit and put it on. 'Tie him up good,' he said, 'and gag him.'

'Please hurry,' Justine fretted, thinking of all the other armed Guardsmen she'd passed in the hallway.

'Let's move,' Barrett said, as she and Carla

300

curled up inside the meal cart. Hobbs grabbed the M16 rifle, and followed behind as Justine pushed the heavy cart. 'Jesus,' she muttered, pushing with all her might. 'I don't know how I'm going to be able to move this. Could one of you maybe get out?'

'There's no way in hell I'm staying here,' Carla whispered.

Hobbs shouldered his rifle and helped Justine wheel the cart out of the room and down the hall.

As they passed, one of the other Guardsmen yelled out at Hobbs, 'Hey, man. We can't leave our posts like that.'

Justine held her breath.

'Lady needs help,' Hobbs said, and then in a conspiratorial voice, added, 'She also told me where I can hook us up with some food. I'll be right back, just keep an eye on my post. Cool?'

'I can't believe they haven't sent around a food cart,' Justine added. 'That's ridiculous.'

'Tell me about it,' the guard said.

'For all you guys do ... I'll find you something good. Give me ten minutes.'

'You're a peach,' the guard said. 'Let me get the door.'

Justine kept her eyes down on the tiled floor as she and Hobbs pushed the heavy cart. 'See if you can get some fresh fruit,' one of the Guardsmen asked.

'There's some apples and oranges,' Justine responded, mentally measuring the distance to the outer door of the locked ward.

As they passed the TV, she meant to keep going, glad for the forward momentum. But Hobbs had stopped pushing.

'Holy shit!' he exclaimed.

On the screen she saw a horrifying image of a dying man; his face was covered with open sores. At first Justine thought it was a dramatization of plague or small pox. But there was a red date stamp at the bottom of the screen indicating that what was being shown was just hours old. A newscaster grimly reported, 'This graphic footage was just received by us. The sender states he is Richard Glash, and the man on the screen is reported to be Homeland Security official Martin Cosway, who was abducted by Glash less than forty-eight hours ago. It was earlier reported that Richard Glash, Martin Cosway and Dr George Houssman had all perished in a car accident; this is now being questioned as we take you to a live press conference with officials of Homeland Security.' The scene shifted and she saw Corbin Zane, in a hazmat suit minus the helmet, attempting to field questions. He was sweating and on the defensive. 'Yes, I'm aware of that videotape. And we believe that it was made in advance by Glash, as a way to confuse us.'

'Isn't it possible,' one of the reporters shot back, 'that what he faked was his death? And that in fact you've gotten everything wrong and Richard Glash is alive and well and in fact carrying out the mass murder which he began?'

Zane stammered and struggled to be heard over the gaggle of reporters, each demanding to have their questions answered. An aide tapped him on the shoulder and whispered something.

Justine froze at the sound of a telephone ringing from the far end of the hallway, from the room where they'd just been. She glanced at Hobbs, and much as they both wanted to hear what else Zane might say, they pushed on toward the outer door.

'Can you buzz us out?' Hobbs called back.

One of the guards, his eyes fixed on the television, hit the button and they safely wheeled through.

'This way ... to the right,' Justine said, pushing the cart down a darkened hallway that led into a wing of administrative offices.

She looked around and then flipped up the plastic flap on the meal tray to free Barrett and Carla.

'Did you hear?' Hobbs asked Barrett, while quickly stripping off the bulky white suit. 'The idiots.'

'Maybe if we got through to them now...' Barrett said, pushing up out of the cart.

'They didn't listen before,' Carla said. 'They're just concerned with how the press is going to handle this.'

'He's got to be with his father,' Hobbs said.

'Of course,' Barrett added, 'that's the only thing that makes sense. He's been in constant contact with someone ... I just realized something else.'

303

'What?' Carla asked.

'Why Glash needed two hostages. One to write everything down and the other...'

'To test the plague,' Carla finished. 'That was meant to be us ... he was planning to infect me. That's why he didn't kill me.'

They turned at the sound of a growing commotion coming from the locked ward.

'Let's move,' Justine urged. 'This way.' And they all tore off in the direction of a side stairwell. Behind they heard the door to the unit slam open and excited voices. 'There's the cart!' a man shouted.

They flew down the stairs. Barrett shouted back, 'One of us should stay and try to make them listen.'

'I'll do it,' Justine said. 'What's the address for the father's store?'

Hobbs didn't break pace as he shouted it and also the cell phone numbers for both his supervisor and FBI agent Anderson. 'Try them both,' he said. 'Somebody has got to believe us.'

Above them, footsteps raced closer, clomping down the stairs. A voice shouted, 'Stop, now. This is an order!'

Barrett landed first on the ground floor. In front of her was a red-and-black painted door with a sign that read *Alarmed, for Emergencies Only*.

She threw her hip against the release lever, a piercing siren went off and she, Hobbs and Carla sprinted into the street.

Thirty-One

Chained to the cot and still naked under the tarp, George Houssman knew his time was running out. He averted his eyes from Cosway's ravaged body and looked over to Richard Glash, at the distant end of the cellar working on his computer.

Cosway had died about half an hour ago in a fit of coughing that had brought bright red blood gushing out of his mouth. It had pooled on the floor, as Cosway gasped, with lungs that no longer functioned. George had watched helplessly. The final look of wide-eyed panic on Cosway's face as he'd tried to breathe, but instead choked on his own blood, stayed seared in George's mind.

'Richard,' Houssman gently called across the space, the words muffled by his mask. 'It's not too late. You don't have to do this. I could even help you get away, so that they wouldn't put you back in prison.'

Glash stiffened and turned. His face contorted and a scream rattled the dust and the spider webs. 'You lied to me!' he shrieked.

George pressed back on the bed. The hatred on Glash's face drew his thoughts back to those horrible visits at Albomar. The little boy clinging to his legs, kicking him, screaming, inconsolable. As Glash now shrieked *'Liar!'*, George wondered if he'd gone too far. He prepared for the worst, ready to die, wondering if being shot or bludgeoned to death might not be preferable to the nightmare Glash intended to release.

'You lied to me! You lie now. You'd lock me up. You'd make them shoot me. I see the things you've written about me. You lie.' Glash stood; he seemed unsteady, as though the blood wasn't making it to his head. He pointed at Houssman. 'You were supposed to be my father.'

Houssman shuddered as he got a clear look at Richard's face and the cracking flesh of his hands. 'You're sick, Richard. You need to get to a hospital ... you need antibiotics. It's not too late, Richard.'

Glash stared at him. He went back to the worktable and retrieved a sketchpad and a fistful of charcoal pencils. He stuffed the pencils into the breast pocket of his denim shirt and pulled up a chair directly across from Houssman. With his mouth contorting, as though deep in concentration, he drew at a furious pace. He ripped off the first page – a line drawing – and let it fall face-up at the old man's feet. 'Don't touch it,' he warned.

George stared down. The artwork was incredibly clear for something drawn in seconds. It showed University Hospital and on the broad marble steps that led up to the main entrance a huge pile of bodies. The detail was amazing, down to a rat that peeked out from the corner of the building.

'You can't become infected ... not yet,' Glash said, his fingers smudging the charcoal on the page. 'Anyway, you're already old; you'll die soon. I think your heart will break as your daughters and your grandchildren get sick and die. I have their phone numbers,' he continued, not looking up from his pad. 'I called Stephanie just this morning to be certain that she and little Faye haven't left town.' He ripped the next page, already with a new drawing, from the pad; he threw it next to the first. 'They hadn't.'

'No,' Houssman gasped, his heart pounding, feeling as though it were being ripped out of him. 'I'm begging you, please don't do this.' He stared at Glash's image of his grand-daughter's face, her normally pudgy cheeks drawn and covered with sores. Her lips had cracked and the capillaries in her eyes had burst. She was clutching a Raggedy Ann doll.

'Did you talk to her?' George asked, terri-fied at the level of detail Glash had about his family.

'No, just heard her voice ... I do that some-times. I used to do that with you and your wife.' His hands never stopped. 'When I was at Albomar they'd let us use the phone for fifteen minutes every week. I'd call you up. I never spoke, because I knew you'd lie and then they wouldn't let me call. They'd say it wasn't therapeutic; it wasn't in my best inter-est.' He tore off the next page; it showed

Barrett, dying in a hospital bed. Glash snorted as he pulled a reddish pencil from his pocket. His hands flew in broad strokes over the pad. The image he now hurriedly completed was more cartoonish and less detailed, but the scene was clear, a favorite of photographers and painters: a long view up Fifth Avenue through the marble arch at Washington Square Park. It showed a man in a medieval cap and tunic ringing a bell in the foreground. Behind him, stretching for infinity uptown, lay piles of corpses. Rats scurried from heap to heap and below the image Glash had written in block letters BRING OUT YOUR DEAD.

'Son,' Peter Glash called from the top of the stairs. 'It's time. I've got the van.'

'Coming,' he said. He looked down at the pad, and coughed. He turned from Houssman as convulsive bursts wracked his body. George watched his face turn bright red; he couldn't catch his breath. 'One more,' he whispered. He pulled out two pencils, one dark gray and the other red.

George watched as Glash feverishly, for a second time, drew University Hospital. In front grew a monstrous mound of bodies. Next to it, he drew himself, staring straight out of the page and holding a lit torch that had just ignited the arm of Faye's Raggedy Ann doll. With a final flourish Glash crushed the two pencils tight in his fist and wrote ASHES, ASHES. He covered his mouth, as though another fit of coughing were about to start. He waited and then stood, letting the sketchpad slip to the floor. He looked at George. 'There is a two thirds probability that I will die.'

Houssman said nothing.

'If I don't, I intend to get married...'

George just stared at him.

'She told me that she'd marry me ... Mary will marry me. If I invite you, will you come?'

'Of course,' George said, grasping at the bizarre glimmer of hope, that perhaps this Mary could prevent the nightmare in Richard's drawings from coming true.

'Richard!' Peter shouted down from the stairs. 'It's time.'

'Yes, Father.'

'Richard,' George said, keeping his voice low so that it wouldn't be heard by Peter, 'why not increase the probability that you'll survive? We could get you to a hospital. We could get you treated. Wouldn't you rather get married ... maybe even have a family? That's what you want. That's what you've always wanted; I didn't see it before; I didn't know. Yes, I'll go to your wedding. I'll be happy to go to your wedding. And so would Faye and Stephanie and Alice, and her two boys. You wanted a family. You wanted me to be your father. I really screwed up. People do that. Let me make it better now. Let me be your father. Let me give you a family.'

Glash paused, seeming to consider George's words. He looked up the stairs at his biological father, Peter. 'The probability that you're lying to me, to try and save yourself and everyone else, is very high. It's nearly one hundred percent. I am going to be very famous. You will write about me, and if I survive, I will invite you to my wedding.'

Thirty-Two

Barrett's rubber-soled slippers pounded the pavement of Seventh Avenue; she was running flat out, pushing past startled pedestrians and not caring that she probably looked like an escaped mental patient in her ripped trousers and pajama top. Hobbs, with the guard's M16 slung across his back, was a few yards ahead and she couldn't stop to see how far behind Carla had fallen. With all Zane's incompetence she'd felt she had no choice but to ignore the warning bullets and chase after Hobbs.

She'd heard Justine try to hold back the Guardsmen at the hospital. That had bought them a tiny bit of time, and the fact that the guards were impaired by their bulky suits was in their favor, at least for the first few seconds.

'We need to split up,' she shouted, catching a glimpse of a camouflage-painted humvee pulling out of the chain-link-fenced parking lot across from the hospital.

'All roads lead to Delancey,' he yelled back as he sprinted left down West 12th Street.

She realized he'd played the gentleman and had given her and Carla the more direct option of Greenwich Avenue, which made a hypotenuse through the Village to Sixth. She was running on pure adrenalin after days with little sleep, and a sickening fear that either they were too late or ... She glanced behind as sirens roared to life.

There was no way she'd be able to outrun them. She tried her best to blend in, just another crazy New Yorker out for a run in the middle of the morning. Of course, that she was wearing a pair of ripped navy pants, hospital slippers, and a light-green pajama top with PROPERTY OF UNIVERSITY HOSPITAL emblazoned on the back didn't help.

She'd made it to West 10th when she glanced back to see a humvee turn the corner east on to Greenwich.

'Shit!' She ducked under the awning of what looked like a large gay club. Inside was dark; she tried the door anyway. To her relief it opened. She looked at the bar and the empty dance floor. A cleaning crew was vacuuming. A muscular man in a tight tee-shirt emblazoned with the club's logo was behind the bar, checking the stock. He looked up at her.

'We're closed,' he shouted over the roar of the vacuum and the sirens that were now screaming down Greenwich.

'I'm being followed,' she said, 'is there a back way out?'

As though he'd heard this a thousand times, he pointed toward an exit sign at the far end of the dance floor.

'Thanks.' She ran, came to the back door and gently pushed it open. She peered out on an alley that opened on to Sixth Avenue. The busy thoroughfare seemed broad and exposed. She heard sirens to the north heading east. She figured they were after Hobbs. So how could she get across the avenue without attracting a posse of her own? Still hidden, she ducked back inside. A door to her right had a sign – EMPLOYEES ONLY. She tried the handle and let herself into a small break room. She grabbed a Yankees cap from an open locker and felt a pang of guilt as she helped herself to a distressed and well-loved bombardier jacket and threw it over her top.

She went back to the exit, took a deep breath, jogged the length of the alley, and keeping her eyes straight ahead, began to cross the avenue.

'There she is!' a woman's voice shouted.

Barrett's heart sank as her head whipped around. She saw Carla running flat out a block south on Waverly. The Guardsmen were in hot pursuit of her, but that maybe would buy Barrett a bit of time. She somehow got safely across Sixth and tried to figure the route. With cops both to the north and south she couldn't see a lot of options. Still over a mile from Glash's building on Delancey, she had an awful feeling. This was never going to work. As she started to jog east on Fifth Street, doubts flooded her. What if Hobbs was wrong and Glash wasn't with his father?

What if we're too late?

Her eye caught on a bread delivery truck parked in front of Emilio's restaurant. The driver, his arms laden with two large brown paper sacks of rolls and loaves, was being led inside. Barrett sprinted to the driver's side. She checked the ignition – no key. Her hand flew up to the sun visor.

'Hey, lady!' a voice shouted. The driver, a young man dressed in white, ran over. 'What you think you doing?' he demanded.

'I'm desperate,' she said, taking in the stocky, dark-haired young man in his tee-shirt, apron and baker's pants. 'I have to get to Delancey.'

'You ever heard of a cab? Stealing trucks is kind of hardcore – you don't look the type.'

Sirens turned off the avenue and headed toward them.

'Please,' she pleaded.

'What did you do?' he insisted, blocking her exit with his body.

'Listen, Richard Glash, the nut who plans to spread plague, is holed up in Delancey Street,' she blurted. 'No one believes me, and I've got to try and stop him.'

The smile faded from the young man's face. 'Even if you're shitting me, I'll take you. Move over.'

'Thank God!' She shifted over to the passenger's side, and then pressed back into the seat, lowering the cap over her face as two police cars with lights and sirens blaring slowly cruised past.

The driver turned to her. 'They're really looking for you, aren't they?'

She nodded. 'Yes, please hurry.'

'What's your name?' he asked, pulling the ignition key from his pocket.

'Barrett.'

'I'm Marco, Barrett.' He checked the mirrors and pulled out behind the last cruiser. 'You sure you're not an escaped mental patient?' he asked, as they inched with the heavy traffic down the block.

Barrett could barely breathe. The bread truck seemed too exposed; all it would take was for one of the cops to turn around. But then again, did they even know what she looked like?

'It's a fucking zoo!' Marco said as the light changed. 'Shit!' He turned right and they were met by a hurriedly erected police blockade that stretched across Sixth. Pedestrians were quickly gathering, making a thick circle around the frantic redhead, who was surrounded by Guardsmen in hazmat suits and uniformed police. Carla was screaming, 'Richard Glash isn't dead. He's staying with his father on Delancey Street!' She could be heard yelling out the address, as the armed personnel closed in on her. 'You've got to believe me!'

Marco looked at Barrett, as a cop tried to move them down the street and off the avenue on to an already congested 8th Street. 'Friend of yours?'

'There were three of us,' she said, realizing

with a crushing certainty that no one was paying attention to what Carla was saying.

'Wait a minute,' Marco said. 'You were one of the hostages. I saw your picture on TV ... she was the other one. That red hair ... she's kind of hot, in a pushy, deranged sort of way ... so are you.'

Barrett quickly weighed the options – run for it, or ... Everything felt like a single roll of the dice. 'How big are your balls?' she asked.

'Big,' Marco said.

'Big enough to plow through this mess?'

'You got it.' He turned the wheel hard to the right, surprising the hell out of the nearest cop who had to jump back to avoid getting hit. Marco's body tensed as he focused on the dense circle of Guardsmen.

Barrett watched him as he laid on the horn and barreled toward the armed Guardsmen.

She rolled down her window and unlatched the door. She screamed out, 'Carla!' She turned to Marco. 'If there's a chance we can grab her let's do it, but don't stop.'

'You want them to follow us,' he stated.

'Hell, yes.'

'Delancey Street?'

'Hell, yes.'

'Hang on!'

Carla, seizing the moment, had slipped through the clumsily suited Guardsmen and now ran toward them.

Twenty feet away from her Marco shouted, 'Hold on!' He slammed his foot on the break. Loaves of bread shot forward from the back, as Barrett wedged her feet hard under the dash to keep from flying through the windshield. The she pushed her door open, as Carla dove head first across her lap.

Marco didn't wait, and with Carla's legs still hanging comically out of the door, he made a beeline past the Guardsmen down Fifth. Glancing in the rear-view, he commented, 'It's like the fucking Keystone Cops.' He slowed down. 'You want them to follow, right?'

'Yes,' Barrett said, as she helped Carla get off their laps. 'You OK?' she asked.

'Yes ... you?'

'I think so.'

Carla looked in the side mirror. 'Here they come.'

'Yup,' Marco said. 'Oh, shit!'

'You've got to be kidding,' Barrett said, watching several patrol cars head north in their direction up Fifth Avenue.

'Here we go!' Marco said, jamming his foot on the gas. The truck shot forward and before the advancing patrol cars could effectively block off the avenue they barreled past.

'Keep going,' Barrett said, 'they're not going to lose us.'

'You guys must be really important,' Marco added, his hands tense on the wheel, as a helicopter roared overhead.

'Do you think they got Ed?' Carla asked.

'I don't know,' Barrett said, her eyes fixed on the avenue as they flew downtown. 'I think he tried to pull them off of us ... at least they're not firing.'

'They're not,' Carla said. 'I guess maybe someone wants to keep us alive. They know Glash isn't dead,' she added. 'I just pray we get there in time.'

'What if he's not there?' Barrett asked, giving voice to her fear.

'Then we're all fucked,' Carla said, and then added, 'and I'll go down in history as the woman who let it happen.'

A squad car tried to edge them off the road. 'Ladies,' Marco said, 'hang on!' He shot ahead. In front of them the light turned red at the intersection with Houston Street. Cars zipped back and forth along the four-lane thoroughfare that separated the Village from SoHo.

'You can't stop,' Barrett said, holding her breath and willing the light to change color.

A megaphone blasted from the closest patrol car. *'Pull over. Pull over immediately. This is not a warning; pull your vehicle over immediately. You are aiding and abetting escaped felons. You are committing a felony. Pull over immediately.'*

'Here we go!' Marco said, his eyes fixed on the rushing traffic. He hit the brakes hard and then accelerated, dodging through the two lanes of oncoming westbound. At the median, a taxicab nearly clipped the front of the truck. Horns blared. Two pedestrians trapped in the center of Houston looked on in horror as Marco barreled toward them. They dove out of the way as the truck bounced over the

318

median and he floored the gas. 'Good thing traffic is light,' he quipped as a cabbie swore at them. 'So how far down on Delancey?' he asked.

She gave him the number.

'My guess is it's three blocks. If we get stopped,' he said, 'just run for it ... but here's a question,' he said, hanging a right on to the one-way, single-lane Orchard. 'What you plan to do if this guy is there? ... Oh fuck, I'm heading the wrong way.'

Carla looked at Barrett as they stared down the street crammed with sidewalk stalls, but luckily no cars coming in the opposite direction. 'There's only one thing to do,' she said dryly. 'Richard Glash has to be stopped ... at any cost.'

'You're not packing, are you?' Marco asked, as they bounced down the narrow, pockmarked street, which even in the midst of the city's crisis was thronged with shoppers. 'In the glove compartment,' he said.

Barrett clicked it open, and saw a handgun nestled under a stack of papers. She glanced in the rear-view and saw a row of police cars, lights and sirens following close.

'Take it,' he said, 'it's loaded. You know how to use one?'

'Yes,' Barrett said, hefting the small pistol, checking the safety and then securing it in the pocket of her stolen bomber jacket.

'Barrett, look!' Carla shouted and pointed at a tall man with an M16 strapped across his back running down the street less than half a block away. 'It's Hobbs.'

'Stop the truck!' Barrett said.

'Boy, am I in trouble,' Marco groaned as he pulled to a stop at the corner of Rivington.

'No,' Barrett shouted back as she jumped out, following Carla, 'you're a hero.'

Marco looked at the two women and then back at the long line of squad cars and paramilitary vehicles that had bottlenecked the street and the new ones now coming at him from the south. 'Fucking A!' And he jumped out and ran after Barrett and Carla.

'Hobbs!' Barrett shouted, as police, Homeland Security agents and the Guardsmen closed in on them.

Between the sirens and the megaphones demanding that they surrender, it was deafening. The din completely blocked the noise from Hobbs's booted foot as he kicked at an alley gate padlocked from the other side.

'Stand back,' Barrett said, pulling out Marco's gun.

'Where the hell did you get—'

Before she could answer, Barrett squeezed off two shots. It did nothing.

Hobbs shouldered the M16, took aim and shredded the lock. He kicked the gate open.

He sprinted down the alley, took aim, and shot the lock off the door to Peter Glash's apartment. 'They've got to be here somewhere,' he said. 'Move fast, and Barrett ... for God's sake, be careful.'

'You too,' she said, looking around the apartment, finding everything about it horribly familiar. 'He's drawn all this,' she said.

'Yes,' Carla replied. 'He's been here before. Or maybe he remembered it from his childhood.'

The two women looked at each other as cops flooded into the room behind them. 'The basement,' they said in unison.

'There were books of drawings,' Barrett said, 'in a basement, all of the ones where I was dying were in some kind of underground space ... no windows. Hobbs, how do we get down to the basement?'

'Come on,' he said, as they ran through the living room and into the candy store. 'Usually stairs are in the back,' he said, as they heard law-enforcement officers pounding into the house behind them.

'There!' Carla shouted, finding a wooden door. She twisted the handle. Locked.

'Hold on.' Hobbs took aim and fired. The rifle clicked, he tried again. 'Shit!' He hurled himself at the door and as it flew in, he half tumbled down a flight of unlit wooden stairs. A cord overhead tickled his forehead, he pulled on it and a single bare bulb lit the narrow stairwell.

'Don't come down!' a muffled voice shouted from below. 'Stay back! Don't come down!'

'It's George!' Barrett cried, racing Hobbs down with Carla right behind.

'Stay away!' George shot back. 'For God's sake, Barrett, don't come down here! Please!'

The three of them gasped at the fluorescent-lit scene. Cosway's pustule-covered body was more gruesome than anything Hobbs had seen in all his years on Major Crime.

Booted footsteps came down fast and furious. A man in a hazmat shouted, 'Everybody freeze!'

'That's it!' Barrett turned around and faced the cops and agents flooding into the basement. 'Just all of you shut up!' she ordered. And without waiting for a response, asked Houssman, still masked and chained to a cot wearing his blue tarp, 'Where's Glash?'

'They're gone,' he said. 'He infected himself with plague; he's very sick.'

'How long ago?' Hobbs asked.

'They just left,' Houssman said. 'You were so close. It couldn't have been more than a couple of minutes. Didn't you see them? You must have passed them.'

'No,' Hobbs said. 'The alley gate was locked ... something's not making sense...'

'Where are they headed?' Barrett asked.

George looked down at the floor by his cot. It was strewn with layers of Glash's drawings. 'There,' he said.

Barrett's heart sank as she saw the scenes of carnage and the façade of University Hospital.

'Justine,' she gasped.

'He's going back to the beginning,' Houssman said. 'That's where it started. He's starting an epidemic. To infect as many as possible.'

Barrett was frantic, picturing her sister, who'd just helped them escape. 'We've got to go back. Oh my God!' She looked around at the throng who were gawking at Cosway, their faces filled with fear and disgust. 'Who's in charge?' she shouted.

Seconds ticked by, as personnel from the different agencies looked around, waiting for someone to take responsibility.

Hobbs spoke. 'I'm Detective Second Grade Ed Hobbs with the NYPD. We need to clear this space. No one is to come near that body. Dr Houssman needs to be quarantined and we need to get our asses back to University Hospital, now.' He looked at the first of the hazmat-suited Guardsmen. 'You, what's your name?'

'Lieutenant Kane, sir.'

'OK, Kane you handle the situation here. No one is to go near the body, understood?'

'Yes, sir.'

'This entire building needs to be thoroughly searched. There's a chance Glash is still here and is hiding. No one is to approach him. If he attempts to run, shoot to kill.'

'Yes, sir.'

'Good, now we need to get Dr Conyors and Ms Phelps out of here as they're the two who've had the most contact with Glash and have the best chance of identifying him.' He looked up the still clogged stairwell, and barked, 'Move! *Now!*'

To Barrett's amazement, and to Hobbs's as well, they did.

Overhead, a new sound rattled the building, the roar of a motorcycle.

'No fucking way!' Hobbs bolted up the stairs, back through the apartment and out the alley door. Barrett and Carla followed close behind and were just in time to get a glimpse of both the Glashes shooting out of the alley on a black-and-chrome motorcycle. Richard's arms were wrapped tight around his father's waist, clinging to him, his black hair matted to his scalp, his face pressed against his back. He was smiling, and his skin was red and covered with tight, fluid-filled pustules. The older man was wearing a face mask, his body hunched low on the bike as he shot out of the alley and then north, zig-zagging at breakneck speed through the clogged street, twisting and dodging between the patrols cars and the merchant displays on the sidewalks.

Hobbs shouldered the M16, but realized he was out of bullets. 'Shoot him!' he shouted, ditching the rifle; he tore off after them.

Bullets whizzed erratically overhead. Hobbs sprinted to the corner of Orchard and Rivington with Barrett and Carla close behind. They saw the Glashes head west and then north on Bowery.

'The truck,' Barrett said, running past Hobbs, as she yanked opened the driver's side door to Marco's bread truck. He was no-where in sight – probably picked up for aiding and abetting – but the keys were in the ignition.

The three piled in, and with Barrett at the wheel they took off down Rivington. At the Bowery she ran a red and nearly tipped the ungainly vehicle as she sped north.

'I should have taken the wheel,' Hobbs said, his gaze intent on the road ahead, looking for the motorcycle.

'Shut up,' Barrett said. 'Just tell me the quickest way!'

'Left on Houston,' he shouted.

There was a cab tight on her left.

'Just do it,' Hobbs ordered.

She gunned the engine and edged out the cab, clipping its front fender as she ran another red and just missed getting side-swiped by a garbage truck as she roared west on Houston.

'There they are!' Carla shouted, pointing at the barely visible motorcycle that was weaving through traffic two blocks ahead.

'Floor it,' Hobbs said, glad for the sirens behind them; they at least might help clear the traffic.

Barrett focused hard on the road and the three lanes of west-bound traffic. 'Which way is he going to go?'

But before Hobbs could respond, they saw Richard Glash glance back. He said something to his father and the motorcycle bobbed to the right and then disappeared north up Lafayette.

'*Go!*' Carla shouted.

Barrett was trying to out-distance a black Town Car limousine on her right that didn't want to let her pass.

'Lay on the horn and don't stop,' Hobbs said, as he reached over Carla and banged on the passenger-side window and pressed his detective's shield to the glass. The limo driver got the message and just as they hit the intersection with Lafayette he slammed on his brakes, allowing Barrett to hook right.

As they drove, Barrett longed to close her eyes and block out all the pedestrians they were passing; all people that Glash might soon be infecting. Then, suddenly, she caught sight of him. He was coughing and struggling to hang on to his father. But then the motorcycle took a left into the maze of small Greenwich Village streets.

'Keep on him,' Hobbs shouted.

'I can't stand it,' Barrett muttered, her eyes glued to the road. 'We're always one step behind ... Damn!' The Glashes were zipping in the wrong direction down 8th Street.

'Take Ninth,' Hobbs cried, 'see if we can head them off at Sixth Avenue.'

Barrett floored the gas and sped down the beautiful townhouse-lined street. At the intersection, the light was turning yellow.

'Just go!' Carla shouted. 'Don't stop!'

As they shot into the avenue a wall of oncoming traffic screeched and skidded. Horns blared as Hobbs spotted the motorcycle disappearing up Greenwich.

'Damnit!'

Barrett, biting her lower lip, tried to steady the vehicle as she took a sharp left on to Sixth and then spun hard to the right in the direction of Greenwich. The two left tires lifted off the ground, the right wheels scraped against the sidewalk. 'Shit!' She wondered if they were going to tip. She held her breath and kept her foot on the gas as the truck righted itself with all four tires on the road.

'Woman driver,' Hobbs muttered. 'There they are!'

Clumsy as her maneuver had been, they were now less than a block behind. Ahead, the light on Seventh had just turned.

'They're not going to stop,' Barrett said, as she gunned the engine.

Peter Glash glanced back and then shot blindly into the intersection. As he did, the cars racing south screeched; one cab was too late and to avoid hitting the motorcycle smashed into a steel parking meter. An older minivan with spray-painted slogans about the end of the earth was violently rear-ended by an SUV. It fishtailed into the middle of the avenue, its front abruptly facing north and its smashed rear blocking one of the southbound lanes.

Barrett laid on the horn, praying that the stalled traffic would stay that way, and flew into the intersection. She could see the stunned expressions on the faces of the zealots in the crashed minivan, then heard the ripping of steel as the bread truck grazed the front of their vehicle.

'Jesus!' Hobbs said, as they sailed past, now not a hundred feet behind Richard and Peter.

'Where in hell did you learn how to do that?'

Through gritted teeth Barrett replied, 'I've been driving in New York since I was sixteen. No guts, no glory. What's the plan? We're less than a block from the hospital. He's dripping with plague. You've got no bullets. What are we supposed to do?'

Peter Glash again glanced back, as the massive white façade of University Hospital came into view. The bike revved and accelerated, heading straight for the broad marble steps.

Richard Glash feels the breath coming hot out of his mouth. He clutches his father's back, realizing that this is the closest he's ever come to hugging another human being as an adult. Perhaps his mother held him when he was young, but that he can't remember. And what he recalls of George and Delia Houssman's affection turned out to all be lies.

'Just hang on,' his father shouts back as he makes the perilous run through six lanes of oncoming traffic on Sixth.

Richard's head feels light, and all over his body sticky fluid leaks through his clothes. The back of his father's leather jacket is covered with a film of the serum that oozes from the cracking pustules.

He looks behind and sees the bread truck with Dr Conyors and Carla Phelps. He let them live and now they're decreasing their chances of survival by following him. Carla Phelps had been right: she had helped him. If it wasn't for her he'd have never escaped; it wasn't fair for her to be the guinea pig – the Martin Cosway. And Dr Conyors was pregnant and had never cheated on her husband. It was better for Dr Houssman, who he wouldn't think about, to write the book.

'How are you doing?' Father shouts back, as the engine revs in preparation for the sprint across Seventh.

'It's perfect,' Richard says, hugging his father tight, wishing he had a pad of paper and pen to draw each passing moment. 'I'm going to die,' he says, the words barely out of his mouth before hacking coughs rattle through his body. He pictures the delicate tissue of his lungs ripping apart as the deadly bacteria spews out of his mouth and his nose. It reminds him of a dandelion, after the flower has gone and the puffball of seeds is formed; that's what he is. His only regret – and it's big – is that he won't be alive to marry Mary. He wonders if she will miss him. Will she cry?

He tries to keep upright, and get a view of University Hospital. And he struggles to hang on. The clock in his head has stopped; he can't predict with any certainty now how much time remains.

The scene in front of the hospital is not the one he'd predicted; the one he'd drawn countless times. Rows of squad cars and military vehicles are barricading the broad front steps. They stretch in all directions, and he sees cement barriers positioned in front of the emergency-room bays.

He reminds himself that it was here that it started nearly forty years ago. He'd tried to play cowboys and Indians with Mary, and then they'd kept him in a locked room, and made promises. All lies.

He stares at the fast approaching building. He's so close, yet the probability of failure, of being shot to death before he can kill them all, is mounting. '"A" and "B",' he whispers into Father's ear, as he coughs and grips tight, trying to not fall off. He rests his face against his father's back, and feels the vibrations of the motor. '"A" and "B".' His gaze falls on a chain-link-fenced schoolyard, filled with hundreds of children and teachers. It's Friday morning, and the summer day-camp kids are pressed against the fence, to see what the commotion is all about.

The cops are waiting. They'll shoot him and Father dead with a high probability of doing it before he's successfully infected an adequate number. He'd sure fooled them with the reservoir, but then they'd figured it out. Well, maybe he can fool them one last time. Even with Mary, after all those years, he'd found a plan B; he didn't have to kill her. The schoolyard would be perfect. He tries to steady his breath.

'Father...Dad, the schoolyard...' He coughs. 'Plan B. I'll do it there.' He braces himself, digging into the sides of the bike with his thighs, with each movement feeling pustules burst open, the warm and sticky liquid running down his legs, his face, his back, his

330

arms. He'd always wondered what it would be like to attend a normal school – not the barred rooms at Albomar. He thinks about Houssman and that this might have been the school for him, if the old man hadn't lied.

The motorcycle swerves and aims for the unlocked gate of the schoolyard. Richard hears the screams of the kids as they catch sight of them. He lifts his head from his father's back so they can get the full effect.

'He's coming this way!' a little girl shrieks.

A young female counselor dressed casually in jeans races toward the gate and hurriedly attempts to lock it. The bolt jams; she makes eye contact with Peter Glash as he bears down on her. Her fingers wrap in the links; she holds on and braces. Others shout for the children to run inside.

Like stampeding cattle the children try to run back into the redbrick building, but they jam up at the closed doors; no one is calm enough to step back so they can get them open. Patrol cars peel off from the hospital. Richard Glash braces for the impact as his father slows the bike and rams the vintage BMW into the gate.

His eyes connect with the wide-eyed terror of the young teacher attempting to hold the gate shut. He smiles at her as a wave of coughing shakes him. *Yes*, he thinks as they burst through the gate and Father takes aim at a group of little children and their coun-selor huddled in a corner of the playground. *I'm like a dandelion puffball.*

331

Thirty-Three

Barrett braced herself as she stared through the windshield of the speeding bread truck. She felt Carla tense up next to her.

Oh, shit! she thought as alarms rang in her head – this was the city block where April, Carla's seven-year-old, attended P.S.85 summer day-camp.

'Please don't let her be here. Please, Bill, please have listened. Not here...' Carla fretted.

Barrett white-knuckled the wheel. 'What's the plan?' she spat out, as she raced after the Glashes. In the distance stretched University Hospital, barricaded by cop cars and humvees. Sirens rang thick, coming from all directions.

'He's not getting through that,' Hobbs shouted, his attention glued to the motorcycle. 'What are they thinking?'

Carla shuddered. 'Oh my God; he'll go for plan B.'

Barrett gasped as the motorcycle wobbled, Peter Glash's booted leg touched down and the agile bike made a ninety-degree turn to the right.

'He's going for the school!' Barrett shouted.

'*Hold on!*' She slammed on the brakes. The truck screeched, the force lifting the back tires off the ground, and for a second there was the stomach-lurching sensation of gravity and momentum threatening to roll them. The wheels bounced down and they now faced the school yard gate – too small for the truck – but the Glashes had no trouble bursting through.

They saw the Glashes advancing on a group of small children pressed into a corner. Peter was using the lightweight bike with finesse to herd the children and two young day-camp counselors into an ever-tighter wedge at the corner of the yard. The two women were standing in front of their charges, trying somehow to protect them as they got forced up against the chain-link fence.

Carla bolted over Ed's lap and raced from the truck and through the gate.

'What are you doing?' Barrett shrieked, but knew that this was her daughter's school, and that Carla's ex had enrolled her in the summer day camp. In Glash's horrible world everything was connected. She wondered for a second if this hadn't always been the plan, and the hospital – yet again – a feint that they'd fallen for.

Carla didn't answer, her eyes fixed on the Glashes. 'Richard!' she screamed over the revving of the motorcycle. He couldn't hear her, and even if he could there'd be no reasoning with him.

She ran toward them and tripped over a

discarded white plastic whiffle bat. She caught herself from falling and grabbed the bat. She sprinted across the playground.

'Mommy!' a blonde girl trapped in the corner shouted over the herd. *'Mommy!'*

'April!' Carla screamed. 'Stay away from him. *Stay away from him!'*

'Carla!' Barrett shouted, out of the truck and running fast. 'Don't do this!'

Peter Glash revved the engine, his sights fixed on the children and the two frightened counselors.

Carla raised the bat overhead, still running as fast as she could. Barrett watched as Carla threw every ounce of strength into the swing, her focus fixed on the back of Richard's head.

The motorcycle swerved to the right, dangerously close to Carla, as two children on the left side of the pack tried to make a run for it. It foreshortened her swing, costing her precious pounds of force. Still, the hollow plastic bat connected with the right side of Richard's head, grazing his ear and rupturing small pustules. Barrett saw splatters of liquid fly on to Carla's face and her fingers wrapped tight around the bat.

Richard swayed and shook his head. He reached back to try and steady himself, but his hand waved out on empty air. His father, sensing something was wrong, slowed. The bike barely moved, its engine low and throaty, Peter Glash caught sight of Carla in the mirror and pulled a pistol from his jacket. 'Too late!' he shouted, as he took aim from the idling bike.

Carla ducked to the right of the bike and grabbed Richard around the waist; she yanked back hard. The weakened man lost his grip and they tumbled to the asphalt.

Barrett knew that Carla's only concern was to keep him away from her daughter. She heard the little girl's screams: *'Mommy! Mommy!'*

Carla was like a woman possessed. She held tight. Glash struggled like a fish on the line; he was burning with fever and dripping sweat and blood. A bullet pinged overhead.

Barrett turned at the sound of booted feet pounding the playground. A battalion of Guardsmen raced in with weapons drawn.

Horrified, she looked back at Carla wrestling Richard on the ground. Her hands were coated with blood and the sticky yellow fluid that oozed from his sores. Glash started to cough.

The scene was repulsive, intimate and frightening; her heart pounded fast, the rhythm beating through the thin fabric of her pajama shirt. She wanted to help and knew that she mustn't.

'Mommy!'

Richard's coughing worsened and he started to choke.

Barrett winced as a bullet tore the leg of Carla's pants. The redhead gasped, and seemed to redouble her hold on Richard, wrapping her arms tight around his chest, holding him close to her and away from the children.

Blood started to ooze and spread through the dark fabric of her pants.

His cough turned to a gurgle; fluid was rushing out of his lungs. He choked and convulsed in her arms as bright red blood spilled forth from his mouth.

She gripped her left hand over her right and pushed hard into his back. She squeezed, struggling to keep her grip.

Even from a distance, Barrett heard something crack inside of him as a fresh wave of blood gushed out of his mouth.

'Put down the gun!' Hobbs shouted. *'Put down the gun!'*

Peter Glash turned the bike and glared at the advancing throng of law enforcement officers crowding through the open gate. He revved the engine. 'Get up, Richard! Get up, boy!' he shouted. His face was red, his mouth twisted and angry. 'Get up!' But his son had stopped struggling in Carla's blood-soaked arms.

'Put down the gun!' Hobbs ordered. *'Get off the bike! Do it now!'*

Carla kept her grip on Richard's limp body; she looked across at the frightened children huddled like sheep in the corner of the yard. Her eyes connected with her daughter's. 'April,' she gasped, and then shouted, *'Get them out of here!'*

Peter Glash looked down at his son. 'No...' he whispered, too low to be heard. He felt his finger on the trigger, the barrel pointed at the redhead; she was drenched in blood and sweat, her battle with his son would take her life. It was his single most awful moment ever, as he faced the onslaught of armed men, his last remaining seconds of freedom. He felt a queer clarity in that moment, his hand gripping steel as the August sun beat hot on his back. Children sobbed behind him, sirens blared, a little girl shouted, *'Mommy! Mommy!'*

He knew that his next move would be his last. If he put down the gun, they'd put him back in prison – in a sense he'd never left, all those years alone in the building on Delancey, rarely going out. His entire existence these last years had been fixed on finding a way to connect with the child who'd been stolen from him. To stop now would be to fail Richard yet again.

With the first of the cops – Hobbs, the one who'd tried to bully him – less than twenty feet away, he raised his hands over his head.

'Put the gun on the ground!' the cop shouted again.

He felt the fever building in his flesh, as awkwardly he dismounted, his left leg swinging back over the low-slung bike.

'Put down the gun!'

With those children right there and their two frightened counselors behind him, Peter knew they wouldn't fire. His ears had tuned in to the sniffles and the sobs.

It was the redhead on the ground who met his eye and immediately understood.

'Shoot him!' she shrieked.

'Don't shoot,' Peter said, as he edged back toward the children, and the advancing wave of law enforcement and Guardsmen came at him.

'Mommy!'

'Shoot him!' Carla screamed.

The circle of cops grew tighter. Peter saw fear in their young faces as they approached Richard and the redhead, who still clung to his son. He could also see their hunger, their lust for blood, his blood. He edged back from the bike, towards the sound of the children. *An eye for an eye.* His breath felt hot in his mouth; he could feel a moist rattle deep in his lungs.

'Put down the gun! Now!'

Still closing the gap with the kids, Peter Glash started to bend as though about to comply.

'Hobbs!' the redhead shouted. *'He's infected. Keep him away from April! Shoot him!'*

Peter spun around; his eyes focused on the closest boy, a seven-year-old in jeans and a Thomas the Train tee-shirt. He lunged.

The first bullet felt like a rock against the back of his head. At first he didn't know what it was, his brain needing time to comprehend. The second ripped through his throat; the third caught him in the chest.

'April, get back!'

Those were the last words he heard as he fell to the ground; he grasped for the little boy, but found only air. With what life re-

338

mained he managed to turn his head in the direction of his son. He wanted to see Richard's face, but saw only the redhead. His eyes met hers, and the final thought in his dying brain was, *There is nothing a father won't do for his son.*

Thirty-Four

Barrett, dressed in a blue hazmat suit, had not moved from the garishly upholstered floral chair next to Carla's hospital bed. Despite the three potent antibiotics that were being pushed into her through intravenous tubing she was dying. Fluid-filled pustules had erupted all over her. The capillaries in her eyes had started to burst. The coughing that signaled the beginning of the end had begun.

Around University Hospital there were dozens of other vigils, desperate parents watching and waiting to see if their child had contracted Clarence Albert's bubonic plague.

'Check again,' Carla said, her lips parched and cracking.

Barrett dialed the room where Carla's daughter was quarantined. 'How's she doing?' she asked. 'No signs of anything,' she told Carla. 'She's going to be fine.'

'They don't know for sure, yet,' Carla said. 'How much longer till they know?'

To Barrett, whose tears were very close, Carla's question had a second meaning: *How much longer do I need to stay alive to know that my child will be all right?*

There was a knock at the door, and a tall

man in a white hazmat suit entered.

'Carla,' he called out softly.

With effort, she turned her head and squinted to find her ex-husband, his face barely recognizable behind the shiny Plexiglas shield, standing in the doorway. 'Bill? Who's with April?'

'Kelly, she hasn't left her side.'

'I suppose I should be grateful,' Carla said, her every word an effort. 'Does April know that ... I'm dying?'

'No,' Bill said, 'we didn't want to tell her until...'

'Makes sense.' Carla coughed. She struggled to push herself up. She reached for the glass of ice water on the table positioned over her bed. She carefully sipped through the straw.

Barrett helped steady the plastic cup as her hands shook. 'Do you want me to leave?' she asked.

'Please don't,' Carla said. 'Stay with me ... what did you want, Bill?'

'I don't know exactly,' he said, staring at the woman he'd once loved and subsequently abandoned.

Carla, trying hard not to start coughing, spoke slowly. 'I've been so angry, Bill. You didn't even give me a chance.' She took a careful breath. 'You thought that I was somehow defective, you just threw me away.'

'I was frightened,' he said, stepping closer to the bed, but still leaving a good eight feet between them.

'I know that,' she said, 'and I know that I should have told you about my condition. I had so much fear, fear that you'd leave me, fear that I couldn't be a mother. In the end, I don't think any of that matters. I loved you, Bill.'

'I know,' he said. 'I loved you too, Carla.'

She looked at Barrett, and attempted a smile. 'So much for unconditional love.' She coughed violently, and when she finally managed to catch her breath, looked up at her ex. 'Bill, if you want forgiveness, it's yours, just take care of our daughter. Love her better than you loved me. Don't break her heart ... like you did mine. Now, I'm really tired. Please go.'

The two women watched as he left.

'You're a psychiatrist,' Carla said after he'd gone, 'men are just weaker, aren't they?'

'Yes,' she agreed.

'When the going got tough, Bill took off ... I don't want to die,' she whispered.

'I know.'

'I don't have a choice.'

'What you did was heroic,' Barrett said, as tears tracked down her cheeks. 'They came so close ... you stopped them.'

'It's something my mother taught me: "If you make a mess, clean it up." I have a favor to ask, Barrett.'

'Name it.'

'Look in on April. Manic depression runs in my family.' Barrett could see it was getting hard for Carla to breathe, her words were labored. 'If she got it...' She coughed. 'If she got it, I don't know what Bill would do.'

'Don't worry,' Barrett said, 'I'll find a way.'

'I've kept a journal,' she said. 'They're in a box in my closet. And one next to my bed. Take them. When April's old enough, give them to her. She needs to know...' She could not finish the sentence. She coughed, and couldn't catch her breath.

Barrett watched helpless as a stream of blood trickled between Carla's lips. The cough worsened as blood vessels burst in Carla's lungs. Blood poured from her mouth. Her eyes bulged as she gasped for air, but found only blood. There was nothing Barrett could do; she kept her eyes on Carla's and watched as death came and took her. Barrett's tears flowed and condensation formed on her Plexiglas mask.

She stayed seated and pictured Carla's final acts, giving her life to save her daughter's ... to save Barrett's.

She felt a buzzing through her suit and then her cell rang. It was Hobbs.

'How's she doing?' he asked.

'She's gone,' Barrett sobbed.

'I'm sorry...'

Her eyes fixed on Carla's, she asked, 'How's George doing?' She braced for more bad news.

'It's looking good. They think his fever was from dehydration and not the bacteria. It's coming down.'

'Thank God! I'll see if they'll let me

through,' she said, referring to the series of decontamination rooms and hastily thrown together procedures the hospital had instituted to handle so many patients in quarantine.

'Tell me you're OK, Barrett,' Hobbs said.

'I'm not infected.'

'You took an awful risk,' he said. 'You didn't have to stay with her.'

'I did,' she said. 'In that playground someone had to give their life to take down the Glashes. She did.'

'I know ... I've thought about that a lot,' he said.

'Me too. She's the one who ran after him. I didn't.'

'Neither did I.'

'It was an awful death.' Her tears ran as she looked at Carla's ravaged body. 'I'm so tired of all this. I feel like my brain wants to shut down, to block it all out.'

She sensed his pause.

'Tell me if this is the wrong time,' he said, 'but I imagine they could take care of your little problem...'

'Don't!' she said, harsher than she'd intended. 'We have to talk, but not right now.'

'Barrett...'

'No,' she said, her teeth beginning to chatter, 'not now. I need to get through this. Let me see if I can get moved up to your floor. I'll see if Justine can somehow work it.'

'You know that I love you, Barrett,' he said. 'All the time you were with Glash, I couldn't stop thinking about you, and how I wouldn't be able to take it if he hurt you.'

She couldn't take her eyes off Carla; she pictured Ed and then her dead husband. She had loved Ralph, been head over heels for years – even when he'd been unfaithful. As the seconds ticked she knew she had to say something. Had she led Ed on? There was the kiss, all those months ago, before everything had turned to shit. It was too hard to think, to find the right answer. 'I love you too,' she said, and knew that she'd have to sort it out later.

'You're not *in love* with me, though, are you?' There was openness in his voice, no hint of anger, just sadness.

'No, I'm not, Ed.'

'Didn't think so. Had to check. Barrett?'

'Yes?'

'You're thinking about keeping that baby, aren't you?'

'I'm not certain,' she lied, her decision clear. 'We'll talk when I get up there.'

Thirty-Five

For the next month it was as though New York City held its collective breath. Every day *The Times* and the *Post* would list the number of suspected plague cases. Tens of thousands of panicked citizens had clogged emergency rooms. All of the children and the counselors from the P.S.85 day camp had been quarantined, as well as 1,400 others who'd potentially had contact with either of the Glashes.

Barrett was still in quarantine, but along with Hobbs and Houssman she was in the group considered to be out of danger. They were allowed to wander through the locked psychiatric ward, but no further. They'd also not been given a clear discharge date. The various agencies involved in the near-catastrophe were struggling to defend themselves against angry and well-justified criticism over how they'd repeatedly mishandled the incident. It was only now – after the true danger had passed – that they were taking a stance of caution, by extending the quarantine period.

Ten people, three of them children from the playground, had contracted the fatal illness. Like Cosway, Carla and Glash, they died fast and horribly. But for the last fifteen days no active cases had been reported.

For Barrett, dressed in pajamas and still required to wear a facemask, it was a forced departure from life as usual. She'd had time to be alone and to think.

She turned at the sound of a knock.

Ed and George, dressed in matching brown pajamas with hospital-issue white terrycloth robes, came in. Justine – dressed in green scrubs and a white coat – was right behind. They all wore masks.

'Hi, thanks for coming,' Barrett said.

'It's not like we had anywhere else to go,' Hobbs quipped. His eyes searched out hers and then quickly looked away.

Barrett looked at Ed. She sighed and thought how much easier this would be if she were in love with him. She searched for the contours of his burn scars, much of them hidden behind the HEPA mask. He almost looked the way he had before the explosion. 'So, you want to know why I asked you all here?' she began.

'I think we know,' Justine said, sitting next to her sister on the bed.

'I'm going to have the baby,' Barrett blurted out, finding no other way to do this.

'You're sure?' Hobbs asked.

'Yes,' she said, feeling scrutinized.

There was silence.

'There's more,' Barrett said, 'and that's part of why I wanted to talk to all of you. You're the only three who know the truth – four if you count my obstetrician, but she's bound by patient confidentiality ... I'm going to have this baby ... I'm going to say that the father is Ralph.' She looked at each of them in turn; Justine, Ed and finally George.

George was nodding his head. 'You want us to keep this secret.'

'Yes,' she said. 'I realize it's asking a great deal. I'm having the baby regardless, but this will make it better.'

'I'll never tell,' Justine said. 'But ... there are practicalities, Barrett. Ralph was part Latino and Jimmy Martin is as blond as they come.'

'I've thought of that, but I have dark hair and ... Jimmy's locked away. He'll never be released.'

'And if he finds out?' Hobbs asked.

'I'll deal with that when and if it happens,' she said. 'You see, you're my best friends and I know that I've been keeping things from you ... like wanting this baby, not just a little, but I've never wanted anything so much. It seems like my entire life – and this isn't to complain, it's more a realization – I've always made the choice to do the right thing. Even if it wasn't what I wanted.'

'Like giving up the piano to go to medical school?' Justine asked.

'Like that, but that's OK. I made my peace with that a long time ago and I love being a doctor ... except of course when my patients are either kidnapping me or...' She shook her head. 'This is way too hard.'

'Just say it,' Ed urged. 'Whatever it is, it can't be that bad.'

348

'It's not bad it's just ... I've always pictured myself as having a career and having a family. The career I've got, and it's great.' She laughed. 'OK, maybe this isn't one of the highlights. But I look around and,' she put a hand on her belly, 'I want this child so badly. I want to be a mother, and I didn't think it was going to happen for me. This is one time, and if it sounds selfish I don't care: I'm having this child because it's what I want.'

Justine, ignoring the posted signs that warned against physical contact with the patients, wrapped her arms around Barrett. 'Sweets,' she whispered into her ear, 'this is totally your decision. I will be this baby's aunt, and I will totally love him or her. But there's just one thing...'

'What's that?' Barrett asked, feeling as though a huge weight had just been lifted.

'I *will* call you Rosemary.'